Sheena Joughin has twice be
Short Story Competition, and
Times Literary Supplement.
Indoors, was published by Do........ .. ..e lives in
West London with her son.

Praise for *Swimming Underwater:*

'[Joughin] is a sharp transcriber of a contemporary English lostness and melancholia ... the beautifully underplayed ending insists on connectivity, with an art that Joughin is clearly making her own'   Ali Smith, *Guardian*

'Many things are left unsaid in *Swimming Underwater* and the effect is all the more resonant and intriguing'
Elizabeth Buchan, *Sunday Times*

'A deftly crafted study of misalignment and missed opportunities, rich in irony'   *TLS*

'One of Joughin's favourite ruminations is the paradoxical thread between art and life, and she plays it here like a purring cat with a string ... As addictively abrasive as a shot of cold vodka'   *Time Out*

'Don't miss this, a take on the idea that the course of true love never runs smooth'   Alex Clark, *Red*

'Joughin displays her short-story writing gift for minute observation ... a coolly refreshing read'   *The Glasgow Herald*

'Funny, thoughtful and unsettling ... the randomness of the connections between characters, meeting, re-meeting and hurting each other as though in an Anthony Powell novel is brilliantly caught'   Novel of the Week, *The Tablet*

Praise for *Things to Do Indoors*

'She writes like an angel and thinks like the devil. Joughin is a major discovery'   Fay Weldon

'Very funny, very edgy, very acute. I love this book'   Julie Burchill

Also by Sheena Joughin

THINGS TO DO INDOORS

and published by Black Swan

SWIMMING UNDERWATER

Sheena Joughin

BLACK SWAN

SWIMMING UNDERWATER
A BLACK SWAN BOOK: 0552771546
9780552771542

Originally published in Great Britain by Doubleday,
a division of Transworld Publishers

PRINTING HISTORY
Doubleday edition published 2005
Black Swan edition published 2006

1 3 5 7 9 10 8 6 4 2

Set in 11/14pt Melior by
Falcon Oast Graphic Art Ltd.

Black Swan Books are published by Transworld Publishers,
61–63 Uxbridge Road, London W5 5SA,
a division of The Random House Group Ltd,
in Australia by Random House Australia (Pty) Ltd,
20 Alfred Street, Milsons Point, Sydney, NSW 2061, Australia,
in New Zealand by Random House New Zealand Ltd,
18 Poland Road, Glenfield, Auckland 10, New Zealand
and in South Africa by Random House (Pty) Ltd,
Isle of Houghton, Corner of Boundary Road & Carse O'Gowrie,
Houghton 2198, South Africa.

Printed and bound in Great Britain by
Cox & Wyman Ltd, Reading, Berkshire.

Papers used by Transworld Publishers are natural, recyclable products
made from wood grown in sustainable forests. The manufacturing
processes conform to the environmental regulations of the country
of origin.

For Catherine and Dan

Permissions

1

It was a cold spring. Back in London, everyone who
arrived on my doorstep was dressed as if they'd
struggled through November, rather than April, to
reach me. Some wore gloves, which they invariably
forgot, along with umbrellas, which reproduced themselves underneath the coats in my hallway. I'd already
lost two hats since Christmas, and was unwilling to buy
another, so arrived in Hastings bareheaded. Liam had
a knitted cap pulled down over his ears when he met
me from the train, in the flickering light of the station
foyer. The pale hat made his face seem unusually red,
as did the fact that he was cross. The train was almost
an hour late. Some teenagers had smashed a light in
one of the carriages as we were approaching Battle,
and the police were called at that station, so the
delinquents could be placed in safe hands. Grown-up
passengers smoked on the platform, discussing the
hazards of travel. When the police eventually arrived,
there were more of them than us. One of the
constabulary accepted a cigarette from a man in tweed,

who told me, as the young offenders were herded away, that children under sixteen should not be handcuffed. He said it loudly enough for the congregation of travellers to become divided in opinion. Some felt that the trouble-makers should be locked up for ever, others that their parents were to blame.

'These vandals are the sort of people who rob old ladies,' a plump woman explained to a slight man in a corduroy jacket.

'Ridiculous. Handcuffing children,' a donnish gentleman protested. He looked at me but I made no comment, simply stretched my face in a way I hoped covered a variety of reflective responses, then stepped back into the warmth of the dusty carriage where I had left my book and bag. He followed to explain that what we had witnessed should not have happened.

'People under sixteen cannot be criminals. They should not be put in handcuffs.'

I reached into my grip for a bottle of water. 'Probably not,' I conceded, as fizz sprayed on to my jeans. 'People shouldn't die. But they do.' That was enough to move him along from my carriage and into the next, where people were sharing a bottle of wine. He may have thought I was drunk myself.

When Liam told me that Fiona was arriving to stay that night, I was more cross than he'd been about my train. I didn't like his sister or her boyfriend, Frank, who was bound to be with her. They did everything together.

'Why did you invite them when I was coming?' I

said in Liam's cool sitting room, with its view of the sea and its noise of gulls and its original cast-iron fireplace, which was hardly ever used.

'I didn't invite them, Ruth. I said they could come. They've got a day off tomorrow. Calm down. Take your coat off.'

He pulled off his hat, dropped it on to the two-seater couch and started to open a bottle of wine which had been on the mantelpiece next to a clock which ticked too loudly. It was five thirty. Fiona and Frank would be here soon now anyway, he told me, with his face towards the floor and the cork of the bottle. They were coming, so I might as well decide to enjoy myself. We could go for a walk, because although it was as cold as November, it got dark at the usual April time.

'You want to see the sea, don't you?' he said, wiping something from the rim of the glass he was about to fill. I went to the hall and took off my coat, then down to the basement kitchen where I had a mug of water from the stiff tap there. I found a heavy glass which I had bought in a junk shop when Liam first bought his house and I was enthusiastic about such things, then I walked slowly back up the narrow stairs to join him in the room where he was by now sitting down. I poured some wine for myself, although I wouldn't drink it on principle, now that I was supposed to be enjoying myself, in anticipation of an evening with Liam's sister and her boyfriend.

'Fiona and Frank are married now, by the way. They did it a few weeks ago.'

I drank some wine, wondering where they would sleep. There was only one double bed in the house.

'I wish you'd told me you were expecting company,' I said. 'I wouldn't have come if I'd known.'

'Well you're here now. Sit down. Or are you thinking of leaving for somewhere else? Shall I take you back to the station?'

I didn't want to go anywhere else, so I sat down, but didn't lean back. I raised my eyebrows at him and he did it to me in return.

I didn't want to leave Hastings, because if I did I'd have to be home again, living twelve minutes away from where Clare lived. She was my friend, and she was ill, and not getting better.

'Clare's worse,' I said. I drank some wine as Liam did not reply. He did not respond well to sickness, in others or in himself. The wine was sweet and thick, so I drank some more and licked my lips. It was nice to have something so simple as a tongue that worked. Liam watched as I lifted my glass again.

'Not bad, is it?' he said.

'Thicker than water,' I said.

'Have you seen my mother lately?' he asked me then, and I told him yes, the day before. She'd come to visit and told me that it was better for Clare to be in a morphine sleep than to lie awake worrying about the possibility of death. She was seventy-three and not worried much about dying.

'You can only worry about dying when you're

young,' she'd reflected, pulling hard on a Silk Cut Extra Light. 'I worry about staying alive.'

She'd left my kitchen soon after saying that, to go and look at a house she was thinking of buying on the Askew Road. She often thought of buying houses, although she had two already. She gave me a hundred pounds just before she went. I put the cheque into my cutlery drawer, with the one she'd given me last time she came.

'She gave me a hundred pounds,' I told Liam.

He said she'd given him a thousand.

'You could buy a lot of pyjamas with that,' I decided.

He said he didn't wear pyjamas, which I knew since we slept together.

'You need them in hospital,' I said, standing up to pour more wine.

'Stop it,' he said. He hated the idea of sickness. We heard the sound of a car horn.

At first Liam's guests didn't seem like anything except two people who'd been in a car for too long and were glad to be unconfined. They rushed around the house like large dogs released from their Sunday-afternoon estate-car ride, eager to sniff their new territory out.

'Good smell,' Fiona decided, sitting down at last, pushing long dark hair back from her face. 'Slightly musty. I like that.'

Liam liked that too, repeating the notion a few times, making much of wrinkling his nose.

Frank sat in the green chair nearest the bay window

and opened a photocopied leaflet, which I'd opened too when I'd first sat briefly there, before I was told my visit was to be ruined. It was the Parish Newsletter, written mostly by a woman who clearly hated dogs and the mess they made in public places.

'She doesn't like dogs,' I said in the direction of Fiona's new husband, but Frank read on, regardless.

He must have known we were watching because he crossed his legs, and turned a page and dipped his head deeper into the coarse-grained print with the air of a man who knows he is not joining in.

Liam's sister stood and walked to the window, to stand to my left.

'Drink?' Liam asked her. 'There's not much left, but we could go for a walk, if you'd like.'

'Great,' she said. 'How far is the sea?'

'You're coming with us, aren't you, Ruth?'

Fiona looked at me, as he waited for my reply.

'Don't think so,' I decided, hoping to make it clear by my tone that there could be no possibility of it, but my churlishness went unheeded, because Frank stood up to stretch his arms exaggeratedly above his head.

'Walk. Good idea. Bit stiff.'

His wife went to stand behind him and rub his back – a gesture which would have triggered a disbelieving grimace from Liam if anyone else had made it, but which went ostensibly unnoticed that evening.

I walked a lot in London, since someone stole my bicycle just after Christmas. Mostly I walked to Clare's house and back, although often I didn't go in. I'd just walk there, thinking I'd like to see her, and then not want to ring the bell, so walk home again a different way. Back in my study, I'd feel regret and dial her number, and sometimes she'd answer, or sometimes it might be her mother.

'She's asleep at the moment, Ruth,' the mother would normally say. 'I'm not sure she's up to visitors today.'

'I haven't had this many visitors since I came here,' Liam was saying as he pulled on his jacket. He noticed one of his shoe-laces was undone and put his foot on the couch to tie it, talking on as he did so. He had a long and elegant back, which I noticed most when he was tying his laces, which he seemed to do a lot.

'You're going to love my Hastings tour, I can tell you,' he told the room as he straightened up.

'You liked it, didn't you?' he said to me.

I agreed that I had. 'It's lovely. Lots of steps every-where, instead of streets. A bit like Paris.'

Mentioning Paris was a mistake, I could tell. Liam thought I was showing off.

'Well, there you are. It reminds Ruth of Paris. What better recommendation could you wish for? She keeps a diary in French, of course.'

Frank thought he was telling the truth. 'Why do you do that? Can't you spell in English?'

'I can't spell in any language,' I said to him.

'She uses a spell-check,' Liam explained, before

turning his attention to me. 'So you're staying here, then? We can't tempt you down to the sea?' He looked up and down me slowly, the way he did. The way he did not much, any more.

'Don't think so,' I said.

'See you later, then,' Fiona said, walking out of the room, which Frank had already left.

'Have a good walk,' I called to her own elegant back.

'You're sure? You want to be alone?' Liam asked me.

'Well, you'd know all about that,' I said, picking up the Parish Newsletter, looking with interest at words I'd seen before.

He left and the door slammed and I was glad of the noise. It sounded like something I wished I'd said. But all I'd really done was to make Liam say it instead.

After they'd gone, I went to the bedroom on the first floor and lay down. I wasn't tired, but I wanted to be horizontal, and the ceiling was a restful thing to stare at: pale blue, with a central rose that had random pieces missing. Liam and I hadn't had sex for a long time. At first, when I realized what was happening, or not happening, I'd get angry and ask him what was wrong. He'd say nothing was wrong, and be angry too.

'I'm not a machine,' he'd nearly shout. 'I have a lot on my mind just now.'

Then there'd be silence for a while, maybe, before I said something else, which would annoy him even more.

'Do you realize how unattractive men find it, to have women demanding sex?' he'd say.

I did realize that, I told him firmly, but I'd stopped caring how attractive or not he found me any more.

'And I feel unattractive, when we don't make love,' I'd say.

'See an analyst,' was his stock response.

'See one yourself,' was mine.

I must have been lying on the bed for about twenty minutes, enjoying the smell of sheets that have had familiar flesh in them, when I heard the doorbell ring. I ignored it but it rang again so I sat up. It could be one of the visitors, grown tired of the walk and come home to rest. I pulled my jumper into shape as I went downstairs and pushed straggles of hair back into stray clips, one of which dropped to the floor. I left it on the grubby carpet, but brushed away a cobweb from the curve of the stair. I wiped the wisp of the thing on my thigh, then looked at myself in the long mirror in the hall before I opened the door and saw I was not unattractive. A man with a suitcase and a rib-knitted hat was there on the step below me. The suitcase was under his left arm. In his right hand he was holding what had obviously been the handle of the thing. It had bits of black thread hanging from it. His hands were smaller than I would have expected for such a bulky person, but he may have had a lot of clothes underneath his thick tweed coat. I said hello, but didn't open the door any wider than I had to.

'Is that your motorbike?' he said.

I leaned my head around the glass-panelled door and looked in the direction he was pointing. Across the street I saw a strange machine, which was in part still a motorbike but had a corrugated-tin box attached to it somehow at the back. It was painted black and silver and had wide handlebars, which looked as if they should be on a bowling-alley wall, or in some country and western dance-hall, rather than on a machine that moved.

I told my visitor that the bike wasn't mine.

'Whose is it?'

'I don't know. But it doesn't belong to this house.'

He stared at me long and hard. He had small but intense blue eyes, underneath interesting eyebrows, which were graded in shade to fine blond hairs at their top edges. 'I'd like a ride on it,' he said, 'if I knew whose it was.'

I said the person who owned it might still be at work. 'I mean I don't live here, so I can't say. I could ask my boyfriend when he comes back, if you like.'

That was a silly thing to say, I realized as he stared at me again. Now we were in some ongoing situation in which he knew I had a 'boyfriend', which seemed a picky thing to own on this bleak street in this grey and cold early evening.

'He might come back later if I wait, then.'

'Who?' I hoped he wasn't planning to wait for Liam.

'The bloke who owns it. He's still at work, then?'

'Well, he might be at work. I don't know. I'm just visiting.'

I had no shoes on and my feet were cold. I pulled the cuffs of my jumper down into the palms of my hands and held them with my fingers.

'I think he'll come back if I wait,' he said, looking away and back at the exotic machine.

I nearly said whoever 'he' was would come back or not whether anyone waited or not, but something about him was too serious to banter with, so I agreed that whoever owned the thing would have to come back sometime, unless he was away.

'Unless someone's just abandoned it there,' I said.

'Why would they want to do that?' He seemed upset at the idea. As if I'd suggested it somehow deserved to be abandoned, like a pet hamster that disappears the day its family moves house.

'Well perhaps it doesn't move. It might be broken.'

He looked at me piercingly then, and moved his bag to tilt under his right arm instead of his left. 'You don't know what you're talking about,' he said. 'You're talking rubbish, that's what you are.'

Then he turned and walked down the steps of Liam's house and crossed the road, which a large ginger cat was also crossing from the opposite side. I stayed to watch as my curious visitor sat on the pavement beside the ungainly machine. He seemed frail and short by comparison. I shut the door. It seemed rude to watch any longer.

In the upstairs sitting room with its wide view of the sky, the sea and Tesco's car park, I collected glasses together and put the empty wine bottle into a wicker waste-paper basket, which had nothing else inside it so fell over a few times until I got the weight centred properly. I took the glasses down to the darkening kitchen, thought of washing them, but decided not to as the sink was lined with potato peelings. I assembled bits of a newspaper – sheeted on the large oval table – into a readable whole and took it upstairs. I put the light on next to the couch and read an article about outer space. It explained how galaxies are currently rushing away from each other in our expanding universe, which is probably flat rather than round, which means that you could perhaps travel for ever in a straight line if you had a rocket.

The doorbell rang, then rang again as I wondered whether or not to pretend I was out. I didn't want to have another conversation with the motorbike man. But if it was Liam's sister or her husband then I would have to let them in. The bell rang a third time, and as I reached the hall I heard someone shouting.

'She was just there. She hasn't been out.'

It was the voice of the man who wanted a ride on the motorbike. Opening the door, I saw he was calling his information to a woman about ten years younger than me. She walked up the steps as I arrived, and the man shouted 'I told you she'd be there.' He then waved at me, and nodded his head. I waved back. He was sitting on his suitcase rather than beside it, now. The ground must have been cold. The light was fading, but the street-lamps were not yet on.

'Hello. Sorry. Is Liam in?' The woman was holding a handbag against her front in what might have been a self-protective gesture.

I was going to say 'Why?' but did not. The moon was white in the sky above her head.

'He's gone for a walk. He shouldn't be long.'

He could be all night, for all I knew. He was probably in a pub somewhere by now. I smiled, but she didn't. She was biting a nail. The sound her teeth made on the end of her finger continued as my speech trailed off.

'Well could I ask you a favour?'

The man by the motorbike was waving again.

'Shouldn't be long now,' he called. I smiled in his direction.

'He's waiting for someone,' I explained to the woman, who was looking at the steps up to the house next door to Liam's.

'The thing is, I need to feed the cat,' she said. 'And I don't have the keys any more.'

I wondered if Liam might have the keys and asked her that, instead of exactly where the cat might be.

'Oh no. Liam wouldn't have them. Kate wouldn't give them to Liam.'

I'd heard of Kate. She lived next door and played music too loudly and Liam didn't like it, but would not complain either, although I'd told him he should. The woman with the cat to feed explained that she was Kate's cleaner, and that Kate had been in London for the weekend and was due back last night.

'I put the keys through the letterbox yesterday morning. That's what I always do when I've done feeding Mog. But now she's not coming back. I don't know why. They just said to carry on with the feeding.'

'Who did?' I'd opened the door more widely now, so that the light from the hallway – which Liam never switched off – could illuminate our fading conversation.

'I'm Sue, by the way.' She held her hand out for mine to shake.

'Ruth,' I said. 'I'm a friend of Liam's.' I didn't feel very friendly towards Liam at that moment, but the description seemed to please her. Her face cleared considerably.

'My daughter's called Ruth,' she said.

The street-lamps came on in a unanimous burst of red. The world seemed suddenly darker.

By seven o'clock Sue had made her way through Liam's kitchen and out the French windows at the back. She seemed familiar with the territory. She climbed over the precarious fencing in the long unkempt garden and into Kate's house through the French windows there, which led into the bathroom, apparently. She fed Mog, collected the keys she'd posted into Kate's the morning before and returned to tell me that all was well. There had been no phone call from Liam and his rambling guests. The man who wanted a ride on the motorbike was still sitting across the road. I offered Sue a cup of tea, which she accepted, and together we decided that it would be appropriate to take one to our friend with the suitcase, who must be 'chilled to the bone'.

'Nice,' he said, as I handed him the mug with 'Love Is . . . Tea in Bed' written in pink around it. 'I'll bring the cup when I'm done.' He smiled up from his squatting position. 'Can't be long now, I reckon.' He touched one of the back wheels of the contraption he had fallen in love with, perhaps. 'Hope it's got lights.' He chuckled. I nodded and went back to Sue, who was asking about Liam as she looked around his kitchen. She seemed interested in a 1996 calendar on the wall beside the fridge, pinned open on October, which was illustrated with a painting of a lily by Georgia O'Keefe.

'He doesn't go out much, does he?'

'Doesn't he?' He was rarely in when I rang. Rarely answered the telephone, anyway.

'What does he do?'

'Pisses me off,' I could have said, but did not. 'Oh. Lots of things. He writes. For magazines.'

'That's nice,' was all she said, and then that she'd better be off. Her Ruth would be wanting her supper. She thought she'd get fish and chips on the way home. I realized I'd like some fish and chips. Liam and I had them the day he moved in here. We had thick white sliced bread and butter, too, which I decided was what I'd do as soon as Sue had gone.

As she was saying goodbye, again, standing at the top of Liam's front-door steps, the man from across the way brought his empty mug back to me.

'Nice,' he said. 'Thanks. Shouldn't be long now.'

I looked at my watch. It was seven thirty-five. The gulls were getting noisier. A cluster of them swooped down, then up again over our heads. The change of light in the sky highlighted their dirty wings and made their yellowy-grey underbellies seem over-stuffed, like Victorian upholstery. Liam liked seagulls, but I did not. I was brought up with their raucous screeching, on the North Norfolk coast.

As soon as I got back inside the house, I turned the heating on. There were goose-pimples on my arms, below the rolled-up sleeves of Liam's jumper, which I'd pulled on during the last hour or so. I sat on the couch and tried to concentrate on the article about space, which I seemed to be nearing the end of. I wasn't sure what I had learnt so far.

We cannot visit other universes. They are in their own space and time. We would cease to exist on leaving our own.

The next-door cat was howling in their garden. It was a harsher sound than the seagulls. Clare's cat made that same noise sometimes, in her long narrow London garden, which she and I had cleared two summers before, when she was well and strong in a blue-and-white T-shirt and khaki shorts, which kept unrolling down her pale shapely legs. Her legs didn't work any more by that spring, though. One of them was bloated and the other too thin. Her left foot hung

24

limp if she ever stood up. When I looked at it, I thought of the webbed feet of swans, which drag behind them under the surface of the Round Pond in Kensington Gardens. Clare and I used to take her son Conor there, when he was small. He once fell in, reaching for another boy's boat, and Clare waded out to lift him back to safety. She was wearing something red she'd made from billowing silk which she lifted as she moved to scoop up her son, as the loose crowd stilled to watch. One man whistled and another clapped and called 'Bravo!' when the rescue was complete, and she took her time then, splashing back to shore with Conor held high, like a trophy, above her pleased and lovely tilted head.

Outside Liam's, the cat was still sporadically howling. Maybe it was hungry, like me. I'd only had a croissant and some coffee all day. Liam usually liked to feed me when I came to stay. I moved to the window, where there was little to see, since what there is most of outside that house is space. Sometimes there are stars – galaxies, perhaps – but then there was only a heavy blue-black, with the lights of the town tingling in it a long way away. The sea was simply a shine. There was no colour to see any more in the shapes of outside. Cats are colour-blind, Conor had recently told me. He liked increasingly to discuss his cat, as we walked to and from his house or mine, or his school, which I sometimes collected him from. Clare's cat was thin and oddly marked, like a badly printed remnant, and called Pringle, after the crisps rather than the knitting wool, because Conor happened to be opening a pack when the cat first appeared at his window. He asked Clare if he could give it some milk, and after that it arrived back every day, and that was how it came to live with them.

A clock somewhere struck eight. I was cross. Liam should have rung me by now. He wouldn't have treated his sister this way. He'd have been here making spaghetti, if she and Frank had been with me. I shouldn't have come. He should have told me not to. He should at least have arranged for me to be warm and fed. He'd probably expect me to light a fire, but I would not do that this evening. I'd ring the station, instead, and find times of trains back to London, and then I'd walk out of this house and down through the narrow-stepped alleyways, which were nothing like Paris, and I'd arrive at the station to board a swaying train full of talkative people, all glad to be leaving the seaside. All cheerful at the idea of London crowds and the smell of coffee at Victoria Station. I'd be back home and in bed before midnight. I would leave no note and I wouldn't come here again.

The phone was next to Liam's computer. When I lifted it the line was dead, but the computer was humming as it always was. The screen-saver was an animated picture of fish, which glowed and made a blubbery liquid noise from time to time. I replaced the receiver and picked it up, to find no dial tone again. The phone socket had the modem plugged into it. It must have been disconnected all the time. I took off Liam's jumper and plugged in the phone, which I expected to start ringing straight away, but it didn't. I waited a good three minutes in silence as my stomach rumbled and I realized I was terribly hungry, which was no longer unpleasant, now I knew why no one had been in touch.

I went down to the kitchen and opened the fridge. It was empty apart from a lemon, some margarine and a Pyrex dish, which must once have contained stew, since its sides were greasy and crusted with meaty-looking black ridges. Liam was good at stew. He'd probably been trying to phone for hours. Perhaps there had been an accident. It wouldn't surprise me if the three of them had ended up in Casualty. I was glad I'd stayed at home.

I went upstairs to Liam's computer again and looked out of the window. The motorbike man was standing up, his suitcase under his arm. He saw me and waved and I waved back, then had an idea, so ran to the hall and through to the front door and stood outside on the cold stone of the steps, as I shouted across to the shadowy man. 'Come here, please. I'm in trouble.'

There was a van grinding noisily towards us up the rise of the street, and although he could have crossed before it arrived to knock him over, he waited until it had passed before coming to stand below me. I turned to put the latch on the door. I didn't want us both to be locked out.

'Not much point now, is there?' he said. ''S too dark for a ride now, I reckon.'

I didn't answer. I was making reckonings of my own.

'Look,' I said. He was looking very hard, although not at me, exactly. He was looking more at the house next door.

'She didn't know owt about it either, then? The lady with the cat?'

I said no, she didn't. No one knew anything about the motorbike so far, but there was something I'd like him to do for me, if he would. Then I asked him too quickly, so I had to say it again.

'I need to go to the shop.' I spoke as if he was a child I had to explain some potentially dangerous situation to. 'It's not far. Just around that corner.' He followed the line of my pointing finger. 'I have to go to the shop to buy some food. But I can't go anywhere because I don't have a key, and I can't just leave the door open.'

I could see he didn't know what I was talking about, so I went down the steps and took his free arm. It stiffened. He shook me off.

'Please,' I said. I went back up the steps and sat down between the open door and the door-post. 'Could you please just sit here, for a moment.'

He didn't move.

I stood up. 'The people in the shop must know who owns the bike. I can ask them, when I'm there.'

He smiled and put his suitcase down. He walked up the steps and sat down where I'd been. I patted his shoulder and said thanks a lot. I ran back indoors and took the phone off the hook, in case Liam rang, then ran out again as fast as I could. There might be a crisis occurring. Liam and Fiona and Frank might need me. At the very least they'd be wanting to meet me, and I couldn't get to where they were if I had collapsed with hunger.

As I left the shop with its fragile door jingle behind me, I decided to give the man guarding my door a cheese sandwich, when I'd made my own. I had enough bread and cheese now for a small class of primary-school children. I'd have liked to have bought a bottle of wine, but only had five pounds on me, so settled for a litre of milk with my foodstuffs, paid as fast as I could without waiting for change and ran all the way back to Liam's narrow-fronted two-storey mid Victorian terrace. The front door was closed. There was no sign of the man, or the suitcase.

I walked up the steps and rang the bell. Nothing happened, so I rang again. I looked up and saw lights had come on upstairs. I rang again. The upstairs lights went off. Then I rang and kept my finger on the button, so the shrill noise mixed with the screech of seagulls. A car came suddenly round the corner I had just run around myself. I thought of the telephone box outside the shop, and that I could ring Liam's from there and ask the man inside to let me in. But no one could answer the telephone, because I'd taken it off the hook.

I stopped ringing the doorbell and pushed the

letterbox open instead. 'Please,' I called into the musty smell. 'Let me in. Open the door. I've got some food.'

What would the others think, when they got back to find I'd let a stranger take over the house?

'Open the door,' I called into the letterbox again. 'I have the key to the motorbike. You can have a ride. You can have a ride now.'

I turned to look into the street, but there was no one. The moon above was round and clean-edged. A communion-wafer of translucent light. A bedroom window opened with a noise like a sharp gust of wind. I bent to the letterbox, then let it slam and walked across the street. I needed to see from a distance what was happening inside. An upstairs window closed as I stood beside the bike the man had sat next to for hours. I waved, like he'd waved at me.

'Let me in,' I shouted up to the sky, up to the sea-gulls – up to all the galaxies rushing away from each other, perhaps – but he did not appear. He must have gone down to the kitchen, where the light came on, then out into the garden at the back, then over the fence to next door. He was obviously in Kate's house, one way or another. The lights there came on, one by one. Square after square of black glass lit up, reveal-ing different colours in the rooms of the house of Liam's absent neighbour. I sat down next to the motor-bike then, and watched lights flash on in the empty house. It looked like some vast illuminated score card on a television quiz show. The strange thing was, I thought later, that I never once saw the man. He must have left over the back garden fences. But I stayed beside the machine he wanted a ride on long after the windows had stopped slamming open or shut. I stayed to watch through the dark as Liam arrived to open his own front door, and his sister and her husband followed him into the house. I watched as Liam came out of the front door again, then, to stand in the open doorway. He was looking for me, but I didn't wave for a while.

2

Visiting my friend Clare when she was sick was difficult, and I never quite knew when to do it. There was rarely a reason to arrive at any particular time, and since I did nothing when I was with her but sit and talk, there was no natural time to leave. So in May, when Conor joined a football club which met on Tuesdays in Ravenscourt Park, I offered to walk him there from his primary school, which was across the road from my house. I'd then go to Clare's until it was time to bring him home again. I thought this arrangement would structure my sick-visits and also perhaps my working life, which was entering a new and fluid stage. I'd been asked to write about poetry for a book on twentieth-century literature, devised by a friend of a friend. Deadlines were vague, as were the lists of poets I was to include, which came in random e-mail attachments.

It was 1998, and the spring was filling with pale new leaves which shadowed the pavements with shades of grey when rain clouds cleared, as they often did, as I arrived in Conor's school playground. We'd walk almost together, in an awkward unit, to the gates of the park, where I'd wave until he became one of a crowd of small blue T-shirts. Clare's son and I were somewhat uneasy together, alone and out of doors, that year. After football, we bought fish and chips, which we queued for side by side, as I made stabs at conversation and he read the menu on the wall. He carried whatever he'd chosen home and ate his meal from the paper it came in, sprawled on the sitting-room carpet at Clare's, with the television near. At about seven o'clock, his grandmother arrived to begin to persuade him to bed, which generally meant I should leave. She brought him to Clare's room to say goodnight.

I had as little experience of writing about poets as I had of visiting bed-ridden friends, but I saw that the two things might blend quite well. Clare's life was more like a poem than a story, now that she was ill. Her days were filled with repetition, as was her mother's conversation and Conor's nightly litany of what he needed before he could sleep. His reading books were thin on plot and thick with words that sounded the same. A ragged poster on his bedroom wall said *The cat sat on the mat*, a sentence my aunt used to love when I was younger than he was.

The notion of poetry made me think of my aunt Jane, because she wrote it. Being with Conor reminded me of her, too, because she was the person who mostly walked with me around my early world. Her flat shoes were what my small self saw, if I looked down at my own feet moving forward outside the house. So when I sat on Clare's bed, or on the chair beside her window, above the uncut garden and the cherry-blossom tree, and she said 'Tell me something,' in the early days of her illness, as I moved through people and she did not, I thought about Jane, whom I hadn't spoken to for years, but whom I'd spoken to through most of my childhood and adolescence.

My childhood was not like Clare's, except that both were lived through the 1960s and both took place in England. Hers took place in a large brick house off leafy Ealing Common, mine in a small flint-covered cottage on the blowy and treeless North Norfolk coast. When Clare played out, it was a crowded affair, full of suburban detritus and thick with potentially dangerous strangers. When I played outside it was in an empty space, shadowed by my mother's tall shape or that of her equally tall but narrower sister. The greatest unknown of an out-of-doors afternoon for my young self was the volatile weather, which altered the vast washed space of the sea. Sometimes a furious lash of high waves, rearing up before the sharp incline of the stony shore, sometimes dull and flat and greying to nothing.

Before I started school, aged five, Jane was simply a person who was always there. She held my hand to take me to playgroup, and down to the daily sea, and into shops that smelled of cauliflower to buy our evening meal, which we ate when my mother arrived

34

home from work. Jane's long back and elegant shoulders were what I saw when I looked up from puzzles or toys on the swirling green rugs of our low-beamed main room. Her typewriter was on a table there, between two windows with long square panes. Her typewriter's silver-ringed clattering keys were as much a part of my afternoons as her abandoned cigarettes were, with their lipstick-sticky tips, or her soft voice as she typed and talked, and the ice-cubes in her drink at six, which I was allowed to suck after she'd emptied the glass.

At primary school, my relationship to Jane was given a categorical name.

'My mother won't be able to come. She'll be at work,' I'd say, when notes were given out inviting parents to off-key concerts or stuttering plays.

'Well, ask your *aunt*,' they'd say.

My class-mates would frown and glance. Aunts were women who lived with uncles. You weren't supposed to have one at home. Nor was your mother meant to be a doctor, as mine was. Doctors were men you didn't like seeing, not women who dropped you off near the school gates on their way to work in Holt every day, and left you to walk home by yourself.

'Does she have a stethoscope?' a friend asked me once.

She did, of course, but I lied and said she wasn't that sort of a doctor.

'What sort is she, then?'

No one at nursery school had ever asked, and

neither had Gillian, my best friend so far, who went to the Catholic school. Her father owned the local pub and her mother had five or six children, and liked me going to tea as much as I liked to be told it was time to go home. Gillian and I looked after the babies and tried to avoid her big brothers, who had razors in the bathroom and underwear that alarmed me when I saw it hanging to dry. Her smallest sibling was male and wore a nappy we changed, so at least I'd seen a penis and didn't have to lie about that.

'She just talks to people,' I said, when asked what my mother really did. 'And then she decides if they're sick or not.'

This notion of my mother as a disciple of Freud may have been what made my friends' parents watch me, as they did, in the after-school sweetshop. Or more likely it was the fact that I had a father who was dead. I was told he'd died in Spain, on honeymoon with my mother, and although I enjoyed the word 'honeymoon', I didn't like his not being alive, which I felt as a visible gap, like a trench or a stagnant moat, between myself and people around me. It got worse the more public my life became, and made school a sort of daily test in which parents must not be allowed into conversation, and in which I had to learn how to look hard at something while other people looked hard at me.

When I told my mother and Jane that people stared, they looked at me for longer than usual themselves.

'It's because you're so pretty,' my mother decided, which I knew was not the truth.

36

'Stare back,' Jane said, then looked down at the sheets of typing she was writing words across.

'Why don't you have someone home to tea?' my mother said then, fingering her pale hair which she wore in a French pleat at the time. 'Why not invite someone back after school?'

I didn't see that that would stop class-mates staring.

'Stell,' Aunt Jane said, raising her eyebrows. She was licking a stamp, pushing her darker, short hair away from her cheek. My mother's name was Stella, but Jane never said the whole word.

'What?' My mother looked up from the local paper. She liked to look at houses for sale, though in the end she bought the one we lived in, when the woman who owned it died.

'Well, does Ruth *want* to have someone home?'

'Of course she does. She needs other children.'

My mother looked at Jane, not me any more. Jane looked back at her with her grey eyes too wide. They might be going to argue.

'I don't mind,' I said.

'But is it something you long for, Ruth?'

Jane often talked of longing for things, as if I ought to do it. And when she did, she'd usually smoke, which made my mother cough or leave the room. She didn't like Jane smoking. She emptied ashtrays upside-down beside her typewriter, and threw half-empty packs in the bin. There was once a scene with dustbin men as I was leaving for school and Jane arrived down and refused to let our rubbish be taken until she'd retrieved a pack of cigarettes from its depths.

'You're disgusting. Addictions are pitiful,' my mother shouted, as she guided me into my side of the car, which smelled pleasantly dense in early-morning sea air.

'Well, you'd know all about that,' Jane shouted back, as we reversed past several binmen, all holding cigarettes.

My mother and Jane argued most in the mornings, which was probably why Jane took to lying in late, and spent most days writing down more words than she spoke. She was always writing something. Letters, or book reviews, and then poems, of course, which I recognized by the way they were typed, down the centre of white paper. When I got home from school she was usually typing, with a cigarette between her long fingers. Sometimes she'd come to meet me in the hallway with its blue-bird wallpaper and the upright piano that nobody played, but more often she'd carry on typing. Once I went in to her with my coat very wet and the ties of its hood stuck in a sodden knot and she turned and said 'For goodness' sake.' Then she struck a match and watched it burn before helping me untie myself.

'The blood jet is poetry, Ruth,' she said. 'There is no stopping it. Sylvia Plath wrote that.'

I didn't ask what Sylvia Plath meant because I knew my mother didn't like her. She said she was a hysteric and that Jane was too. But Jane made the usual things for supper and she liked to play cards and Scrabble and to watch the television she bought as much as I did and more. She watched it late at night, when she wasn't allowed to type, because the noise came up through the floorboards into my room, my mother said. But the television was just as loud.

The question of someone coming home to tea grew more pressing as my first term at school progressed. My mother and Jane didn't mention it, after their initial altercation, but I could see it had to be done. There was always someone, arriving into our morning classroom flushed and smug, carrying a little stitched bag with neat-looking zips, which they would make much of asking Miss to look after until home-time, when they were going to someone's *'for tea'*. I was asked to tea myself by various friends, but explained that I couldn't go, because my mother wouldn't be able to collect me, which was fine until a plump girl said her dad would bring me home. On the appointed day I pretended to be too ill to go to school, but the girl insisted that she must come to my house in return, anyway, which my mother couldn't see was unfair.

'Because when she's been here, you can go there, Ruthie. Does it make any difference who goes where first, really?'

'A great deal,' Jane said. She was frying sausages, which spat, which she always enjoyed. 'We need to know how they cut their sandwiches.'

She turned and leaned against the cooker, with her

39

shoulders back in her red roll-necked sweater, which stretched across her breasts. She smiled in my direction and took cigarettes from the pocket of her black corduroy trousers. There was mud on the legs, which were unevenly hemmed. Perhaps I could ask the girl to come on a Saturday, when Jane would be out. Or we could have a picnic and Jane would read a book and not speak, but that was unlikely since it was mid November and even Jane didn't picnic in snow.

'*It is a house of female habitation*,' Jane said. '*A house expecting strength, as it is strong.*' She liked Stevie Smith at the time. 'We can't be bullied into tea invitations.' She shook the frying pan vigorously.

'Oh, stop it.' My mother had her telephone voice on, which she used when the surgery rang. 'And stop smoking over the sausages, too.'

'Well fry them yourself, then.' Jane came to sit at the table, crossing her legs up on the chair next to mine. Her socks were green. She'd bought them in London. 'You don't have to do anything you don't want to, Ruth.'

The sausages made small violent sounds. My mother got up and turned down the gas. 'Well sometimes you do, actually, Jane.' She opened the cutlery drawer with a bang. 'I do things I don't want to every day.'

'Me too.' Jane stretched her fingers and studied the neat short nails. 'But we're grown-ups.' She brushed ash from her shoulder. 'Aren't we, Stell?'

'Are you going to lay the table, Ruth?' my mother said.

'I'll do it,' said Jane, 'when the time has come.'

'The time is now.' My mother rattled cutlery as I looked at the clock. It was twenty past six. Outside the rain was hard.

'I'll ask her to tea. I don't mind,' I said.

I'd ask the girl to come on Thursday, I thought. My mother worked late that day.

'Well, do whatever you want, sweetheart.' Jane dropped her cigarette into the sink, where it hissed. My mother left the room, saying that would be lovely.

Jane pulled one of her faces. She poured herself a gin, and didn't bother with ice.

It was a slashing wet afternoon, the day my friend walked home with me. Our journey took longer than it could have done, because we did not stand on any cracks, at my insistence. When we arrived it was almost dark. I opened the unlocked door, which you had to push hard, and told my friend where to put her wet shoes, underneath the storage heater, against the wall in the kitchen. It was where my mother put hers.

We heard Jane typing before she heard us arrive, but when she saw us through the stained glass of the living-room door, she waved and smiled and stood up. She arrived in the kitchen to offer us coffee or tea, which was not what she and I had arranged. She was meant to ask if we wanted Ribena.

'I'm planning a cake,' she said. 'With icing.'

This was welcome news. Jane's cakes could look impressive.

'Now you run along and play something upstairs,' Jane said. 'I'm on the last page of a letter and my ribbon's running out, so there'll be no secretarial work today.'

My friend looked confused. She was holding a blue patent-leather bag, which she'd been concerned should not get wet coming home. She clung to this as I moved to the stairs at the back of the kitchen, then up towards my room, which was the first on the right at the top. I explained as she trudged neatly behind me that my aunt let Gillian and me write letters on her typewriter. These would generally be explanations as to why her poems should be printed, which she dictated as she smoked. Or sometimes invitations to parties in faraway places, to wild celebrations of fantastic achievement, which sometimes were in my honour.

'Who's Gillian?'

'Oh, just one of my friends, who goes to a different school. She has a baby brother.'

I left a few moments for this enviable fact to settle, before opening the door to my bedroom, with its pink curtains that I'd begged Jane and my mother to make. One of them didn't pull properly, but there was no reason to know that unless it was night-time. My friend sat on my bed and opened her bag. I watched with a certain apprehension, but all she produced were two lengths of spotted seersucker ribbon and a large yellow plastic hairbrush.

'Shall I do yours first, or you do mine?' Her soft face

42

looked eagerly at my plaits, which I let her unravel as I sat on my bedroom stool.

'Who does it for you in the mornings?' she asked.

I told her my mother, but not that we often left the plaits in overnight, to save time at breakfast.

'Is that other lady your aunt?'

I nodded as well as I could, while having my hair dragged back.

'She talks a bit funny, doesn't she?'

I'd never thought about Jane's voice. She spoke like my mother, but coughed less often.

'She's from London,' I said.

'Gosh,' she said. 'Do you want to do mine now?'

Hers was long and blond and loose, except for a wide velvet clasp, which she undid gravely before she sat down. I'd never brushed anyone's hair before. It was strangely pleasurable.

'Where were you born, Ruth?'

I carried on brushing, lifting slippery strands upwards from underneath, to begin again at the feathery place which was the nape of her neck.

'Wales,' I said, because it sounded exotic. Jane had been there with her friend, Diane. They'd walked round castle walls and camped in a field, from which you could walk to dunes and a beach. They were going to take me, next time.

'My dad comes from Wales,' my friend said. 'My uncle lives there. Does yours?'

I said I wished my hair was blond. She shook her

43

head, which made brushing hard. She insisted my black was nicer.

'Does your mother have black hair?' she asked.

I suddenly wished she did. And long black lashes too, like Elizabeth Taylor.

'Yes. She can sit on it, if she wants to.'

I moved quickly on from this lie, to ask if she wanted to look at my ribbons. They were in an old cigar box Jane found in London, which was slithering and full and always warm.

'You've got a lot of red ones,' she said, wrapping one around her wrist. I was obviously supposed to offer her one to keep, and was glad that Jane called up. She was going to post a letter, and had to buy eggs for our cake. She warned us not to adjust the fire downstairs, nor to open any windows.

'Be good,' she called up.

'We will,' I called back.

'Yes, we will,' my friend echoed. She looked more pink than before, and moved around faster, after we'd heard the front door slam. She lifted my dressing gown from the end of my bed and moved it up to the pillow. She sat down where it had been, then moved to stand near the window, fingering the curvy lever that held it shut. I went to stand beside her. I was taller than she was. She smiled, and shrugged in a studied way.

'Do you want some Ribena?' I said. 'With ice?'

She was at the door of the room before I was, and then almost running downstairs. As I found glasses, she went through to Jane's desk, where I heard type-writer noises.

'Don't do that,' I said.

She stopped and stared down at some of Jane's papers. 'Funny writing,' she said. 'Can you read it?'

'It's poetry,' I told her.

She wrinkled her nose and sat on Jane's swivel chair, where she pushed herself round with her feet stabbing the carpet. She laughed. The fire made a noise as a log burned through and re-positioned itself. Jane had put the guard in front of it.

'Where does she sleep?' my friend asked then, not stopping her roundabout movement, but slowing to hold my gaze as she moved.

'Who?'

There was a painting on the wall of an old lady, in pale pink, with a young man beside her. He looked unhappy. His shoes were different shades of brown.

'Your aunt.'

'In her bedroom,' I said. 'Don't you want your Ribena?'

'Upstairs?'

I nodded. Everyone slept upstairs. Jane's dressing table was covered with paperclips and biros that leaked. None of her lipsticks had lids on, and the bed would be unmade, and perhaps scattered with biscuit packs.

'You know what I'd like, Ruth?'

I'd tell her we weren't allowed in Jane's room.

'I'd like to play hide and seek.'

'Aren't you thirsty?'

'Your bow's undone.'

She pulled me to sit with my chin down against my blouse, which itched as she tugged my ribbon into shape, dragging the hairs at my nape.

'You count,' she said. 'And I'll hide. Count twenty-five, not twenty.'

She ran and slammed the door behind her. I strained between numbers to hear if Jane's key would turn in the lock. 'Sixteen, seventeen, eighteen, nineteen.' A car engine stalled in the High Street, and would not start again. 'Twenty, twenty-one, twenty-two.' It couldn't be long. Unless there were no eggs in the shop and Jane'd gone to borrow some from the pub. 'Twenty-three, twenty-four, twenty-five.' There was silence except for the sudden screech of a gull, then another one, more violent, but further away.

'Coming,' I called, not moving from the couch. I didn't want to find her, but went through the motions of peering round the sitting room. I passed slowly through the kitchen, where there was nowhere to hide except under the table, then I went to my mother's room, where the fur coat hung on the door of the wardrobe, and the bed was made, with its faded paisley throw, and the shoes were in pairs beside the wall. There was no feeling of another breath there. The Eau de Cologne was on the dark chest of drawers, next to the eyebrow pencil in its saucer, and the lipstick with its gold moulded top, beside the jar of face-cream that I'd often unscrewed. I looked underneath the bed, but knew it would be nothing but musty space.

The door of Jane's room was closed. I opened it and knew right away that my friend was behind the curtains, whose lining was torn. The window was open, and the window box wet. The sheets were crumpled and there was an ashtray on the bedside table. It would be full of long pink-rimmed cigarette stubs, and sweet-wrappers, and pencil shavings too. Newspapers covered the chair to my left, and books with torn paper between their pages were stacked on a footstool. There was a bra on the floor. I walked out and shut the door behind me, and went into my own tidy room.

'I know you're in here,' I called. My voice was apprehensive. 'I know you're here somewhere.'

I looked under the bed. I opened my wardrobe and pressed the hanging clothes there, as if to discover a body.

'I'm he-e-e-re.' Her distant laugh was triumphant. 'I'm in here and you didn't find me.'

I sat on my bed, beside my ribbon box. I pulled a narrow tartan one out. I didn't have to move now. She'd won. I'd hide downstairs, for my turn, then Jane would come back and we could help with the cake.

'Ruth, come and get me. Come and find me, Ruth.'

I stayed where I was. I called out that I was giving up. I said it was her turn now to go downstairs and count.

'No, you come here. We start from where the last person was. You've got to start here, with me.'

She wasn't hiding any more, when I got back to Jane's room. She was stretched on her back, on the floor. Her hands were behind her smiling head. A pair of tights straggled from under her legs.

'It's not very pretty,' she said. 'Does she like this colour?'

The room was dark green. My mother said it was gloomy, but it looked nice at night with the bedside lamp on, when Jane and I played her rhyming game. Jane smelled nice in pyjamas.

'Does she have perfume?'

My friend stood up carefully and smoothed her skirt, before moving to consider Jane's messy chest of drawers, with its oval mirror that was jammed at an angle with newspaper and had photographs propped at the base. There was a photo of me as a small girl, holding a large stone on the beach. A picture of a boy on a horse. A photograph of Jane and my mother, both frowning, both holding kittens.

'Is there any nail varnish?'

I shook my head. 'Jane can't wear it. She's allergic.'

My friend picked up a dried block of mascara.

'Shall we go downstairs? I'd like some juice.' I wanted her to see me get the ice out of the fridge. I was good at getting ice into glasses.

'Who's that?' she said. She was looking at a postcard pinned to the wall. It was a slightly overweight man sitting at a typewriter with a white shirt and a beard. There was a packet of cigarettes on his desk.

'My dad,' I said.

She tiptoed then to look closely. She wrinkled her nose, and turned to me with a twisted mouth. She said he looked like a grandpa. I looked away, to the geraniums in the window box. They were brown at the edges and very wet. I looked at books sliding at the end of Jane's bed, and on the floor and underneath rumpled piles of clothes. The book nearest my foot was by Pablo Neruda: *Residence on Earth*.

'Does he live here?'

'Who?'

'Your dad.'

'Of course he does.'

The door downstairs banged.

'What does he do?'

'He's a policeman.'

Her eyes widened. 'Gosh,' she said.

'I'm home, you two,' Jane's smoky voice called up. 'Hello. Did anything happen?'

We looked at each other. My friend stopped chewing her hair and pushed it back. Her shoulders were square, in her navy blue. Her lips were full and moist in her confident plump pink cheeks.

'I'm home.' Jane sounded further away. 'Come and see what I got. The cake will be miraculous.'

I didn't want to move, but the girl was out of the room and banging down the threadbare stairs to the kitchen, where I arrived behind her to stare at the giant chocolate bar that Jane had put flat on the table.

'We're going to melt it,' she was saying, as my heart banged in my chest. 'We're going to swathe the whole thing in sweet dark oozing sludge. Can you imagine that?'

Jane sat down in front of her mixing bowl. She broke an egg in, and beat it round fast with a wooden spoon. She did the same thing with a second egg, then asked me to pass her the flour. The cupboard handle seemed freezing, and the packet of flour enormous. My aunt lifted the sieve and started to shake flour down into her bowl. Usually I would be helping with this bit. I liked the patterns the talcum-powdery flour made. I would imagine wedding dresses taking shape as the mixture momentarily patterned, or the veils of sad and wintry brides. But on the day of my school-friend's visit, I had more urgent thoughts to sort in my mind. I had to get her out of the house.

I sat down suddenly on a hard chair and put my head on my arms on the table, like we had to in school if we had a headache.

'Ruth. What's wrong?'

I felt Jane's hand on the top of my head. I left it a while before I looked up.

'What is it, Ruth? Don't you feel well, sweetheart?'

I looked up then at her large soft eyes and felt I was going to cry. She bent close to my face, and smoothed my hair. 'Dearie me,' she said. 'You look terribly pale.'

I couldn't bear the long silence and the staring, so I pushed her arm away and ran. I ran as fast as I could upstairs to the bathroom and slammed the door and locked it behind me. I sat on the edge of the bath, and rested my elbows on my knees. I couldn't move or speak as Jane arrived to knock on the door and say my name. I thought of the name Pablo Neruda. I said it under my breath, and was able to focus on the tiles of the floor, with the green ones smaller than the white and the crack underneath the towel-rail where water collected and my mother got cross.

'Ruth, can you open the door? What is it, Ruth? Let me in now to see.'

I opened the door to see her face, intense and gentle and not unconcerned.

'Can you make her go? I don't want her here.'

She touched my cheek. She kissed it. She nodded. 'Of course I can, sweetheart.' She looked more relaxed. 'I'll take her home now. You drink some cold water.'

I tried to say thank you, but it came out a whisper, so she whispered 'That's OK' back.

'And Jane –' The words were not much louder, but she turned and heard as I went on, 'I don't want her to know.'

She smiled. 'I don't either,' she said.

When I'd heard the door slam, I had a drink of water from the plastic cup next to the sink, then I left the cool shapes of the bathroom and went and looked at the picture of the man in Jane's room. He must be somebody's father, I decided, as I went back to my room and saw that my ribbon box had been closed and was back on the shelf. I looked at myself without plaits in the mirror, and was pleased with my pallor and smooth dark hair. I was glad my eyes were blue, like my mother's.

When the front door slammed again, only one person came through it, so I went downstairs to see Jane taking her coat off. She readjusted her belt, and lit a cigarette. I knew she wasn't cross by the way she smiled when she saw me.

'Feeling better?'

I nodded.

'So what went wrong?'

'She asked who that man in your bedroom is, Jane.'

She raised her eyebrows. She smoked, with her head on one side. 'Now which man would that be? Did he speak at all?'

She poured cake mixture into a tin with her free hand. Together we watched the liquid ripple slowly into itself.

'Want to taste?' she said.

I dipped my finger and licked it.

'Nice?' she said, and I nodded.

'Want to get my ice out?' She slid the battered tin into the oven, and pushed the door shut with her hip.

'He's got a beard and a typewriter.'

She licked the back of her hand, then wiped it on her trousers. She lifted the gin from the cupboard it lived in, and frowned at the amount in the bottle, wrinkling her nose.

'It's a photo, on your wall by the mirror, quite high.'

Her face relaxed, and she smiled and moved again to lift a glass from a shelf. 'Oh that. That's Ernest Hemingway. That's Papa, my sweet. He's dead.'

She poured herself a drink, sat down with her feet

on a chair and asked what had been said about him exactly. She patted the seat to her left. She lit another cigarette.

'She thought he must be my dad.'

Jane spat her drink down her nose in a snorting noise. She put her hand flat against her face and she laughed, high and loud, in a way she rarely did at home.

'If only,' she said, when she'd sniffed for a while. 'But unfortunately not.'

She drank for a moment, then looked at me, her eyes blinking and soft. 'What a curious friend,' she decided at last. 'I'm glad she's not here to eat my cake.'

She poured more tonic into her glass. She squeezed a lemon into the mix, and I watched a pip sink before I told Jane I'd like to know more about my father, if I could.

'Well you must ask Stell, sweetheart.' She moved to the window and opened it. The wind came in and was cold. *'To ask the hard question is simple,'* she said. 'That's Auden. You must get to know him.'

She puffed contentedly and waved smoke away from her face, as I asked if he was nice.

'He's dead, sweetheart.' She went to the fridge and got carrots out. 'But you can know dead poets better than live ones.'

She rooted in the vegetable basket and found potatoes, sprouting spindly limbs in peculiar gestures. We peeled them together until my mother came home, when Jane told her we'd all had a lovely time, but that our guest had felt ill and had to leave. My mother frowned. There was a gastric flu going round, and she hoped I hadn't caught it. She felt my forehead, seemed reassured, and asked questions about the afternoon, which Jane answered for me if I looked at her hard. I said I was tired, and it was true. Too tired to ask any questions. Too tired for a bath, which my mother understood.

'Making new friends is tiring,' she said.

I heard them talking downstairs for a long time that night. They laughed more than normal. My school-friend who didn't quite stay to tea had made them cheerful, it seemed, for a while, at least.

3

By the late May of 1998 I'd started to spend time with some twentieth-century poets. I chose those I wrote about randomly, and was attempting Fernando Pessoa one Tuesday afternoon. He wrote under four different names, which made him hard to explain in eight hundred words. 'His love life was inhibited. The few friends he had committed suicide or went mad.'

In the reflection of windows on the other side of the street, I watched a neighbour on my side brushing his path. I listened to hard and steady strokes of bristle on concrete, and the sound of an aeroplane leaving the country. Pessoa lived in Lisbon, but often wrote in English. A woman on a bicycle arrived to visit the house on the corner with the very high hedge that Liam said was haunted.

'To be a poet is no ambition ofmine.
It is my way ofstaying alone.'

My doorbell rang, then rang again sharply. I went down to find Liam's mother, Colette, looking flushed and rather regal. Her steel-grey hair was in delicate

55

hollow rolls from ear to ear. Her hairdresser was round the corner from me.

'Ruth. Thank goodness. I'm cold.'

She and her walking stick moved into my hallway, trailing wafts of citrus shampoo and stale cigarettes.

'Can you give me a coffee? I'm on my way to the Askew Road house, but I had to warm up.'

She was halfway up the stairs.

'I've bought it now. Exhausting. I think Fiona might live there. She'll pay rent, at least. Not like Liam in Milson Road.'

'Tell me about it upstairs,' I shouted to her back. She found it hard enough to keep breathing as she negotiated the gradient, without making conversation. I shuffled through estate agents' leaflets, offers of help with ironing, minicab cards and pizza flyers to find an unwelcome letter from my bank, then followed Colette's three-legged shape into my kitchen.

'I was saying I don't want it to be like Milson Road all over again. Are your ears all right, Ruth? You can get them syringed, you know.'

I lit the gas fire and moved a chair near it, relieved that she was wearing trousers. She'd once set a skirt on fire, sitting too close to the heat there one cold autumn night. I filled the kettle with a heavy heart. Milson Road was where Liam had been living when we were first involved. His mother owned the house, and had a habit of arriving on Saturday mornings to sit in the garden there, which she'd bring small shrubs into but forget to plant. Colette had seemed to want to know

56

me, which I found flattering until I realized it was because she used to know my mother, from their time together at Oxford. After I'd discovered that, I avoided weekends in Milson Road, but there were things of mine left there when Liam moved out, so Colette took to visiting me with teapots and shoes or forgotten old blouses. Since she'd started using a walking stick, I'd found it harder to say I was busy.

I washed mugs and realized I'd run out of sugar. I told Colette this fact and she made a face. Then looked around the kitchen as if she might be considering buying my home, as well.

'Is there milk, at least?' She sank her head into her tartan jacket, affecting her defeated pose. 'Or shall we go out? I feel so weak.'

The kettle boiled energetically. I opened the window as she lit her first cigarette. Smoke drifted towards my paper lampshade. She pulled her jacket around narrow stooped shoulders, dropping her lighted Silk Cut momentarily on to her knees.

'Well as long as it's warm, I suppose. How was Hastings?'

'Fine.'

I'd already decided not to mention the unknown man and his temporary occupation of the house there. She'd think it was all my fault, as Liam had done, and that the watch that had disappeared must be claimed for on the house insurance. The watch had been in Liam's bedside drawer ever since I'd known him. It wasn't broken, but he didn't wear it. It had belonged to his father, and Fiona said it would be best not to tell Colette that it had been stolen.

'Is Liam surviving?'

'Seems to be. Fiona and Frank were there too.'

She didn't seem to like that. 'I thought they weren't getting on.'

'Who?'

'Fiona and Frank.'

'They just got married.'

'I know.' Her tone was determined. 'But why rush and do that, in secret, if everything was fine? Frank is a waste of time. I hope Fiona will see sense and live in my new house.'

Frank and Fiona had lived together for longer than I had known Liam.

'I think they like it in Barnes. They've got all that space. For Fiona's pots and everything.'

Fiona made ceramic figures for exhibitions and shop windows, and private clients sometimes, too. I thought of them as pots, which Liam advised me not to say out loud.

'Ruth, you've got to start living in the real world. They're paying rent. I don't know what he does exactly. Though I've heard he does a good impression of me.'

I'd never seen it, and told her so. 'I hardly know him.'

'Well, you know enough people, Ruth. Everyone I know is dead. That's the trouble with living. There comes a time when you haven't any old friends left.'

She took the coffee I handed her and put it on the floor, sloshing most of it on to my carpet. I didn't have to pretend I hadn't noticed, because she was unaware of the mess. I sat down at the table, with my black tea. Liam was always spilling things too. Liam ought to have rung me up. My tea was too hot, and the chair too high. I couldn't think of anything to say, but wasn't really trying.

'To think is uncomfortable, like walking in the rain.'

'Anyway. My new house.' Colette lit another Silk Cut. 'Have I told you all about it yet?'

'Don't think so.' I'd be hearing again, whether she had or not.

'Well, it's a little house on the Askew Road. Small rooms, but a good bathroom and an attic that's almost converted.' She squinted at me through smoke. 'And this will interest you, Ruth.' She coughed. She blew her nose on a paper handkerchief that shredded as she pushed it back in her pocket. 'The house used to belong to Diane.'

She knocked ash almost into the ashtray and waited for me to react.

'I haven't told you that already, have I? It's where Diane was living, before she died.'

I wished I smoked then too. I needed something to do while my amazement waned.

Diane had been my aunt Jane's closest friend. I knew she was dead. She'd had a heart attack. Her son, Gray, whose real name was Graham, had written to me to let me know. He'd told me when the funeral was, but I

59

didn't go. I'd said I was sick, which I wasn't. I didn't want to see Diane's coffin, or the people who gathered to crowd it away.

Without Diane, my childhood would have been different. More ordinary, I used to think. Certainly more peaceful, on the frequent evenings her calls to Jane came from London and subsequent arguments raged through the house or made its silences squeak. Without Diane as a friend, Jane may not have visited London, and I wouldn't have encountered the city as early as I did, and wouldn't have felt so out of place, either there or at home by the sea. I wouldn't have known Gray, or any of the large London houses that held Diane's companions and their noisy fun.

Without Diane, Jane's poems would not be what they were. Many of them were about or for her, though never explicitly so. Without Diane, Jane wouldn't have been the person I knew. And now Colette had bought her house.

'Yes, it's Diane's old place.'

Colette wasn't looking at me, but inspecting her rings.

'Though I don't think I knew that when I bought it. I mean Diane and I weren't exactly friends, as I suppose you know? I did what I could in the old days, of course, to help my friends, when I was specifically asked.' She smoked for a moment, and gave me a careful look. 'You tend not to enjoy women who seduce your fiancé, Ruth.'

I'd heard about Diane 'seducing' a man who was

once engaged to Colette. It was an anecdote my aunt and even my mother enjoyed, on the rare occasions they discussed their past, when they'd all been at Oxford, with all the young men arrived back from the war. The story was that Colette got engaged to one of these creatures, who then decided he'd rather marry Diane. But Diane didn't actually know this mercurial person. She'd never even met him. He saw a photograph of her in Jane's room, and decided on the strength of that to cancel all other engagements. As a seduction, it was impressive. And quite believable too, if you'd ever met Diane.

Colette was smoking again, reflectively.

'Betrayal hurts when you're young, Ruth. At least it did in my day. As I've often told Liam, and Fiona too, commitment is very important.'

I forbore to mention that her daughter's commitment to Frank didn't seem to mean much to her. I'd long since learnt not to pursue what Pessoa called 'melody of thought' with Colette. She was too keen on calling the tunes. I asked if her coffee was OK, and wondered how long she was planning on staying. I was due to collect Conor in less than an hour. I wanted to finish Pessoa this afternoon and move on to Neruda.

'Oh, coffee. I never like coffee any more unless it's in the place near me. Although that Shepherd's Bush Road café isn't too bad. Except they give you too much. Like soup. Is it Tuesday today?'

It was, and I told her so.

'I've got a patient at three. I'll give up on the house

for today, I think. Perhaps you might call me a cab?'

I got up, but was asked to sit down.

'Not this minute, Ruth. These people are never on time.'

Liam's mother was a doctor, like mine had been, and saw patients privately now she'd retired. She was supposed to be a brilliant diagnostician. She certainly knew Clare needed more than an osteopath when she'd met her on my stairs, some months before. 'That girl should have a scan,' she'd said. 'And sooner rather than later.'

I never asked Colette's opinion of any symptoms I had. She may decide I should be on a critical list myself. 'We've all got to die of something' was one of her favourite pronouncements.

She lit another cigarette. She inhaled and looked at her feet in their scuffed red boots. She was one of those people who's been wealthy for too long to notice that they've started to look destitute. That their expensive clothes should be replaced. Or washed, at least.

'And now I've got Diane's house. I wonder why I bought it.'

'You must like it, I suppose.'

She didn't need it, that was for sure.

'Well, I think I do.' She pushed her glasses up into the pale fine creases at the top of her nose. 'But what I wanted to discuss with you, Ruth, why I came today I think, was to tell you the attic is still full of things. Things of Diane's, from what I can see.'

I stood up, but there was nowhere to go. The other chair was stacked with unread newspapers and things I'd printed about poets from the Internet. The accumulation of information was satisfying, at this stage. When Pessoa died they found a trunk with twenty-five thousand items in it: fragments and poems and journals and letters. He didn't leave much else.

'*To have is to delay.*'

If Diane's possessions were anyone's now, they must be Gray's. But he didn't like things. Or used not to. I hadn't seen him lately, to ask.

'What sort of things?'

'Well.' She inhaled robustly. She scratched her stately head. 'Well, the papers there, I suppose, would interest you most.'

I swallowed some tea-leaves, which caught in my throat. Colette waited while I choked.

'I mean there's so much for me to deal with. But the papers might be worth saving. I think Jane may want you to have some.' She stubbed her cigarette. 'What do you think?'

'Why?' It was the first word that came into my head. I'd got crates of Jane's papers already, since the Norfolk house was re-let and I'd had to clear the third bedroom. Piles of notebooks covered with her sturdy handwriting were now in my attic, where they languished, unread, alongside the collected contents of my mother's bedroom desk. Since both women had been careful not to allow their intimate lives to mingle when they shared a house, I enjoyed the notion of them maybe cross-fertilizing in the silence of my dark upstairs. But I had no urge to sort through the boxes; to read first drafts of Jane's old poems, or rambling descriptions of what my mother had seen at the seaside on her regular afternoon walks.

My mother loved to walk by the sea, and liked to record what was happening there, in small notebooks she kept in the glove compartment of her car. There were pages full of observations in the Morris Minor she crashed in the frozen-fog twilight of the November afternoon that she died. She smelled of the sea when I got to Norwich General. You wouldn't have known she'd been in an accident. Her thick hair was salty and gusted. They'd put her in a hospital robe with sprigs of washed-out roses all over it, but her short fingers were sticky and the nails clogged with sand. She must have been gathering seaweed. The boot of her crumpled car was full of the stuff, pale brown and still wet in flat semi-transparent ribbons, or darker and budded with swollen pockets of air that she'd taught me to enjoy squeezing until they popped. She collected seaweed on any and every beach. She thought it was good for the garden, although it generally stayed in the yard in collapsing bin-liners, steaming the air with a greeny smell, which pressed into my bedroom's open window on warm summer evenings.

I complained that it smelled like the shower-block on the campsite Jane and I had been to in North Wales. Diane had come too, and she and my aunt stayed in a room above the showers. I used to untie the flaps of my low insect-skimmed tent in the early hours, getting pyjama legs wet with dew and fat blades of grass between my toes, as I made my way through shadows and deeply ridged bark to find my way to the grown-ups.

Jane and Diane would be deeply asleep in the enormous bed of their shared room. I had to negotiate their strewn clothes and books and scattered footwear, with heels that stuck into my feet, as I tiptoed across to arrive at soft-smelling Jane, who slept on the outside, luckily. Diane would be curled up, close to the wall. By the time I woke up, she would have gone for a swim, leaving Jane and myself to snuggle together, as light moved to shine in our faces as we talked about Jane's dreams, which always included me, in the telling, though I knew they didn't really. When Diane arrived back with cups of tea and wet hair, we'd spend a long time deciding what to do next. Diane would want to walk or drive or hire bicycles or fishing rods, which Jane protested would be exhausting, but would not refuse. Diane liked moving, more than talking, when she was on holiday. In London she talked and moved quickly at the same time, all the time.

'Ruth? Are you listening? What do you think?'

'Sorry?'

'The papers, Ruth. In my new house. Don't you want them?'

'Well, Jane's left so much here already.'

Liam's mother looked puzzled. There wasn't anything of value in my kitchen. Though some of the rent from the house in Norfolk now paid for these rooms in London. And I had all Jane's books upstairs, of course. Lately these arrived in soft packages with a Boston postmark, with newspaper cuttings instead of the card she used to send asking where I was going and what I was doing and how I was. I told myself I hadn't replied to these because she never wrote her address on them. I was cross, though – or more than cross – that she'd gone to America three days after my mother's funeral and left me to organize myself, with what felt like no relatives left on the planet. Her last collection was dedicated to my mother. *For Stell*, it said, *with love*. I put it on the shelf with my others. Liam used to read them, though he didn't any more.

'Well, I've got more signed first editions of Jane's than I need, as it is.'

Colette snorted. 'Diane wouldn't have begrudged you those, my dear.'

I couldn't imagine Diane begrudging me anything of Jane's. She was a generous woman, so far as material things went. She gave presents, for no reason, most times I saw her. She gave me my first camera. My first transistor radio. My first dress that stood up by itself. She used to tell Jane we must indulge these whimsical gifts – she had no daughter, she'd say, and couldn't resist. There was once a walkie-talkie doll waiting for me in her Highgate house, which made a bleating noise and marched a few steps. Its insides lurched heavily if you turned it upside down, which alarmed me, so I left it hidden in the room next to the bathroom

66

when Jane and I went home. I hoped Diane never discovered it, because she meant to be kind, I assumed.
She always suggested I go in the front of the car with
Jane, when we were together. I got carsick in the back.
She was always asking if I was all right – which no one
else did much. Always taking her coat off for me to
wear on top of my own if we went for walks when I
was small. Her coats smelled of perfume which was
connected for me with the heavy cream blossom on
wet chestnut trees, probably because I only saw those
when we went to stay with her. I didn't actually like
wearing Diane's coats on top of my own, because I
couldn't walk in them. Jane once said I should borrow
something of Gray's, but Diane said I couldn't, which
pleased me. I think she knew, as Jane seemed not to,
that to wear a boy's things would be worse than
tripping over. And I was sure, in some mysterious way,
that Gray would know I had worn his coat and would
sneer if I ever met him, which I supposed I one day
would. Though he went to boarding school, and spent
holidays with his father, he was Diane's son, and she
wanted me to meet him, which probably meant I must.

I liked the notion of Diane without a son best, when
I was young, and my mother seemed to as well. Not
that my mother was ever around if Diane was. She'd
go and stay with friends when Diane came, which she
rarely did. I once cried when my mother was about
to leave, and she stayed until after I'd gone to bed to
cheer me up. Jane and Diane went out to a pub.

'But you might have to learn to like people more,

Ruthie,' my mother had said as she stroked my head in my room, which she only came into before I went to sleep, or if I was sick. She had a smoother smell than Diane or Jane, which I associated with her surgery and with my curtains being pulled with a rattling noise and with pillows and sheets and being persuaded to sleep.

'How can you expect people to like you, if you don't like them, sweetheart?'

'I don't like Gray.' It was the first and last time I ever said anything directly about him to her, and I felt bad straight away and hoped she wouldn't ask me why, which I would find hard to answer, since we'd never met. She was silent for a while and then told me that everyone has something nice about them, if you look for it hard enough. She said that about any friend I quarrelled with. Sometimes she said it when Jane was there and Jane would imitate her in a high voice and tell her not to be sentimental.

'Don't be disingenuous, Stell,' my aunt would say. 'Most people are worse than you imagine they'll be, once you get to know them. Which is why I don't bother with people much, Ruth. Books are nicer. Especially books by people who've been dead for some time.'

There would follow one of the silences that I quite enjoyed, since it wasn't about me any more. And I liked to hear Jane say you didn't have to like everyone. I didn't see how you could.

Now Liam's mother was staring, with something like

intensity. 'So what do you think, Ruth? I'd like to get this sorted out. The whole thing is exhausting me.'

'Sorry? I don't quite understand.'

She stubbed her cigarette. She did it violently, like Jane used to sometimes, after Diane's calls from London.

'The papers, Ruth. In Diane's. In my house. Do you want them?'

I didn't think I did. Thinking about Diane made me surprisingly tired.

'I have to say that I think Jane might like to think of them going to a good home for now.'

I couldn't see that Jane would care either way what happened to someone else's old bank statements and gas bills, but I didn't want to discuss my aunt just now. Liam's mother didn't seem to like her. The idea of her, at any rate.

'But won't Gray want them? Have you been in touch with him?'

'No, I have not. His mother's solicitors are dealing with everything, which doesn't surprise me. Gray couldn't cope with selling a house. I lent that boy a hundred pounds in 1982, and didn't hear from him again until July in 1987, when he phoned to ask if I could lend him some more. I'm not a bank, Ruth.'

'No.'

'And how's the literature book coming along? Liam told me you've started. I don't understand why he's not involved. He could be making money, for a change.'

69

'He's busy. And anyway, it doesn't pay very well.'

That was a silly thing to say. It might lead to having to explain what Liam was busy with, which I wasn't entirely sure of.

'Anyway, it's coming along. I'm doing Fernando Pessoa today.'

She raised her eyebrows. I told her he died of cirrhosis of the liver.

'I'm sure he did.' She looked at her watch. She was fond of gin, which she drank neat, with a sliver of lime and great chunks of ice, which she bought in bags which jammed her freezer's door. 'I'm surprised Diane didn't go that way too. But hearts run in her family. Her father collapsed stepping out of a taxi, coming to see her just before finals. She blamed her third on the grief.' Colette sighed. 'But these things run in families. Like strokes run in yours, Ruth.'

Since my mother had died in a car and Jane was still alive, this generalization seemed reckless.

Colette stretched her head now, moving it gingerly from left to right as if she'd been in an accident herself.

'Well, Ruth, I'm sorry you're not interested in all those lovely letters. I thought you'd be so pleased.'

I sat up in my chair. Colette looked at my fridge.

'Not that anyone would be interested in publishing Jane's prose at this stage – even if she gave her permission.'

She seemed to be almost about to move from her chair. The neighbour's wisteria was thriving. Great stringy handfuls of pushy green cord were making their way into the cracks between my kitchen window-frame and the wall.

'So anyway, Ruth. The house. I'll have to get a skip, I suppose. Is that terribly vulgar of me?'

'Don't think so.'

Not as vulgar as owning three houses, I thought. I wondered why she hadn't bought one for Liam yet. She generally seemed slightly offended that he'd bought one for himself, although it had been a good investment. But Colette didn't seem to like her children making good; liked perhaps to think that Liam had done the opposite, by getting involved with me.

'Well, Ruth. You don't seem to be able to make up your mind. As Liam says, you could prevaricate for England.'

She pushed her sculpted hair around her head, looking dissatisfied. Then went on to say that she had thought I might be grateful for the offer of some fragments of the past.

' "These fragments have I shored against my ruins",' she misquoted, smiling brightly at me. 'David adored "The Waste Land", before he got involved with Diane, of course. Is Eliot in your book?'

'Suppose so. Everybody has to be.'

'But not your aunt Jane, presumably?'

'Probably not. But I think I would like the letters, Colette. I mean, I might as well keep whatever there is, until someone decides they want it. If anyone ever does.'

She sniffed. Said that was unlikely, but was a

generous thought. I must mull it over and let her know, she decided. But now I must call her a cab.

After she'd left, in a flurry of banknotes and rhetorical questions about lost boxes of matches, the house seemed larger and more silent than it had before she arrived. I washed cups, wiped surfaces, retied my hair, then went into my study and dialled Colette's number. She wouldn't be back yet, but I wanted to tell her that I would like to have Diane's papers. The message I left sounded oddly strained and inconclusive, because I'd been wary of sounding too keen. I ought to leave another, but that would seem demanding. I moved to sit at my desk, with no particular thoughts of what to do next. My head was empty except for a vague anticipation, then a sudden memory of Diane's voice, calling down the stairs from a landing about twenty-five years before. She was calling for Jane, who was in a room with me, looking out at rain from a high bay window. The walls of the room were papered. Between Jane and myself was a chair that had a wooden back with birds engraved in it. I drew it as part of my art O-level project. I drew it twice: first empty, and then with Gray sitting in it, wearing a shirt with birds flying across the front and holding a vase of crocuses. The vase was his idea, and my art teacher loved it.

I sat on my red swivel chair and stared at the screen-saver. It was a picture of a car screeching into a dark city-scape, its tail-lights like rockets, from left to right. Conor had installed it a few weeks before. I blew crumbs from my keyboard and thought of Jane's high typewriter on its desk in front of the windows in the room at home, where'd she sat on her own swivel chair, with its arm-rests and its torn seat. I thought of the noise of Jane typing late at night, which stopped when my mother went down to join her, to be replaced by talking or shouting or laughter, before my mother went up to the bathroom, when I'd hear water, and doors and windows closing, and then Jane typing again.

When Jane wrote letters, she typed very fast, and dragged them from the matt-black roller to cram into envelopes and rush to the post. Letters to London gave Jane's face a different look than her poems did. Those were typed slowly, and were often removed to be marked with pencil, then biro, then Tipp-Ex, and then more small black words on top. I didn't feel like working any more. I lifted a printed page at random from my desk and read something familiar:

'And so, to amuse our minds
Round again to the start
On its circular railway winds
That toy train called the heart.'

I rang Colette's number again, but didn't leave another message. She probably wouldn't answer the phone again today. She rarely heard it ring.

I typed slowly, as I wrote to Liam's mother that afternoon. Jane's letters to Diane began with the words 'Darling Di'. I knew that because I'd seen the tops of them sometimes, if I walked near her, until she noticed and said, 'We don't read other people's writing unless they ask us to, Ruthie.'

I'd blush then and wish my mother was home. She didn't care if I read what she wrote. My note to Colette said I'd be very pleased to have any papers that Diane had left in her attic. I could collect them any time that suited. It had been nice to see her, I said, and I hoped her patient had found her at home. Not being in the habit of writing to Liam's mother, I prevaricated over the closing regards. *Best wishes, Ruth*, I decided at last. That's what Jane used to write in letters to school, explaining why I'd been absent, or late. I had no idea how she ended letters to Diane, on the typewriter underneath my bedroom, where my mother stroked my head and told me to like people more than I did.

As I walked to the postbox, on the way to collect Conor, I wondered if Liam knew whose house his mother had bought. I thought he would not. I also had a feeling that he wouldn't approve of my reading my aunt's letters to someone in faraway days. I decided I wouldn't tell him, unless he asked. There was no need to tell anyone, really, whatever I did with the papers I may still not be allowed to have. It was all in Colette's hands now. And it had been her idea, not mine, in the first place.

4

I could have spent days reading stray letters from torn envelopes in the water-marked suitcase that Colette left on my doorstep, exactly a week after her visit to me. There were dozens of letters addressed to Diane; dozens of dozens, though not all from Jane. Even Jane couldn't have written so many letters, unless she'd done nothing but that for a couple of years. Diane seemed to have kept everything that came through her door, ever, though in no particular order. Pages explaining how things were in Norfolk, when I was three and my mother was absent or ill, were mingled with crumpled descriptions of my teenage years, and poems Jane was working on, which slid out from Diane's old telephone bills and mis-spelt notes from Gray at boarding school.

My fingers were grubby with dust and ink by the time I'd finished the odd pages I read on the first day I got them, but I didn't stop reading because of that. I stopped because the phone rang and it was the man I was writing about poetry for, asking how it was coming along. He was one of those people who says your name a lot, as if your attention might be wandering as he talks.

'So how's progress, Ruth?'

'Fine. Just about to start on some more of the Russians.'

I said that randomly, skimming the list of poets I had and seeing the name of Osip Mandelstam, about whom I knew nothing except that he was a Russian and lived through the Revolution.

'Ah, so that's where you're up to. Great stuff. Anything ready for send-off today?'

'Did you get the War Poets attachment last night?'

He said he had indeed, and that it was tremendous, which I doubted.

'OK, Ruth. Well, I'll let you get on. Good luck with the Russians. Let's talk again soon.'

We said goodbye and I took the list of poets from my study wall and looked at it hard. I wished I'd said I was about to do Eliot and Pound. I knew who they were, at least. I did once meet a man called Osip, but he was Welsh. We were introduced one morning in Diane's house in Highgate, where she lived when I was a child. He was eating breakfast, wearing a pink shirt, which I'd never seen a man doing before, and he ate his boiled egg by peeling it completely, then mashing it on to a piece of toast spread with mustard, then folding the toast in half and biting into it, like a sandwich.

Life at Diane's was strange by nature, when I went for weekends with Jane, because it was in London. The sky was different from the wide skies of Norfolk, and the trees were taller and the houses made of flat, painted bricks, not set with the little round stones that made our blue-grey cottage seem cobbled all over. Arriving to see Diane seemed something like arriving inside a television set. Into the News, perhaps: a place where men wore suits and people stood near each other and everyone talked as if they had some drama to report in a limited time. London was a place where there were buses and bus stops, with queues at them, and on the buses you could see people's mouths moving underneath the warm shine of little opaque bulbous lights.

Jane and I would normally arrive at twilight, when the birds would be noisy as we came out of the Tube, which made me cough, which I liked, and we'd walk up a hill with ivy on high walls to get to Diane's, where the doorbell was large and circled with brass. The bell said RING on it, in black, and that was my job then, when it was something I had to stretch up to reach. Jane used to lift me to ring it at some stage – or maybe that was somewhere else we went, when I felt her fingers digging into my waist from behind.

My earliest memories of Diane's Highgate house are slidey splices of fragmented vistas, which jerk like clips of hand-held camera film. A stone staircase I walked up holding a hand, with pebble-dashed wall panning along to my left. A large wet-lipped white dog with cold blue eyes nosing my legs in the red-papered hallway. Nettles, blowing and lethal by a slatted fence you could crawl underneath, into longer grass. The airless brown space of the larder with its heavy door into shelves that had checked waxed paper on them, which smelled of old cheese. The sunny blade of Diane's stunted bread knife as it cut a thick slice and she buttered it for me, as it rained outside and people talked. The fine orderly shadow of a Venetian blind on the green study wall, where the spidery typewriter lived.

These snatches are pasted on to a more general memory background of incoherent interior spaces with voices and mirrors and picture frames on coloured walls, of reeling patterns on chair-backs, the velvet smell of couches with covered buttons along their backs, the carved banister rail which curved round corners, and the upstairs landing carpet which rolled for miles, like one of those airport moving walkways, into the bathroom, which I seemed to spend a lot of time inside. There were tall brass taps there, which dripped. The water smelled of burning as it filled the bath, and was browner than tap water at home. London water tasted different, too. I was reluctant to drink it, but Diane didn't mind that.

'I never drink water, either, if I can possibly help it,' she used to say, over my head.

Her bath was long and narrow and high-sided, with a top that rolled over sharply after the languid ascent of its rough stained walls, which I could barely see over as I filled and squeezed the ragged sponge. That pale and porous natural sponge was one of the many domestic objects owned by Diane that I'd never seen before. Our sponge at home was blue, ungiving, and bought in Home Supplies, the local shop, which Jane once wrote a poem about.

Diane was as different from any woman I'd ever been near as her bath was from any other I'd encountered. She was cool and upholstered-looking, with brightly coloured, wide-belted trousers and a wet red smile. Her warm wide fingers had rings on them. One of these was in the shape of a ladybird, with silver antennae and two gold spots. I found myself staring at this a lot, since when Diane took my hand, as she often did, she held it for a long time while she talked to someone above my head. When she kissed me, as she did when we met and parted, her face was soft and matt, and her neck was too. She was fleshy, where my mother and aunt were not. Seen from a distance she was solid, replete, as after a good large lunch which she hadn't cooked herself. She liked dancing to the jazz records she left lying about on her couches, and she liked talking on the telephone, sitting at the hall table with her legs stretched out on to the black and white checks of the floor. I liked her laugh, although not to be too near it, and I liked the way she said 'Jane, you don't mean that' when my aunt was talking. I only really heard Jane talking to my mother – apart from myself and my friends – and my mother would never have said 'You don't mean that' to Jane, unless she was about to leave the room and slam the door. But Diane said it between laughing and lifting a glass to her mouth. She left half-full glasses around wherever she was, which made it seem as if she was always filling one up. She must have had dozens of glasses. I sometimes washed them, which I liked, since they were heavy and cut with diamond shapes, which caught soap bubbles in surprising ways and glinted as you rinsed them. They looked their best filled with tonic water, which Diane introduced me to. Her fridge was well stocked with small bottles of the *Sch . . . You Know Who* stuff, for the gin she drank with ice and lime. Limes were another thing I hadn't seen at home. My mother drank whisky, with water. I liked the smell of gin better.

Diane's Highgate house, which belonged to her father, had a long unkempt garden, with a daisy-strewn lawn and lots of dock leaves, which every garden of childhood seemed thick with. There seemed to be more nettles in those days, too. There was a sweeping copper beech, and another tree at the end of the lawn with pale-pink blossom, which dropped like confetti through every wet spring, and some sort of evergreen hedge at the back, which I used to hide underneath to have a pee when I couldn't be bothered to go back through people in the house to the cloak-room next to the kitchen, where I couldn't flush the chain.

From the end of the garden you could see the window of Gray's bedroom. This room had no handle, so there were some pliers on the bookshelves outside to twist the catch open. I had managed these a few times and had a good look before I ever met Gray. When he was still just a name, rather than a person who belonged in Diane's house. His room had a wooden seat running around the bay window. The wallpaper had aeroplanes on it the first time I went in, but then later the paper was yellowy plain and the ceiling navy blue, which I thought was odd. He had a mirror that stretched the length of his door. That was odd, too. One part of it made you look fat, and the other too thin. I suppose it was meant to be like that, but at the time I thought it was a grotesque mistake. I liked Gray's dressing table, which had watches on it, dismantled into slivery bits, and little drawers on each side. I liked the way these drawers were locked.

In the wardrobe in Gray's room there were trousers hanging limply from coat-hangers, with miniature clothes pegs on each side of the hook bit, and a few ties, which didn't interest me. What I liked to feel was the checked dressing gown, abandoned and long at the end of the bed. This had tissues in the pocket and a gold signet ring slithering in with them too. I tried the ring on all my fingers, but it only fitted my thumb, and wouldn't stay there unless I lifted my hand to point high up. The ceiling of Gray's room was the floor of my own, because I slept in the attic.

My room in Diane's Highgate house smelled of warm felt carpet and tea-chests, which were piled below the skylight. I liked the dense air there, and the sloping ceiling with its uncurtained window, where there was the faraway dark of sky at night, and clouds amid blue in the mornings. The bed had flower-print sheets, with matching pillows. There were too many pillows for one person, and a green eiderdown which would not have been wide enough to cover two bodies, although it was a double bed with a wooden headrest, with swooping shapes inlaid. I stared up at that headrest a long time whenever I went to bed there. The bedside table matched it. This would have a glass of water on it which I would regularly empty into the pot of a straggling rubber plant that pressed its torn-looking leaves up to the skylight. It seemed important that I should appear to have drunk the water during the night.

There was usually talking downstairs – and on the stairs too, when I slept in Diane's attic. The light above the skylight would be a paler navy than the light outside my room at home, because of the street-lamps in London. Outside, cars stopped and started a lot, and people got in and out of them, slamming doors and talking and clattering the pavement with high-heels. These were Diane's friends, who came in the evenings to laugh and talk downstairs, after I was in bed. Sometimes visitors would arrive in the afternoons, and when they did my name was said more than anywhere else, except perhaps on bad days at school. I was spoken about more than I was spoken to.

'Ruth is . . .'
'Ruth must be . . .'
'Ruth likes . . .'
'Ruth is *so* like . . .'

Throughout these speculations, my hot hand was held for too long and I would be worried about the sweat and suspicious that anyone holding it must wish they could stop. The worst was when women visitors smoothed my hair back and tilted my head to evaluate something – my hat size, perhaps. If I'd been a blusher, I would have been beetroot for hours, but I wasn't. I didn't blush or faint, or have period pains that made me sick, like some girls did, later on. I was tolerant of being discussed, because it went with being at Diane's, like sitting still went with the dentist's. I knew the touching would stop sooner or later and I'd get away out to the garden, where I'd take a tennis racquet and a ball to the high brick wall at the side of the house. I liked to see how many hits I could do without stopping. My highest score was eighty-seven, and I could have gone on for ever the day I got that.

Jane once decided to see how many times she could get the ball back and forth. Her heavy fringe flopped as she energetically lunged, and I was surprised at how strong she looked, in the cultivated clutter of a suburban garden. I watched her long pale neck and her narrow wrist as the man's watch she wore glinted in the afternoon sun. I wondered if I looked nicer in London, like she did, and if I could ask her, and decided I could, when we were back home. Diane sat on a tree-stump and smoked and watched. She had tanned bare feet and painted toenails, which she pulled at as she counted Jane's rangy strokes. My aunt got up to twenty-three.

'I think you should stick to banging the typewriter, darling. And I'm sure Ruth agrees. Don't you, Ruth?'

'Ruth needs a person to hit the ball to, really.'

'Well, it can't be you, that's pretty clear.'

'We must get her together with Gray.'

They often said they must get Gray to meet me. Usually as we were all saying goodbye, when Jane would say, 'Wouldn't that be fun,' in the way she only said things to Diane, but I hoped they wouldn't bother. I liked Gray having a bedroom, and sometimes wondered about him, but I liked Diane's as it was. I knew how to amuse myself. I was allowed to eat ice, and leftover chocolate mousse on the mornings after people had been. I was familiar with a few faces, and one or two names. There was Osip, of course, and someone called Red, who was often asleep on a couch when I came down in the mornings. I used to dare myself to wake him by clattering bottles together, but he never did wake until Diane arrived, in her pyjamas, to roll him from the couch on to the floor. If he remained asleep, she'd invite me to sit on him, which I did not, though I once helped her tie his shoelaces together. Jane thought it was my idea, and I was alarmed that Diane let her think it was.

'Keep away from sleeping men, Ruth,' my aunt said. 'They roar if they're disturbed.'

'Can turn quite violent,' Diane continued. 'And their smell lingers on you, like bleach.'

'Poor Ruth,' they said, 'with no one to play with.'

'I'll get Gray here next time, I promise. He'll play tennis when you come in July.'

Jane looked at Diane, who made a face, and sort of snorted. 'See what your sister makes of that delightful plan,' she said, then snorted again.

Red and I stared. He told her to keep sudden noises to a minimum, please, till he'd smoked his first cigarette.

Gray was not as I had imagined during explorations of his bedroom. His fingers were thinner than mine. The ring in his dressing-gown pocket would have slipped off them right away, but they were probably good for playing the guitar he owned, which lay in its case in the hallway, the first time he and I were in the same house overnight. He wore narrow black trousers and had fine fair hair. He didn't talk or laugh like his mother. When he stood up to shake my hand, I saw he was taller than she was. It was the last Saturday of July in 1969, when men had just walked on the moon. We'd had the Pope's message read out in assembly, and the television showed Neil Armstrong stumbling about like a helium Michelin Man, and Jane and my mother had a row, as they did increasingly through slow evenings at home. My mother thought it was stupid sending men to the moon, and Jane thought it wasn't, so they kept switching the TV on and off between them, as the coverage of mankind's giant step rolled on.

'We owe it to History to watch all night,' Jane kept

saying, and my mother said she owed it to her patients to get some sleep.

'Can you stop thinking like a machine for a moment?'

'Well one of us has to. We can't both sit round writing poems all day.'

'Ah. So that's what I've been doing for the last ten years. I thought I'd been minding your daughter.'

'Odd way to mind a child. Sneaking off to London whenever you get half a chance.'

Drinks would be poured as this exchange took place, with the fridge door often slammed, and ice banged out. I used to watch spilled ice-cubes thawing into small wet pools as my mother and aunt argued in the adjacent room. I associated wet patches on kitchen floors with noisy disagreements, although it some-times meant people were having fun. Which could be just as loud.

'Well, you remember, Stell, that I'm only in this graveyard because you did some pretty serious sneak-ing off of your own.'

When Jane started on this tack, as she often did, I had by then started leaving the house. Gillian lived above the next-door pub, and her parents never minded if I slept over. I liked the noise from down-stairs there. It was something like staying at Diane's, without the chocolate mousse.

Gray and I did not play tennis together on the Saturday I met him, or any other time after that. His hand was so limp when he first shook mine that I doubted he could lift a racquet, although later events showed that he could have. He didn't hold my hand for more than a moment, but put both of his into his pockets and sat down as soon as he'd mumbled hello. Then Diane said he ought to show me the fish, which seemed to please him. He smiled at her, not me, and started out of the room. When I caught up, he stopped to hold the door open for me, which no one had done before. I said thank you too quietly, so he said 'Sorry?' and I said 'Nothing.' Jane said, 'Ruth's so shy.'

It was the weekend before my eleventh birthday, which was partly why Jane and I were in London. She was going to buy me a dress. My mother had already given me a record-player. She never gave presents on the exact day they were due, which was one reason I thought Jane was wrong to say she thought like a machine. Machines would have been more accurate. A machine wouldn't have done nothing for whole weekends without getting dressed, either, like my mother did once a month or so, which meant Jane and I were trapped in the village, since Jane didn't yet drive the car. The birthday record-player was an exotic addition to my bedroom, though, and made more so by the fact that I had no records to play. So far I had simply enjoyed the ridged precision of the rubber turntable, and the jerky mechanism of the arm. Jane said Diane would let me play her records, so I could decide what sort of thing I might buy.

'I'll ask her as soon as we get there. We can have a

record party,' she'd said on the train, but when we arrived Gray was there.

It was raining, or had been, as he led me into the garden to look at the fish, which Diane had bought for her new pond. My shoes got wet and the stitching turned dull brown, instead of the bright yellow it was meant to be. The edge of the pond was muddy, but we stood side by side in the squelch and watched. He had his hands in his pockets again. I liked his white shirt, rolled up round firm smooth forearms, and his man's laced shoes, dark with wet at the front. The fish were regal and long with slow willowy tails.

'Imagine what it would be like if one of those swam between your legs.'

I didn't know what to say to that, so said nothing. Then he said, 'I mean if you were in this pond now, with your bathing suit on.'

I could think of nothing more horrible than standing in the murky pond in my swimming costume. It didn't sit right at the neck any more and strained underneath my arms. We'd get a new one for the summer, my mother said. She thought there was no point until it was hot again.

'Can you swim?' Gray said.

'Of course I can. We live by a beach.'

He threw a stone into the pond and watched the ripples it made, as he said, 'Oh yes, I forgot. You're the girl with no father who lives by the sea.'

Then he moved off and started to climb a thick-limbed chestnut tree that had branches overhanging into the garden next door, and he called me over to see something, but when I got there he shook the thing violently. I was covered in heavy drips. Dark blotches formed on my pale-blue skirt and my blouse turned transparent on the shoulders and arms.

'Watch out, it's an electric storm,' he said. 'We might have to sleep in the shed.'

My hair was splatted with what felt like enormous bird-droppings but was only water, so I didn't move. I looked towards the house and saw Diane in a window, laughing at something a tall man was saying. I saw Jane too, leaning forward to light a cigarette from a flame held by a woman I'd seen before. She wrote poetry too, and was called something French. More drips fell fast from overhead foliage.

'Do you mind?' I said, which seemed the right thing to say when someone unknown was wetting one's clothes.

'Do you?'

'What do you think?'

I turned and went back to the fishpond to watch twigs drift, until he came over and said he was sorry.

'I'm wet too.' His trouser legs were sopping and his shoelaces heavy and trailing mud. 'Feel that,' he said, touching the top of his head. I did, and it was cold and hard and damp. I wiped my hand on my skirt.

He suggested we go and have a walk round inside, but I could tell he didn't want to by the way he looked at the house. The French windows were open. Diane and Jane were just visible in a group of glasses and cigarettes in moving hands.

'Do you like Jane?' he said.

I stared involuntarily, wide-eyed, to see his face, but he was looking away, towards my aunt and his mother. How could he think I might not like Jane?

'Of course I do.'

'Why?' he said.

'She writes poems.'

'Well, they're not hard. They only last about a page.'

'Jane's the cleverest person I know.'

My arms were cold. His face was red in the rainy light.

'Except me, of course. You know me now.' He was looking away, up into sky.

'Who says you're clever?'

I waited for him to say 'Everyone,' so I could say 'Except me,' but he stayed silent as a hand-in-hand couple came out on to the wooden steps which led down into the garden. They looked across at us in a vague way, then lit each other's cigarettes and blew smoke out and talked, until Diane came out too and the talking stopped.

'That woman in the blue dress hates my mother,' Gray told me. 'I heard her saying so last time she came.'

I stared and he told me not to. He asked if I wanted a drink, and I nodded, as if I was asked that all the time, so he went into the house, but didn't come back.

I discovered him later watching *The Des O'Connor Show* in the room next to the kitchen. He was drinking something fizzy, but didn't offer me any. He was pretending not to have seen me. I lifted a newspaper from the floor, then walked across the room to another door, which was behind his chair, but he still didn't turn round. He chewed gum absorbedly, wrinkling his pale nose from time to time to make small sniffing noises, lifting his hands to clasp together on the top of his head. His hair was dry and soft-looking again.

The music in the room behind me where the grown-ups were was suddenly louder. Gray turned towards the door I was standing in to give me a look that made me say 'What?', before I rushed across to the other side of the room and almost ran into the kitchen, where Jane was opening the fridge.

'Ruthie!' She was humming to herself and looked very pink. 'We're dancing, Ruth. Come and join the fun. Where's Gray? Do you like Gray, sweetie?'

She called me sweetie when she'd had a drink. It was a word Diane said a lot. I didn't answer the question.

'I think you will like him, you know.' She was piling a glass plate with slices of lemon, which kept falling on to the floor. I helped her collect the uneven pieces and balance them in a delicate pyramid shape, which pleased me, but she was unable to lift the plate from the counter, because of her drink and two bottles of tonic. Her jacket was slightly off her shoulder. She had two small bones at the base of her neck, which other people seemed not to.

'You bring that for me, would you, sweetie? Come and meet my old friends. They're asking what's happened to Ruth.'

She put everything she was holding down on the large dark wooden table. She lit a cigarette and stroked my head, which made me drop my plate. Lemons hit our feet. Jane held her cigarette with her teeth as she bent to lift a few, then she gave up, and leaned back and examined me closely, in a way she had when slightly drunk. I knew she was going to say I looked tired, because she always did at this stage. She touched my cheek, then my hair again, and said maybe I should think about heading for bed.

'Unless you want to keep Gray company for a while?'

I shook my head. She frowned, in a curious way.

'I don't not like Gray,' I told her then. 'But I don't think he likes me.'

'Well I think you're just a tired girl, Ruth. Run up to bed now, and I'll come and tuck you in later.'

She always said that at Diane's, but she never did come up, and I wouldn't have seen her again that night if I hadn't gone back downstairs, after I'd been up to my room and not wanted to stay there. I decided to tell everyone that I'd felt sick, which wasn't an absolute lie. My bed hadn't looked like it should. The covers were rumpled, and the green eiderdown squashed. There was a dark ring on the inlaid wood table, where a glass had made it wet. I thought of the drips on my skirt in the afternoon and took it off quickly, along with my blouse. I left my underwear on, underneath my pyjamas, then went down the long staircase and into the room with the music and people, who were standing in clusters, or sitting and smoking. The talk was loud, and I didn't move in at first, but watched the record on the player next to the door going smoothly round and round, with vibraphone music like an ice-cream van's jangle.

Diane found me, before I could find Jane. She took my hand and we walked together to the couch, where a long man was lying. The window was open, with a good cool breeze. Diane told the man to sit up and make room, then she eased me into wide velvet cushions and draped a few jackets around me. It wasn't very comfortable, but as camouflage it worked well. No one noticed me for ages. And when they did, I pretended to be asleep, as they stood and discussed what to do with me next.

'I want her upstairs. Let's carry her, Di. She can sleep in your bed. It's far too big.'

Jane's voice was too loud. The clock in the hall struck two. Someone put a cigarette out near my face. I tried not to cough. I didn't want to speak.

'Jane, you can't mean that. Leave the child alone.'

A bottle was emptied into a glass behind my head. A man's voice agreed with Diane.

'Let sleeping dogs lie,' he said.

Then Jane decided she must lie down on the floor next to me, and someone must bring her some blankets.

'Ruth needs me near her,' I heard her say in a not unfamiliar late-night way. She sat on my legs and slid on to me almost, but Diane must have pulled her up.

'You don't mean that, Janey. You know you don't.'

The door was opened and closed a few times, and there were reassuring thuds in the hallway. People moved up and down the stairs. People in what I had made my new bedroom told each other to shush between whispery giggles, then there was the blanket, tucked round my neck again, and something heavier down near my feet, and then silence, except for rain outside and the rhythmic large purr of someone snoring near by.

When I woke up the lamp on the floor beside me, which was an asymmetrical one that Diane had made, was still lit, but not giving out any light compared to that of the sun, which streamed through badly pulled curtains to splatter over rugs and the dark wooden floor. I sat up and found I was stiff, with forearms ridged from the cushion's black piping. I had no idea what time it was, but decided I needed a bath. My mother thought hot baths the solution to most of life's crises. It was about the only straightforward opinion she had that I completely understood. I soaked a long time that morning. People tried the door-handle and went away, and I didn't tell them I wouldn't be long, or say I was sorry they couldn't come in. I said nothing, but was pleased to be there, alone and soaping my limbs with Diane's creamy soap. When the water got cold I still sat for a while, then I put my pyjamas back on and went downstairs.

I was glad to be told as I entered the sitting room that

Gray had a sore throat and was staying in bed. Diane was debating a call to her doctor, and banging the window shut as I watched. Her blouse pulled out of her red patent belt to show firm creamy skin. Jane said it was best not to be hasty with these things.

'Soluble aspirin works wonders for any child, in my experience, Di. Doctors hate to be called out on Sundays.'

My aunt was sitting on the floor, leaning against the couch with my blanket still on it, pulling a hair from the marmalade on her thickly buttered toast. She hadn't noticed me.

'Gray's hardly a child, Jane. You can't mean that.'

Jane laughed, and shrugged her green slinky shoulders. She had new pyjamas. Diane turned and winked at me, before folding herself down on to a rolled-up rug.

'I suppose what you're trying to say is that we don't want to hang round all morning, to see if he dies or not.'

Diane patted the seat of a footstool, near the spot she was now cross-legged on, but I found I wasn't moving towards her. She selected a piece of black-crusted toast from a haphazard stack on a plate on the floor, then felt under the frill of a chair for a knife, which she found as she talked on to Jane.

'And I think you're absolutely right. He'll live. Don't you think so, Ruth?'

Jane smiled as she saw me then, and offered me some of her toast, which I took as Diane went on that she must now agree with both of us, and not call a doctor for Gray. 'And you know what I think?' She played with an ashtray, then pushed it away from her, wrinkling her fine long nose. 'I think we three ought to drive into town. I feel like being trapped in heavy traffic. It will be a cleansing experience. I'm appalled by the amount of empties, Jane. Why didn't we stick to gin?'

Jane made a small groaning sound and took a cigarette from a pack near Diane's bare feet. She picked a silver lighter from her friend's top pocket. She said she'd always wondered what pyjama pockets were for.

'And now I know.' She inhaled, and closed her eyes. 'Let's go to a film. Can we see a film before we buy you a dress, Ruth? A matinée, that's what I need. Something pure and uplifting, with no talking in it. I haven't talked so much for years.'

Jane and Diane were addressing each other now, like they always did, but Jane ran her hand through my hair and pushed the toast plate towards me, as Diane lit her own cigarette. We heard a lavatory flushing upstairs, and footsteps, not coming down to us. Gray's bedroom door closed with a bang.

Jane and Diane took me to see *The Sound of Music*. I'd seen it in Norwich with my mother before. When it was over and we clambered back into Diane's red Saab, they sang 'How Do You Solve A Problem Like Maria?' all the way to Fenwicks in Bond Street, where we bought a dress of red and white chiffon with layers of petticoats. It was slightly too big for me, but there weren't any smaller, and they said it would fit by Christmas, when we'd all be together again. Then we had tea, with coiled Danish pastries, in the top-floor café where Jane wrote our three names in the mottled condensation on the windows. Outside again, Diane kissed Jane and me goodbye, and we got a taxi to Liverpool Street. On the train I sat next to Jane and put my head on her lap, which smelled of cigarettes and Diane. I slept almost all the way home.

My mother was only slightly late to meet our train. Jane and I waited by the wall in the car park, as we always did, for our familiar timbered blue car to arrive. My mother was dressed, and cheerful, which was a relief. Her arms around me were firmer than I'd expected, and the smell of her nice, and I was glad to be back and to hear her asking 'Did you have a lovely time?' She always said that, wherever I'd been. Even after a day at school, or a walk down by the boats on the nearest shore.

'Sort of,' I said. That's what I mostly said, and mostly it was sort of true.

'Get any records for your amazing machine?'

I'd forgotten all about my record-player. The thought of it seemed sad as I sat in the dank back seat on our journey home, with Jane and my mother not talking, in the front, near the windscreen wipers. I said that was why I was crying, when we got out of the car into the grey car park with its empty litter-bin and its smell of the sea, and its noise of gulls overhead.

'I wanted some records. I didn't want a dress.' My mother was locking the door. Jane was trying to make her cigarette-lighter work.

'We'll get some this weekend. That's your birthday, after all,' my mother said, and for once she was keen to do what we'd planned. We went into Norwich and chose Dusty Springfield. I played 'You Don't Have To Say You Love Me' so often that Jane hid it underneath the couch and made me pay her to tell me where it was. But I never wore the dress from Fenwicks, and never went again to the house where I first met Gray. Diane was always moving house, and Jane and I went most places she lived, except the Askew Road house, of course, because by the time I knew she'd lived there, Diane was dead, and Liam's mother was in receipt of an attic full of my past. In receipt of a suit-case of letters from my aunt Jane, at least, which I didn't read much, the afternoon I first got them, because I had to write about a poet called Osip Mandelstam. I don't remember seeing the man called Osip again. But I always remembered the way he ate breakfast as one of the many odd things that happened at Diane's. It was an untroubling memory to have. Like those muffled and ponderous men on the moon, who Jane seemed to think had changed our lives.

5

Jane took me with her to visit Diane in London wherever she lived and whoever was there. The first time I saw Gray in the last of her houses I knew, he was frying an egg, back-lit by late-afternoon sunshine that made the small kitchen there glow. It was August 1974.

'That gas is way too high, Gray.'

Diane opened the fridge, and her son turned briefly as she banged ice out of its tray on to the Formica work surface. Some skidded down on to the red-tiled floor. Gray glanced at ice-cubes near his feet, then went back to frying his egg, on the other side of the long narrow pine table which was in all Diane's kitchens, and mostly covered in the same chaos as it was that day. There was a vase of large peonies amid its clutter that afternoon, and a pile of *Swimming Underwater*, which was Jane's first collection. There was to be a party that night to celebrate its publication. A book launch of sorts, I'd been told, in some independent bookshop off the Portobello Road. My mother said she'd like to be

99

there, and might make an effort to catch a late train. We knew she wouldn't, though. She never came to London any more.

'Gray, you remember Ruth?' Diane said as she lifted bottles of tonic from a crate on the floor next to the fridge. She opened a drawer and dragged rattling things in it from side to side with manicured fingers. She lifted a potato-masher with a wooden handle. She lifted out an egg-slicer, a carving knife, a ball of string and several wooden spoons.

'You know what I'm going to do?' she asked the room then. 'I'm going to get one of those little chains, like the thing we have on the bathroom plug, and I'm going to get some pliers and open the last link on the chain and hook the end of the bottle-opener into that link and squeeze it tight shut and padlock the damned thing on to a big hook on the wall.'

She took a pair of scissors with orange handles out of the drawer and dropped them on to the worktop in front of her shiny green blouse. The fabric stretched over her breasts, where she luxuriously swelled. One of the small covered buttons was undone at the point of most strain, I noticed as I tried to look past her to Gray. She turned to look at me looking, and smiled in a small way, then looked at my own breasts, which were still 32A. I was wearing a purple scoop-necked T-shirt, which I'd tie-dyed myself and of which I was proud, but it seemed somehow neat in this kitchen, rather than boldly subversive. My breasts seemed neat too, and the way I'd laced my suede boots. Gray had

100

bare feet, and Diane wore faded red espadrilles, one of which was coming untied round her ankle, below the cuff of her baggy silk pants.

Jane was over on the other side of the table now, pushing spoons and forks and biros around, taking part in the search for the lost bottle-opener. Gray reached to unhook a fish slice from an array of jangled implements hanging on the wall above the cooker, which made the sleeve of his top slither back down past his elbow. He scooped his egg elegantly up from the pan and on to a plate, where bread was buttered and waiting. He left the gas high, but pushed the frying pan off it, then ground pepper carefully over the shapes on his plate. Knotted tape trailed from his shirt at both his wrists. His fingers were long and tanned and on one was a silver ring with a flat black stone. He sat on a stool that you could wind higher or lower, like those in photo-booths, and as he lowered his plate to the table he lifted a steel corkscrew, with a bottle-opener at one end of it, and held it out towards Diane.

'Here,' he said.

She made a small whining noise, that had a snarl somewhere in it, took the thing and opened bottles, poured tonic on to gin, drank deeply and asked her son to say hello to her guests as she handed my aunt a drink of her own.

'Hi, Jane. Hi, Ruth.'

He said 'Ruth' as if it had a question mark at the end of it, as if it was something he'd struggled to remember, which made it sound somehow intriguing.

'You remember Ruth, don't you Gray?' his mother said, picking at a pistachio nut. 'You met her last in . . .'

'Highgate,' Gray said. 'Yeah. Hi, Ruth.'

He smiled to himself, rather than me, and forked egg yolk into his mouth. He mopped grease with bread, pushed strands of sandy curls from his shoulders. His collar bone was showing. He had freckles on his nose, and the soft beginnings of a beard.

'God, Jane, you're not going to your launch like that, are you?'

Diane stopped dropping ice into a different glass from the one she'd started on to stare at my aunt, as if she'd just entered the room wearing something no human had attempted before.

'I mean I know you're a genius, but even so. You'd better borrow my black.'

Jane was having trouble with her cigarette-lighter. The flame kept fading just as she touched it to the end of her John Player Special. She was wearing grey flannel trousers and a blouse of my mother's, with a striped tie knotted around her waist as a belt.

'Di, I'm a poet, not an advert for perfume. Have you got a light, Gray, by any chance?'

He felt in the embroidered pocket of his shirt and found a brass object, which Jane knew what to do with. She was exhaling with satisfaction when the door behind her opened and a willowy figure came through, with large green eyes and sleepy fair hair parted in the middle to curtain her face. Her long skirt trailed, as did the fringed threads of her crumpled blouse and fine lines of her pale long arms. Her neck was pale too, above a wanton neckline, interrupted by languid strands of glass beads. She drew a bony hand across her forehead on seeing the room so crowded and moved backwards, saying 'Hi.' I immediately wished I could say 'Hi' like that.

'Clare. Don't rush off. We don't bite.' Diane patted the table-top near where she sat. 'And we have Jane Myers, the poet, in our midst.'

The girl's eyes were on Gray, but moved slowly to Jane.

'Hi.' She nodded almost imperceptibly. She lifted a hand, as if it had something soft and weighty in it, and pointed it vaguely back towards the door. 'I've got a bus,' she said. She almost smiled. 'I'm . . .' She stroked one hand with the fine fingers of the other. She looked at the corner of the ceiling, behind Gray's head. 'I'm singing. I'll see you.' Her eyebrows were raised as she left, still facing us all.

Gray scraped his stool back to follow her. We heard her voice again, briefly, though not what she said, and then the front door slammed.

'My, that was decisive.' Diane raised her fine dark brows in my direction. 'Don't worry, he'll be back. He didn't ask me for anything, so he's bound to be.'

I tried to shrug, in an offhand way, but it came out feeling somehow deformed, as if I'd developed a sudden hump. Diane wasn't supposed to know I wanted Gray to come back. Though it was a sort of relief to have him out of the room, with the girl.

'The trouble with these heavenly creatures is their lack of sentence structure,' Jane said.

'Heavenly creatures?' Diane was rinsing the end of a smoked cigarette under water that gurgled in a twisted drizzle from the one tap over the porcelain sink. 'Insect population, more like. And don't mention butterflies.'

'But that one's astonishing. She can't be getting a bus. Surely she has wings, folded somewhere about her?'

Diane half smiled, her lips pressed together. She winked at me. 'Maybe,' she said. 'Or maybe she simply drifts.'

The clock in the plant-filled dark hall struck five, and our hostess decided she needed a bath. Jane said she'd like to freshen up too.

'What will you do, Ruth? Do you want to unpack? Have you got anything to unpack?'

'I'm sure she has nothing so banal,' said Diane, giving me one of her easiest smiles. 'You know what I'd do if I were you, Ruth? I'd sit here and see what comes through the door next. I sense that the great unwashed are waking. They generally try and make toast.'

'Ruth makes very good toast.'

'I'm sure she does. She must have inherited some of her mother's glamorous talents.'

'Now, Di. Your toast is superlative.'

'Jane, you say the nicest things. Come and scrub my back.'

104

Music drifted from somewhere nearby. A cool watery flute sound with eerie singing mingled in.

'Ah, that sounds like the underworld stirring. The best place for us is behind closed doors now, Jane. And darling, you can't go like that. You look like a parcel, doesn't she, Ruth? A badly wrapped spider, that's what you look like today.'

The music got louder as a door opened and closed. Someone coughed, and someone else laughed. I began to feel nervous.

'Don't worry, they're harmless. More's the pity.' Diane touched the top of my head, then she took my aunt's fingers and led her out. 'Come along, sweetheart. You shall go to the ball.'

'Emily Brontë didn't wear Jean Muir,' Jane said, and I heard Diane explaining that she would have if she could, as they made their way towards the steep brass-rodded stairs. I crossed my legs then uncrossed them again, wishing they were longer. I watched the gas Gray had left burning, blue-white against the black of the hob, then I watched all the glasses shining around the worktops and table, and after a while I poured what was left of a bottle of tonic over the ice Diane had left in one of hers. I dribbled some gin into the tingling liquid as well, since the bottle was still on the table.

By the time I'd poured my second glass of gin and opened more tonic, which I thought Diane would approve of in the circumstances, I was feeling as warm all over as the glowing kitchen appeared to be. I pulled my feet up under my legs and began to feel at home. Music drifted from across the hallway; or not music, exactly, but a man's voice droning over a slow low beat, which I later discovered was Lou Reed and learnt to love. It was about someone wrapping himself up and sending himself to his girlfriend, who jabs a knife into the box he's packed into and kills him by mistake.

The front door slammed as people left. I heard voices fade as they descended the stairs which led down and out of the building. Diane's sprawling quarters spread over the top two floors of the house. Then the kitchen door opened and two people came in, not together, but as a unit, somehow. The girl was smoking what I assumed was cannabis. The new people didn't speak to me, but the male nodded his head in my direction as the female opened the fridge.

'Mmmn. Cheese,' she said. 'Cheese on toast is good.'

'Sure,' he said. 'How do we do it?'

There was silence then for a moment. He noticed the gin bottle on the table, looked at me and my empty glass, shook his head and sat down in the chair on my left.

'Bad stuff,' he said. 'Bad for your head. Want some of this?' He waved the joint the girl had passed him in front of my face. 'I guess we make toast, then put cheese on and heat it until it gets gooey. Any chocolate round?'

The girl was looking at me, as if I knew something she didn't.

'I'm Ruth,' I said. 'I could make toasted cheese, if you like.'

The girl sat down. She said 'Amazing.' She dragged lank hair back from her authentically ethereal pallor. 'I burn a boiled egg.'

The man laughed and coughed and laughed some more. 'You burn, Josie. You just burn, you know?'

'I'm feverish. You don't understand.'

Then Gray came in and the atmosphere changed, which may have been because he was the only person standing up. I felt better that he was there.

'Hey,' the man at my left said. He had a flowery shirt on, which should have tied at the neck, but was open, showing a hairless expanse of flesh.

Gray opened the fridge, so I looked at it then and the light inside that made the room darker.

'Where's Clare?' the girl asked. She was pulling at the frayed hem of her cheesecloth blouse. 'Where's Jake?'

'Clare split. Jake's over there,' Gray said.

The man next to me waved at the girl across the table from him.

The doorbell rang as we watched smoke spirals rise, and Diane called down that she'd get it. There were fast footsteps on the stairs, and her crying 'Well, at last!', and a male saying that he'd almost had a heart attack walking to get here, and couldn't she live somewhere flatter.

'Like Norfolk, you mean? Like Jane, I suppose?'

We heard them moving through into the room across the hallway, where the music had come from before. I'd have liked another glass of gin, but didn't want to pour it in front of Jake, who thought it was bad for my head. The sunlight was lower now on the table, and softer on the wall across from me. Gray was standing with his lighter in one hand, burning a small dark object between his other thumb and forefinger. I didn't want to watch him, but he seemed so engrossed in the activity that it was hard not to look, so I stared as he blew the flamed thing in his hand and waved it around, before crumbling bits of it on to the counter. I could see his backbone through the loose weave of his shirt. It looked as if he wasn't going to sit down with us.

'Want to make for the park?' he asked his fingers, as they flattened Rizlas together. He turned round and narrowed his eyes in my direction as he licked the length of the long cigarette he'd constructed. 'Want to see what the day says?'

I hoped no one did.

'Do you play any instruments, Ruth?'

Gray was talking to me, but looking out of the window. The girl looked at my face, and Jake did too.

'The piano. A bit.'

'We have a piano,' Gray said, which I knew, then he rolled his stool over to perch between Jake and me. He inhaled with a sound like a short sharp sniff, closed his eyes with their lashes, exhaled slowly, then leaned into my shoulder and said, 'Want some of this?'

I wished I could have made some noise which sounded seriously grateful and taken it from him, like the other girl would have, but I didn't know how to smoke, so I shook my head. He shook his head too, in a wry, indulgent way. He took my hand and opened my fingers, as if fingers were something quite new to him. He closed them over the rolled cardboard end of the smoking thing, and held my hand in both of his, to steer it towards my mouth and place it between my lips. It was his fingers against my face that I was most aware of as he told me to inhale.

'Close your eyes and breathe in,' he said. 'Imagine it's oxygen and you're dying.'

I closed my eyes and breathed in. I couldn't imagine I was dying, because I didn't want to. I felt I was nearer to properly living than I'd ever been before. I breathed in and smelled Gray's cupped palm, and his hair, and the open bottle of gin and the sweet unwashed yet soapy scent of the girl and boy on my left.

'OK, breathe out.'

I breathed out. Gray's hand was a bit away from my face. The ring on his finger was big, just in front of my nose.

'I like your ring,' I said, and he said, 'Breathe in again now, Ruth. Ready?' I would have exploded if he'd asked me to. His fingers touched my face around my mouth again. 'Breathe out first. Breathe in now.'

Jake was laughing as I drew on Gray's large cigarette, and the girl was scraping butter with a long-bladed knife on to a Jacob's Cream Cracker. Everything sounded loud as I exhaled.

'Now look at the window,' Gray said.

The window seemed long, and impossibly bright.

Dust was moving slowly. Gray's hair was exquisitely near my cheek. Diane's voice was distant yet loud, and getting louder. The door of the room opened like something in Disney. A vast flat plane of luminescent otherness, crushing my kitchen world into high-flying bits of coloured dust.

'Ruth. We're leaving in ten minutes. Jane is locked in the bathroom. You have to ring your mother.'

Her voice was a screechy blur. The name of my mother seemed funny. Everything swirled, and I held Gray's wrist, then the flashed fabric of his upper arm.

'You have to ring your mother, Ruth,' the girl's voice said in my ear. She was blowing smoke in my face. 'You're leaving in ten minutes.'

Then she laughed, or the man did, or it could have been me. A random laugh was in the room, very loud, and somewhere else.

'Gray,' I said. I remember that, because I said it a least half a dozen times.

Then I remember too how golden he seemed, how soft, how saturated, how faraway. And then a hand on my head, an arm round my waist, underneath me, and myself feather light, suspended across acres of hallway carpet into walls of swirls, mile-high walls of red moving shapes, and voices from outside the windows. Voices saying my name and 'Leave her alone,' and through it all the shape of Gray's face, near mine. Even as I thought I was going to vomit, the smell of his neck so near me was nice.

* * *

110

When I woke up, I was in the sitting room, on a couch with paisley velvet ends. The room was gloomy and there was no one there, and I was hungry and thought for a while of the egg Gray had fried, and I thought too of my mother and that she hadn't phoned. Then there were voices, and light, and Diane talking loudly, sounding cross. I pulled my knees up into my breasts and thought that I'd like to try moving. I rolled on to my side and looked at the gold in the leaf-pattern on the carpet. I saw the top half of the body of a man in a yellow shirt, against the coarse grain of a wide-armed wicker chair across from my couch. He had something like a length of string in his mouth. He had a moustache and a beard. His long dark fringe fell into his surprised-looking eyes. He didn't notice I was awake.

'But you could have said. You could have told me he was *invited*.'

That was Jane. Her voice wasn't often like that, but when it was, it could go on for a while. She had that voice with my mother sometimes. My mother sometimes wept.

'I mean, come on Di, you know what I'm talking about. I mean, *David*. It might have been polite to just explain that he'd be at my book launch. No?'

A glass was lifted from the table beside my shoulder. Music started from a speaker just to my left, so Jane talked more loudly, and more slowly, too.

'But then you'd have to have told me what friends the pair of you are, now. And then you might not have been at my book launch yourself.'

Diane's perfume seemed strong as she lifted a bottle from the floor I was by then looking down on.

'Well then you'd have been rather stuck for a bed for the night, sweetheart. Can we stop now? This is boring.'

The music was suddenly louder. Nat King Cole sang that he was lost, and the man in the yellow shirt sang along for a while. Then he said, 'Do we have to listen to this shit?' and I saw his knees turn into legs and the legs walked out of my view.

'No, but Di, listen. I mean, you know I don't invite him any more. You know that. I mean, Stell probably wouldn't have let me come if we'd known.'

And Diane gave one of her nasty laughs. The kind I couldn't describe even to my best friend, who asked about such things.

'Oh, Stella decides what you come to now, does she? Come on now. You can't mean that, Jane.'

I turned my head to look at the ceiling and saw Diane standing right above me, slashing a match against its box over and over, trying to make it ignite.

'David's fun. And he's looking so good these days. I thought he added to the event.'

'Yes. You made that very clear.'

The man in yellow was looming then, lighting Diane's cigarette with a chunky lighter that lived on top of the piano.

'Dance with me,' he said to Diane.

'I might just do that, you octopus.'

I lay on my back and watched the ceiling move

112

nearer, and then recede, as the music almost made sense.

'Isn't this ridiculous, Ruthie?' Jane had come to sit on my legs. She rarely called me Ruthie. 'You know what? I'd like to go home.'

Her back was against my front. She was wearing a black dress, tight around her, which left her shoulders bare. Her neck looked warm and smooth below her slashed hairline. I kissed it because it was there and I wanted to kiss some flesh.

'What do you think, sweetie? Shall we go home right now?'

Jane never asked me what we should do. And she never decided to leave Diane's in the middle of a party. The fabric of skirts brushed the couch we were on, as women danced near by.

'I like it here,' I said. 'But we can go if you want to.'

I couldn't think of moving, exactly, but the idea of a train swaying and closed was nice so I smiled into Jane's pale eyes, and then Diane's trouser legs were in front of my face, and she was pulling my aunt upright.

'Let's twist again,' she said. 'Like we did last summer.'

The other end of my couch was suddenly empty so I moved my legs into the free space and listened to Eartha Kitt, singing that her heart belonged to daddy, and then to the man in yellow asking who I was and why I wasn't enjoying myself.

He offered me a glass of sparkling wine, which I took and drank, like lemonade.

'You're a thirsty girl,' he said. His breath smelled of cigarettes and flaky pastry. Like sausage rolls, perhaps. 'I'd better find you a bottle.'

When he came back he sat where Jane had been, beside where my legs were, and seemed too big to be so near.

'Now tell me all about yourself,' he said, passing me a fresh glass of wine. He put his hand on my ankle. I hoped Jane wouldn't see. She'd once thrown a glass of water over a man who held my hand in the local pub. My mother was there and she was cross with Jane, who told her she was craven. I remembered the word, because I liked it a lot. I liked the words Jane said when she and my mother had rows.

'You must belong to someone here,' the man said. 'Now let me guess who it is.'

I'd finished my second glass of wine and begun to want to go to the bathroom.

'Excuse me,' I said to the man on my couch. My legs didn't go where I'd thought they would. They ended up over his knees, and his face was near mine then and his arms up round my shoulders, so I bit the part of his cheek that was nearest my mouth, which must have been his moustache because it felt like a tooth-brush between my teeth, briefly. Then I got off the couch and tripped into someone's spangled heel and I didn't wait to hear what that person said as she fell over. I saw the door-handle ahead of me, and was out of the room, into the empty hall, and the coat hooks bulky with hats and scarves. I climbed the stairs slowly, watching my feet achieve one step after the other, holding the high bannister rail, wanting to be where Gray might be, although I'd no idea where that was.

Outside the bathroom I met the girl from the kitchen who'd wanted cheese on toast a long time ago. She was going into the room with its high and mirrored surfaces as I left it. She said 'Hi, Ruth,' and I wanted to answer, but couldn't remember the word 'Josie' in time. I waited outside the bathroom until she came out, and then I followed her. I followed her up the stairs beside Diane's bedroom door, then along the top corridor of the flat, past an old knife-sharpening machine, past pictures with their backs to us, past stacked chair-legs and boxes of books and a disconnected gas fire and past a hundred unwatered plants to a dull green door which I followed her through. It felt something like walking into heaven. There were candles everywhere, and incense, hanging in spirals from unlit lamps. There was music, but not like the music downstairs. A man on a cushion over the floorboards from me was playing a guitar. He was wearing what I thought was a dress, because I'd never seen Afghan shirts before, or smelled the coats those people brought back from their travels either. The room was oily with fabrics, and thick with the smell of grass and sweet perfume which must have been jasmine, or musk. A smooth-skinned man in a brimmed white hat took my hand, and offered me what he was smoking. I took it and breathed in as if it was oxygen and I was dying, and then I lay down on a mattress which seemed to be the floor. Then it was different and someone in beads was saying they must paint my face, and Gray was there just in front of me, or beside me as my face was painted, I suppose, because the next morning I had a large flower on my cheek. I also had a silver chain around my left ankle. I think Josie put it there. I remembered how small and cold her fingers had felt, compared with Gray's, which were curiously warm.

The next morning, the room was silent and the drifting smoke in the air had stopped moving somehow, to hang in the atmosphere pleasingly, vague densities below the ceiling, as solid but untouchably soft as the numbness just behind my eyes, which was not a headache, but more of a feeling that something pale and viscous had been smeared on the inside of my skull. I stayed horizontal and thought of nothing, until the door opened and bare feet walked across the boards towards me. Diane was holding a cup. She said it was tea, with sugar, and that it would do me good.

I didn't say I didn't take sugar, and she didn't mention that my face was blurred with colour, or that I was no longer wearing all my clothes. I pulled sheets up around me and surveyed the roomful of people in sleeping bags. Gray was not where he'd been before.

Diane watched me sip tea for a while in silence, before half whispering to me, 'I'm glad you found some fun, Ruth.'

She lifted a guitar from the end of my mattress and sat down to finger the fringe of the bedspread, as she told me I ought to be making a move, because Jane had decided to leave. She leaned back and took my tea and had a sip of it herself. 'Unless you want to stay here, of course, sweetheart.' She turned then and gave me one of her smiles. The kind that comes before a wink. Then she got up from my soft space and walked out of the room.

I got the twelve forty-nine from Liverpool Street Station with Jane. I had school the next day, and anyway, no one asked me not to go home. (That only happened in dreams I had for weeks afterwards, where I stayed in Gray's room, for ever.) When we said good-bye he was in the kitchen, buttering toast. The table was crowded. He said, 'See you soon.' Everyone in that room smiled. I smiled back, but my mouth was out of the habit already, so it may have looked odd. The flower on my face was washed off. The colours of it in the bathroom sink had been murky and left a greasy film. As Jane and I stepped down together into the hot light street from Diane's cool dark doorway, I saw the girl called Clare moving towards us. She was outside the paper shop, and carrying a music case. She had a different garment on – something long and flowery. Her head was down, and the sun was on it. I was glad Jane didn't notice her, or say anything. I didn't want to be noticed, walking away with my aunt.

On the train to Norwich, Jane read the *Observer* for

the whole of our journey, except when the tea-trolley came laboriously through, when she stopped reading and bought a black coffee.

'Want anything?' she asked me, as she stirred packs of sugar into the ridged white plastic cup. I shook my head. I wanted her to cheer up, and not be cross with Diane. But she laughed bitterly and left the newspaper limp on her knees as she said, 'Want anything?' a few times to herself, as the landscape sped uneventfully by. When she started to read again, I leaned across from my seat, which was the one facing backwards, and I patted her knee, which I'd never done before unless it was part of a game. I did it then, though, because I could tell she was sad. Jane didn't react. She mightn't have noticed. She was someone who noticed what people said, more than what they did. But I was only sixteen, and knew nothing yet of beginning to know that someone you love likes someone else more.

6

One late afternoon at the beginning of June in 1998, I was beginning to enjoy Philip Larkin.

'Talking in bed ought to be easiest
Lying together there goes back so far . . . '

I hadn't talked to anyone in bed for too long. On the night of the motorbike man in Hastings, I'd slept in the attic, alone. Fiona and Frank had Liam's room. I heard them talking, on my way up from the bathroom. Fiona thought I was mad, she'd said, and wondered why Liam put up with me. One of them then pulled the curtains, so I couldn't hear Frank's response. I heard Fiona tell him that the watch the man stole was worth hundreds of pounds, which might have been true. Though that wasn't the reason Liam was upset it had gone. He was upset because it had been his father's. But that probably wasn't why he'd fallen asleep on the couch that night before anyone else mentioned bed. Liam had a way of falling asleep when things went wrong, which I found frustrating. And he was being frustrating now. He was supposed to have rung me on my afternoon with Larkin. He was supposed to be arriving in London.

It had been raining, briefly but hard and loud, on leaves outside my study, which now hung wet, dishevelled, but plumply veined, and extraordinarily green in the steel of the sky. Like lime-yellow rags they sagged against black branches, where a fat pigeon was grooming, seeming sated rather than battered by it all.

The light was changing, though it wouldn't be dark for hours. It was only just after seven.

When the telephone rang it wasn't Liam, it was Clare. She was back in Charing Cross Hospital, which she'd been in and out of on a regular basis for months.

'Am I interrupting anything?'

The pigeon flew off with a smacking sound, like shoes being slapped together after a sandy walk.

'I'm just working.' I was aware that it sounded suitably dull.

'Good day?'

Someone ran fast up the stairs on the other side of the wall of my room.

'What are days for? Days are where we live.'

I said I had a pen at the ready. 'Say it slowly,' I said.

Clare's number would be a long one. Hospital telephones were usually about as useless as her medicines seemed to be, but the existence of both was some comfort, and I wrote the trailing numbers of bedside phones down as diligently as I walked to late-night chemists with prescriptions, clotted with lists of odd symbols, impossible names and the inevitable scrawl of some GP's signature, looping wearily over the whole. Doing something was better than nothing.

'Mum's going to ring you about Conor's plans,' Clare told me.

Clare had never been one for 'plans', in health. I'd often helped with any that had to be made about Conor, as and when they were necessary. Perhaps it was because I was not a mother, or because I'd known her before she was one, that Clare took my advice. We never discussed why I gave my opinion of things that might affect Conor's life, but I did, and she normally took it. Together we'd decided which local nursery was the nicest one, and what hours would be best for her son to attend. Together we'd agreed that he must have packed lunches, although school food was free. When he needed name-tapes, we chose the colour and script together, and took turns at sewing them on. Also together, while talking about childhood one afternoon, Clare and I had realized that Conor must go to the zoo, though Liam came with me, on the long-promised day, because Clare got some unexpected work. The zoo trip was the only thing Liam and I had done with Conor, so far, and wasn't altogether a happy event, because Liam forgot to tell me that he hated captive animals. He didn't mind the aquarium, with its back-lit shreds of slow and muscular fish. He wouldn't go on the carousel, but did take a picture of Conor and me on a red-and-white horse, which Clare still had on her bathroom wall.

Liam disliked hospitals as much as zoos, whereas I found it easier to see Clare in a ward than at home. She was mostly separate from Conor there, of course, but it wasn't just that I found a relief.

A person in hospital is surrounded by sick people, rather than evidence of the life they could be engaged in if they had the use of their limbs. I didn't have to sit among Clare's unworn clothes when she was in Charing Cross. I didn't have to walk into the kitchen to make tea with the kettle she no longer filled, or to open the fridge with the photographs of our Cornwall holiday stuck to its door. To see the sitting-room wall she'd once almost painted, while I'd watched her shapely back stretch and her bare feet stick to the emulsion she invariably dripped on to the floor, to pad through in incoherent imprints on to the pale hall carpet. Those blotched traces of footprints made me aware of her feet when I sat beside her at home. These would be dangled out from the duvet, because she hated them to be hot. Sometimes we'd wonder at the fact that useless feet could still feel hot. Sometimes it was as easy to discuss them as it might have been to discuss a broken vacuum cleaner. Other times it was difficult.

In hospital one had the place itself to rely on for conversation. The latest nursing bungle, the newest flowers, the whereabouts of the smoking room, the nocturnal noises of adjacent inmates, the details of any new treatment. In hospital it was normal to be talking to someone in bed. It was in her own home that Clare seemed increasingly out of place. Pain is not hospitable.

After Clare's call on that moist June evening, I decided to give up on work for the day. I rang Liam's number and got his answering machine, with the message that sounded as if he'd got his hand trapped in a door, just out of reach of the phone. I tried not be cross.

'We should be careful
of each other, we should be kind
while there is still time.'

I pushed the 'play' button on my answering machine, and it said I had no new messages. The mechanical yet fruity voice reminded me of the receptionist in my mother's surgery, who used to ask, 'Who shall I say is calling Dr Myers?', although she knew very well it was me.

I decided to open the bottle of Sancerre in my fridge. Sounds of my neighbours and the smell of their barbecue filtered into my kitchen as the telephone started its liquidy trill again. I rushed back through to answer, but wished I hadn't when I heard Clare's mother's voice.

'Ruth.' She sounded relieved, as if she'd expected someone infinitely sinister to be awaiting her call. 'Ruth, have you heard the latest?'

I said that her daughter had rung me, and that I'd be visiting the next afternoon.

'Are you going alone?' Now she sounded suspicious. 'Has . . .' She cleared her throat, then left a gap. 'Has anyone asked ... to go with you?'

I said no, and why? I wished someone had. Although Clare preferred her visitors single.

'Well, Ruth, I don't know. Someone rang a while ago and asked if I thought Clare might agree to see Gray.'

She said his name in almost a whisper.

'Who rang?' I wished I'd brought my wine through with me. 'Did they say he's in London? Did you ask where he is?' Gray was still living in Paris. I'd had a Christmas card, saying he might be over in the spring. Before that I'd had a birthday card, saying he'd probably be over in October.

'I didn't, Ruth. I told whoever he was not to ring me again. Clare doesn't need any shocks just now.'

'No.' There was a silence as I wondered if Gray could have my number, and realized he could, if he'd tried. I asked how Conor was, so I could carry on thinking my thoughts.

'Well, it gets a bit much for him sometimes, Ruth.' After a brief pause she went on in a brighter voice. 'He tells me you have a new kettle.'

I didn't answer. I'd had my kettle for years.

'Oh well.' A longer pause. 'He's very tired, Ruth.'

'Yes. You must be as well.'

Tiredness was a concept we often dwelled on together, for want of anything specific. 'A good rest' was something Clare's mother approved of. My own mother had been the same. My childhood in retrospect seemed thronged with people telling each other they needed more rest.

There was a short strained silence, before Clare's mother conceded that she was indeed tired, and said goodbye in a weary way. We weren't easy on the telephone, which was odd, since we'd spent hours at Clare's together, doing practical things which lead to an intimate manner, if not emotional closeness. She talked there non-stop, but carefully, somehow. Too carefully for a woman of my generation. For a woman of my background, at least. Jane and my mother weren't careful talkers. Diane could sometimes become one, if she wanted something particular to happen next, which involved a degree of persuasion. But Clare's mother had nothing to want, at present. If she wanted anything it was perhaps for the present to go on for ever. For ever and ever, as the Lord's Prayer used to say when we were at school, with our eyes shut and our hands clasped, and the smell of each other's cardigans filling the hall with navy-blue warmth.

In my kitchen I repossessed my drink, and heard the neighbours' music shimmering into the fading day.

'Shall we dance?' the wife said. She often said that.

'Have some more fizz,' her husband told her.

Then their garden was silent and I thought of Clare again, who used to like dancing a lot. She had a way of lifting her arms as she turned to the music that was as pleasing to see as a mechanical toy of some sort, fully sprung and swirling. Anyone else looked clumsy if Clare was dancing, at parties in the Old Schoolhouse, where she lived on and off with a ragged bunch of fellow musicians throughout the early eighties. And most people sounded tone-deaf when she sang, as she often did in her discoloured kitchen in the morning, wearing the kimono which still hung in faded folds over the door of crammed cupboards in her room.

Clare and I found that we lived near each other in the summer of 1982, after I'd moved into Amor Road, which was my second London home. Everyone I knew had painted floorboards, so I wanted them in that place. This bold move towards clean late-twentieth-century living involved lifting layers of heavy patterned carpet. Underneath were sheets of newspaper, creased with fine dust from disintegrating underlay. The newspapers dated from 1965, but I didn't read them. I was too busy organizing my new environment to care what had happened when I was seven years old, although I do remember an advert for a cooker which looked like one my mother bought about that time. It was the first major change in my childhood home, and one of the few things we had completely new. The man who came to install it chewed spearmint gum, and Jane said the smell of it made her feel sick.

Having lifted newspapers from my Amor Road floor, I decided to burn them in the grate of the largest room of my new quarters, before venturing out with the carpet, which I'd have to put in a skip. There were plenty of skips in London streets in 1982, but you had to avail yourself of them after the pubs had shut. Some people got their boyfriends to help, but I didn't have one just then. Liam was my longest relationship so far, and I hardly ever saw him, which I considered a great success or a terrible failure, depending on my mood and if he was in when I rang him up.

It was through burning old newspapers in Amor Road that I met a woman called Robin, who turned out to already know Clare. I was drinking green tea late at night, watching roaring flames, feeling organized and vaguely daring, when the doorbell rang in a prolonged and violent way. Robin was outside, wearing a jumper that stopped just above her knees and a pair of grubby socks. She'd come because smoke was billowing through from my chimney breast into hers, and seeping through the grilles of her gas fire into the limited air of her bedroom.

'I thought I was being asphyxiated,' she explained as I asked her in. 'I couldn't understand it, till I remembered someone had moved in here.'

I was horrified, and poured water into my grate. I offered her my couch to sleep on, my own mattress even, which was wide enough for both of us, but she went off home cheerfully, saying to come round for tea in the morning. I brought flowers and chocolate biscuits and many apologies for her broken night, which became shrill as I realized the fire in my grate had discoloured her bedroom. The chimney breast was black, while other walls were pale cream. I was appalled that something I'd done should have affected

127

another person's environment in so direct a way, but Robin said that was city life.

'I mean, we're all breathing the same air, more or less. That's what I like about London.' She lit a joss stick, which made me sneeze. 'And anyhow, now we've met. You could have lived there for years without my knowing, if you hadn't lit a fire.'

That was typical of Robin. She saw the best in things. The bus that didn't come meant you had to walk and see the stars; the job you didn't get meant you could stay in bed and read; the bottle of wine that turned out to be corked meant you wouldn't be hungover. Even Clare's illness was something we must use to make our own lives 'more precious', as far as Robin was concerned. It wasn't a world-view I shared, but it affected my life for a while. It was Robin who eventually took me to Clare's, though I said I might not be welcome.

'Clare likes everyone, silly,' she'd said.

I could see from her smile that to disagree would indeed be silly.

'. . . the big wish
Is to have people nice to you . . .'

I wanted Clare to want to be nice to me. I wanted to be part of her world. But that didn't really happen until Conor arrived into her life, and, by coincidence, mine.

After my first glass of cold but indifferent wine, on my evening with Larkin, I rang Liam's Hastings number

128

again. There was no answer so I had another drink, and was thinking of food, when the music drifting into my kitchen from the neighbours' garden stopped. Their doorbell rang its optimistic chime and talkative guests moved through to the barbecue, whose familiar charcoal smell was smearing the communal air. Now there would be a loud appreciation of the scent of the honeysuckle, which was always discussed by outdoor guests of my immediate neighbours.

'It's altogether luscious,' one of the guests decided.

I heard a cork being pulled, and glass against glass as liquid refreshment was handed round.

'Isn't it exquisite?' the hostess agreed. 'You don't even need a drink to feel heady.'

'Cheers,' her husband said cheerfully. He was a cheerful man.

The neighbours walked to the wall at the back, which my own garden shared, to view the honey-suckle's roots and marvel at its growth. They'd crane their necks to look up at the climbing roses next. I knew my neighbours well, considering we never spoke. They probably knew my habits too. Had doubt-less heard my arguments with Liam, the taxis I called, the friends who arrived and almost left.

I found olives in the fridge and ate them. Robin's long-ago garden was full of voices. The inevitable company there ate sun-warm raspberries from the tangle of bushes at the back, beyond the rabbit hutch and the bare earth around it, and the dandelions, and the bird-table which nobody could make stay perpendicular. After the raspberry season there were blackberries, and bitter apples, small and dry on the tongue. We made a sort of jelly with them, which we ate on toast when the year turned cold.

Robin had no barbecues, but occasional bonfires in the garden that mine used to overlook. I went thoughtlessly and almost daily there, my first summer in Amor Road, to lie barefoot on blankets after the hot bus journey home from work. I had an undemanding job in a bookshop, which Robin thought was exotic. She worked in the library on the Shepherd's Bush Road, near Clare's ramshackle establishment, and aspired to selling books rather than lending them to the public. She thought it would indicate a more independent cast of mind, and I encouraged her to think of my life as more glamorous than it was by dwelling on the evening readings we had in the shop, rather than my menial position there. I didn't tell Robin that Jane had got me the job, or that my mother rang me there about twice a week to see if I needed more money than I earned, which I did, and which she sent.

In 1982, my mother was taking a sabbatical in Normandy. Her phone calls were less frequent and more muffled than when she was at home. She wrote long and surprisingly lyrical letters, detailing the health of her hens and the progress of the reference book she was writing. The hens were robust, but unproductive. The book was a dictionary of family ailments, called *Be Your Own Doctor*. Clare owned it, many years later, as did most mothers she knew, which gave me a feeling of unearned pride, and a sense of something like shame as well, because I got the royalties. These were not hefty, but were more than Jane got from her poetry, so far. Poetry doesn't pay bills, as my mother often told my aunt, though it might help keep people healthy, as Jane insisted it could. I was impressed anyway with the way my mother wrote, alone in Normandy. She went about her book in a more methodical way than I did, with my history of poets, or Jane had with her poems. She was more used to hard work than either of us, although she'd never been given much credit for that by my aunt or myself when she supported us both. We felt we deserved to be supported, of course, and perhaps we did, but my mother then perhaps deserved to be thanked in a way she never was. Perhaps that's why she decided to write a book designed to keep mothers at home with their children, rather than bothering doctors. Jane always said *Be Your Own Doctor* was meant as a kind of reproach, but I thought of it more as a compensation. It couldn't do much to help Clare now, of course. I don't think poetry helped that much either, although the fact that I was writing about it gave us something to discuss.

I finished my olives and ate pasta salad. I must tell Clare about Larkin on my visit the next afternoon. I could tell her I was enjoying the man from Hull more than I'd expected to. The noise from the neighbours' garden increased as their outdoor spotlights came on, and their conversation moved to house prices south of the river, and the possibility of finding reliable builders in Fulham.

'How high they build hospitals!
Lighted cliffs, against dawns
Of days people will die on.
I can see one from here.'

I could see no hospital from my kitchen. I could see the darkening creeper at the end of the garden, which was a dense tangle of crimson in autumn, and past that I could see the backs of houses. A man was sitting at a computer in one of the illuminated windows there, and in another two children were jumping on beds. I poured myself a third glass of wine as the neighbours' sausages sizzled, and the husband told his wife they would take half an hour, and she expressed the opinion that they would take longer. The guests were silent. Perhaps they were in love. Or perhaps they had sore throats, like Clare did the day I found her at Robin's, in a ripped chiffon blouse and checked trousers with a red leather rim at their cuffs, which she'd had to add since her legs were longer than average. Clare was almost six foot, but that wasn't apparent when I walked into Robin's, with my fingers white with dried paint and my T-shirt reeking of turpentine, to see her sitting on the couch.

Robin was standing by the kettle, which was coming to the boil.

'Ruth, this is Clare,' she said. 'Clare, this is my new neighbour, Ruth.'

132

We looked at each other, then away again, then back, as Robin watched. Clare's hair was cut in a finely waved crop, and her face was fuller than it had been the last time I'd seen her, but I knew exactly who she was.

'Clare's a singer,' Robin told me, turning away from us, across the room from each other, locked into our awkward introduction.

'With a throat infection,' Clare added. 'Don't come too close, if you value your health.'

She looked almost into my eyes. I felt like I was in a play and had forgotten my lines. Clare's physical presence was always a shock to me in those early days. I wanted to look at her for longer than I thought I could.

'Tea, Ruth? There's no more Lemsip. D'you want hot water and honey, Clare?'

'I'm fine.'

Clare tilted a cup she'd lifted from the scuffed but gloss-painted floorboards. She looked over at me again, as I didn't sit down, because to do that would have brought me nearer her inspection. She took Robin's cigarettes and lifted them to our hostess with an enquiring air.

'I shouldn't, I know, but can I?'

Robin nodded and I watched Clare light up. She squinted through the smoke, then took the cigarette out of her mouth and turned it in her fingers, watching that delicate movement.

'Ruth works in a bookshop in Camden.' Robin

handed me coffee and rooted for a teaspoon in the sink. 'She sits at the till in the window.'

'Yeah. Hi, Ruth. You're looking good.' I felt my sticky palms moisten as Robin turned, her eyes wide with surprise. Clare gave a sort of laugh that turned into a cough, then smiled and nodded, widening her own shining eyes. Having a fever suited her. 'Yes, we know each other, Robin. And I know about the bookshop too. Gray saw you at the Ishiguro reading, he said.'

I used to send invitations to all our shop's readings to Diane's, hoping that Gray would find one on one of his trips back from Paris, or – wildly – that Diane would send them on over to him and he might plan a visit. When he finally did show up, it didn't go as I'd planned – however that was. He left before the book-signing, just after the man responsible for buying American fiction had asked me to go for a drink. Later, I wished I'd asked Gray to come too. He must have thought I was busy. Or maybe he had somewhere else to go. Somewhere else where Clare was.

Robin was still staring. 'So you've met? That's amazing. Isn't London small?'

Clare nodded. So did I. Robin sat down and folded her arms, looking from me to Clare.

'Life never ceases to amaze me, you know?' She took a cigarette and smoked, looking happy and more amazed than usual. 'So, what? You met through the mysterious Gray? Or does he just happen to know you both?'

Clare looked at me, with raised brows and pale eyes. 'How did we meet, Ruth? It's so long ago.'

I had a flash then of her in the doorway at Diane's, the day I first saw her, when Jane said she looked like an angel. I remembered her too with wet hair and skin in Leeds, outside a pub with Gray. I'd felt sick, so he walked me home. Anyone who knew Gray in the seventies couldn't help knowing Clare too, in a way. If you visited Princedale Road, you were aware of Clare, somewhere, being talked to or about by somebody else. Clare's name was part of his presence, as much as the oily smell of his clothes and his warm, infrequent laugh.

'We both know Diane, I suppose.' My voice was high, so I cleared my throat and explained, for Robin's benefit, that my aunt and Gray's mother used to be friends.

'They were an odd pair, weren't they? I used to dread finding them in the kitchen.' Clare coughed. She stubbed her cigarette violently into a saucer. 'God, I shouldn't have done that.' She unwrapped a throat sweet and sucked hard, as Robin said how much she loved Jane's work, which I knew, because she had two of the three books she'd written so far.

'So, what? You met at Diane's? How long have you known Gray, Clare?'

'Not as long as Ruth has.'

She stretched her arms above her head. She did it the same way Gray did. She yawned. 'Too long, anyway, however long that is.' She crunched her sweet, which I thought was foolish. If she had a sore throat, she ought to suck it.

'But I thought you were planning to move to France?'

'Well, I might be. But France is a big place.'

'Yes.' Robin smiled indulgently. 'And so is Gray's flat, you said?'

Clare shrugged. 'We'll see,' she said. Then she turned to me. 'So Ruth, you're living round here now?'

Gray hadn't asked where I was living when I saw him at the bookshop. Because someone else was taking me out for a drink, maybe. I picked at paint on the back of my thumb and said I'd only been living next to Robin a fortnight. I'd been up near King's Cross, before.

'Mmmn. Gray said.'

'I hate decorating,' I said, after a moment of silence. I tried to look suitably limp, rather than elated that Gray had known where I'd lived. Perhaps he'd been planning a visit. He must have asked Diane. They must have talked about me, at least.

Robin said it was good to have connections. 'I was in a squat for two years when I arrived from darkest Devon.' She laughed, then went on that I was obviously someone who landed on my feet. 'She almost killed me, the night she moved in. But she made a friend instead.'

Clare sniffed and nodded, seeming more relaxed now the conversation had shifted away from herself. She felt the glands in her neck, stretching it up and back. She said she shouldn't have got out of bed. She didn't feel like a party.

'Have an afternoon nap.' Robin was shaking a bottle of nail varnish. 'Or get drunk beforehand, and dance it away.'

She took off one of her socks, saying she'd decided to dress up for the night and that might mean red toe-nails. She asked if I'd seen Clare dancing yet. I liked the 'yet'. It seemed to imply that I would, sometime soon. I shook my head. Clare was looking out of the window. Diane's friends danced at Princedale Road. Gray's upstairs people were languorous, and rarely vertical.

Clare said she couldn't imagine that anyone would see her dance again. Her legs felt like worn-out rubber, she told us, and smoothed the fabric of her trousers with long capable hands. Then she unfolded herself, in her careless yet deliberate way, and said she'd better be getting back home. Someone was coming to check out the stereo at three.

'Would that be Matt?' Robin looked up from squeezing tissue paper between her toes. She said she liked the look of Matt. 'Do you know him too, Ruth?'

Clare was pulling a large Fair Isle jumper over her head, although it was a warm July day. I waited to see whether she answered Robin's question before I did. Matt was my best friend through my first year at Leeds. Clare had met him there, with me, and knew how close we were. So if she didn't say anything about him now, then I wouldn't either.

'See you around, anyway.' She smiled, and nodded in my direction. She arranged the cuffs of her jumper. She bent to tie a lace in one of her baseball boots, though it wasn't undone as far as I could see.

'See you at the ball,' Robin said to the long curve of Clare's spine, as she retied her other shoelace.

Something about the silence that followed made me feel awkward.

'So.' Clare's face was flushed as she stood tall again. Her eyes seemed darker against the pink now. 'Nice to see you, Ruth.' She lifted an embroidered bag from the couch and dragged at a thread that hung from its fringe. She snapped it off. 'Don't see me out, Robin. I know the way.' She was almost out of the door when she turned and paused, and stayed on the brink of words for just long enough to make me think an invitation was coming my way.

'Good luck with the decorating, Ruth.' She smiled decisively after that, and left and didn't return. The room felt smaller. I felt too hot, too short and almost ashamed, somehow. Robin turned to me and raised her brows.

'Well, I'm not her new neighbour, am I?' I said, with what I hoped was a careless shrug.

'She'll expect you to come with me, silly.'

But I didn't go with Robin that night. I went to the first of many parties in the Schoolhouse the Christmas after I'd met Clare again. And that was because Matt had a room there by then, and he'd met Robin, and they were in love. I left my beaded cardigan behind, at the first of those dizzy affairs I went to, and so I went back the next day and Clare offered me a coffee that I didn't accept. When I got home I wished I had.

My own neighbours were playing Van Morrison and I was absorbed by the time my brooding telephone eventually rang.

'What meeting made us feel,
So new, and gentle-sharp and strange.'

The blackbirds had finished their noisy home-comings and I'd replaced the bulb of the kitchen light. The phone was Liam, who wanted to meet me. I told him I'd been thinking about meeting Clare in Robin's kitchen, years ago, and how she didn't ask me to her party. I didn't tell him that I'd found out the next day that Gray had been there, on his way for a dawn ferry from Dover.

Liam sighed heavily. I heard noises like a party or a pub in the background. 'So you're in that sort of mood.'

'What sort?'

'A past-tense mood. It's so perverse. I'm ringing you up to ask you out.'

Gray had asked Robin to remind me that night trains still took people to Paris. 'Tell Ruth I'm still where I was,' he'd asked her to say. It cheered me up for weeks, though I didn't tell her about my distant Paris week-end. I'd never told Liam either.

'Why didn't you tell me what you were doing?' I asked him then. 'I've been ringing you for hours.'

'Well now I'm ringing you.'

He sighed. I listened to warm sounds all around him.

'Well, do you want to see me?' My voice sounded cross, so I took a deep breath and tried again. 'I mean, where are you?'

We should be kind . . .

'The Prince of Wales. Out at the back. Fiona and Frank are here. They'd like to see you too.'

I doubted that, but I looked at Clare's latest hospital number, on a torn card jammed into a shelf above the phone. I looked at my computer's screen-saver, floating small shapes around. They grouped hummingly together, then burst apart, like cheerful, dancing things.

'I'll be there in ten minutes. I'll come on my bike.'

'Bring your lights. Don't dice with death.'

The neighbours were on their front doorstep as I wheeled my bicycle on to the pavement. They were holding fine-stemmed glasses and looking up at the moon, which was white and round and full. I didn't wait to hear the words they'd find to describe it. I was glad to be simply spinning along and away, moving smoothly over the turning world, with my legs up and down in a satisfactory motion. I was glad Liam had rung. He wanted to see me.

7

The longest time I ever spent alone with Gray was in Paris in the August of 1975, when the bar on the corner of the street was shut for the annual *vacances*, but the Arab shop opposite our building was open almost all the time. We bought dried figs there, coated with thick white powder that looked like flour but wasn't. We bought tins of sardines with red-and-blue labels and large dark loaves of bread which we spread with runny butter and warm strawberry jam. There was no fridge in the flat on the Rue Pierre Lescot, which was noisy with pneumatic drills from early morning until late afternoon because the Beaubourg was being constructed a few hundred yards from our door. The sprawling site was called 'Le Trou'; a huge scooped agitation filled with machines and bare-backed workmen. You had to stop talking if you were walking around it, because the noise it produced was enormous. You couldn't hear what the men's hot red faces were shouting as you passed, but they looked pleased, so any comments were presumably complimentary.

*   *   *

I wasn't supposed to be in Paris. I wasn't supposed to be in London either, although that's where my mother thought I'd gone. London was where I'd been headed, when I'd called a taxi to take me away from home. As I was closing the door of the vehicle, Jane came out and handed me twenty pounds. I didn't want to take it, but I did.

It was the summer the Americans and Russians went into space together, to hold hands through their hatches and mouth each other's language, like huge-headed sea creatures on our television set. The only interesting male I knew had gone to stay in my best friend's parents' caravan.

'This isn't *life*, this is a death sentence,' I said to Jane as she drifted through to the kitchen, where I was playing patience with a set of cards that annoyed me. Their backs were printed with nineteenth-century paintings. She said she'd been going to suggest we go for a swim, which surprised me, since she hated to be in the sea; was happy at her typewriter through the hot afternoons, and long cool evenings too. *Swimming Underwater* had been very well reviewed.

'I mean we might as well be dead as live here,' I continued, glad of her attention. I wished it was time for her gin. There was no ice in the fridge. 'And if you want to be famous, that might be an idea. You could just kill yourself, like Sylvia Plath.'

I'd started reading *The Bell Jar*. My aunt filled the kettle and spooned instant coffee into the mug she refilled every half-hour or so. She drank it black, so there was no point in taunting her with the fact that we'd run out of milk, as well as ice. Her nose was peeling from Sunday afternoon on our back doorstep with the papers.

'Well, I don't approve of suicide, Ruth, as you know.' She squinted at steam as water boiled. She had a way of squinting at things as she talked, so you never knew if she was talking to you or herself. 'And besides, I quite like my life. Don't you?'

'I don't like yours, if that's what you mean. I don't like living with two old women much either. It's like being in prison.'

She'd made her coffee by now and was walking away.

'It's worse than prison, because there's no one to talk to. Prison would be better.'

Jane stopped walking and turned to look at me hard. She sipped her coffee, frowned down at the mug, then suggested we do something together, later on.

'We could go to Holkham beach for a picnic when Stell gets back, if you like.'

I said I could think of nothing more boring. 'Do you know what it's like, stuck in the middle of nowhere with you?'

Jane went out of the room, towards her typewriter.

I followed, and talked to her back. 'You want me to be bored to death, don't you?'

She didn't answer, but she didn't start typing.

'Why can't I go to London?' The notion came to me as the words to voice it did.

She turned round. 'London? But it's Thursday afternoon.'

'So?'

'Well, we haven't planned anything, Ruth. It's a working week for most adults.'

'Oh, so you're working, are you? Typing with two fingers is keeping you from having fun, I suppose? Why did you show me London in the first place, if you were going to make sure I stayed here the rest of my life?'

Jane lit a cigarette. It took her a few matches to do it. 'I took you to London because I thought you'd enjoy it, and to give your mother a break.'

'Break from what? From you in her house all the time?'

Jane stood up. I could see from her nostrils that she was breathing differently. 'Ruth, that's enough.'

'Enough of what?'

'I've had enough of being attacked.'

She put another cigarette between her lips, but didn't light it right away. She was looking out of the window.

'Oh, I see. Well, what about other people having enough? Have you ever thought of that?'

She snatched her cigarette out of her mouth and said my name in a way I hadn't heard it before. A sound like a slap, and her eyes drilling into me then as she moved towards me and shouted, and I wasn't afraid, I was pleased. My heart banged with the noise, the response to something I'd said, as I watched her explain that she'd given up most of what she once had for people who didn't have 'enough'.

'I know all about other people and what they take if you let them, Ruth.'

She lit her cigarette then, and was silent for a moment as she squinted at smoke, then went on in a quieter way that she'd once disliked being here as much as I seemed to now, but was in this house because she'd been asked to come and asked to stay.

'People don't always do what they want for themselves, Ruth. Sometimes we just make the best of a bad situation. Try doing that for a change.'

She sat down and started to type. I wished I had something to bang. I said I didn't like her being there any more than she did. The typewriter drove me mad, I said, and poetry was a waste of time.

'Well if you don't like it then leave, Ruth,' she told me. 'Don't waste your breath shouting at me.'

I took my toothbrush from the bathroom where the window was swinging, and went along the echoing landing to my own room, where I took my London bag from under the bed. I put in some jeans and a blouse and some knickers from the top left-hand drawer, which was where I kept my passport, so I took that too and a birthday card with a ten-pound note in it, and I decided to go to London. I hated Jane, and she hated me. I'd go to Diane's and see Gray and his bedroom and not tell Jane and my mother.

I rang for a taxi from the telephone beside my mother's bed. I waited for Jane to rush into the hall and ask what was going on, but she didn't. She carried on typing, so I went downstairs with my red leather bag, with the sleeve of my silk blouse hanging loose over the top of it, like an unworn arm on an amputee.

'I'm leaving, then, since that's what you want. Tell Mum I'll be in touch.'

I moved as quickly as I could without running out of the front door, leaving it open behind me.

The taxi-man drove fast along the high-hedged, long-shadowed afternoon roads, and by the time we were in the city centre I'd decided not to ring from the station and explain. It'd be worse for Jane that way.

Diane didn't seem as surprised as she should have been to find me on her doorstep. As we arrived in her kitchen, she picked up a shoe and started dragging the lace from it, explaining that she needed it to mend a belt she wanted to wear.

'They're Gray's, of course.' She dropped the shoe next to its pair, upside-down on the table. 'But he won't miss them. He's in Paris.'

I sat down, although she hadn't asked me to. She lifted a belt from a chair-back and wandered into the hall, calling back through that Gray was in need of company. He was hanging about, waiting for Jake to arrive. I followed her voice.

'If you want to see Gray, you must go to Paris, my sweet. You could get the night-boat, if you hurry along.'

She was applying lipstick as this was said, which

meant she had her back to me, but my face was reflected in the hall mirror, with hers. She had a glass of gin on the table, and another on the kitchen counter, where there was a smell of roast chicken and a stack of dirty plates. The top one was covered by cold roast potatoes, set in a pool of jellied gravy. I thought it would be best if I got a train back home in the morning, rather than one to Paris tonight, but I didn't say that. I was too surprised.

'I'd ask you to stay here, darling, but I'm on my way out and it'd be rather dull for you. Though of course if you want to, you must.'

She finished one of her drinks. She poured another, and asked if I'd care to join her, which she hadn't done before. She and Jane drank the gin when I arrived with my aunt. I usually went up to see who was in Gray's room, and where whoever was there would be going next.

'Smoke?' Diane held a packet of Silk Cut in my direction. 'Stell would be horrified, I know, but you have a decision to make.'

I shook my head and said, 'No thanks, I don't smoke,' like my mother would. I didn't want to be in Diane's kitchen any more. I should have known that Gray would be somewhere else. I watched a wasp negotiate a pool of spilled liquid on the table, then circle up with its slight but solid noise, then down again on to a teaspoon. It reminded me of home.

'How long is he staying in Paris?'

'Well, in theory not very long. He's supposed to be

grape-picking in a week or so, although I have pointed out that no one picks grapes until the end of September. Still, my son is nothing if not optimistic.'

I realized the buttons on my blouse were done up the wrong way, so the bottom one had no hole. I started rearranging them as Diane rattled the ice in her glass.

'Anyway, darling, I'm going to have to make a move. Now do you want to see Gray or not? Do you want to see *Paree*?'

I watched the wasp banging against the glass of the window.

'I mean I can't imagine you've come all this way to see me, my sweet. Have you been to Paris before?'

Then the phone rang in the hallway and she went through to get it, so I ate a potato, hoping the call would be my mother. Diane must be drunk, though I'd seen her much drunker.

She got back from the hall and told me it had been a wrong number, although she'd been away for a good three minutes.

'So have we made a lovely plan? Is it all decided? You're going on the night train. God, you're a lucky girl.'

She gave one of her laughs, the throaty kind, that sounded more like low growls. I hoped the train would be calm, and the sea-crossing flat. And that it would be warm enough not to need more than a long-sleeved silk blouse when I arrived in France.

* * *

Gray looked sleepy but pleased when he met me at eight o'clock in the morning in shorts and a paisley shirt. I'd forgotten how tall he was. He stooped to kiss my cheek, which seemed to go with the Gare du Nord and its shafts of light, and suitcases moving through the noise of slurred sentences from loudspeakers, way up above. I kissed him back, on both cheeks, which meant his fine long hair got caught in my earring and I had to hold my head still while he eased it free. Then we looked at each other.

'Great,' he said. 'Jane said you'd be here.' He had a way of blinking that managed to be soft but intense at the same time.

'Jane said I'd be here?'

'Yep. She rang at four this morning. Guess she knew I'd be up.' I couldn't see how Jane had been up at that time herself.

'Did she sound OK?'

'Sure. Sounded fine.'

His smile was red against his tanned face, and his hair bleached more blond than it had been at Easter.

'How did she know I was coming?'

He shrugged. 'I didn't ask. Guess she just did, if you didn't tell her.'

I nodded. If Gray wasn't worried, I wouldn't be either.

'Thirsty? Hungry?'

I should have been. I'd slept through the buffet closing on the boat, and hadn't changed my money either, so couldn't buy anything on the green-seated train, where everyone else seemed to have picnics.

'Not really.' My stomach felt full of little beating wings.

'You look tired,' he said.

He took my hand, in a way he had sometimes before. I was glad of the long fingers against my own, which now felt like somebody else's. I was glad too when he led me out to a taxi rank and told the man where to go, in an accent that sounded authentic. We drove through high buildings in hard shadowed light, and clambered out into a hazed white place and the smell of dust and stale urine, and the sound of water, gushing the sides of the street, and the laborious beginnings of work in the Trou. Gray lifted my bag out of the soft seat we'd shared. He gave the man money, then we were on cobbles together and he found keys to open a heavy brown door, up into a cold flight of stone stairs, where he stopped on a landing to find a key under a jam-jar on a window-ledge, then we went on up to the top, where he put my bag down in the segmented light from a high tiny window and opened the door on to a narrow kitchen, with a blue and white checked floor, which we walked over into a larger room with rugs and couches and a marble fireplace and books on every high-windowed wall. I had to squint in the light of it, after the stairwell.

'Want to brush your teeth?' he said.

I said I did, and went to the bathroom. I was having the end of a period and wanted to check my tampon. I only had one spare with me, and didn't want to have to ask Gray how to get more, so I was glad to see I might not need any. I washed my face, which looked paler than at Diane's, which seemed like days ago, then I went out to find Gray, who was making coffee, shaking the dark-chocolate smell of ground beans into a battered tin jug. Every surface seemed to be covered in checks, like school-uniform dresses, but larger.

'It's very clean here,' I said, for something to say.

'There's a *femme de ménage*.'

I'd never quite been alone with Gray's lean body in a room before, so I backed out and into the adjacent one, where the mantelpiece had photographs of women with different smiles, in different frames next to each other.

I sat on a rug-covered couch while Gray arrived with coffee, and some biscuits in packets strung together like beads.

'So you didn't tell Jane you were coming?' he said. He poured dark liquid into wide cups with gold at their rims.

'Not really,' I said. The biscuits were ginger. I dipped one into my coffee. It seemed like sawdust on my tongue.

'Does your mother know you're here, though?'

I told him I hardly ever saw her, which wasn't true, but didn't feel like a lie. 'Have you ever seen her?'

'Who?' Gray was pulling his shoes off.

'My mother.'

I was thinking that the couch would be long enough for me to sleep on, if I bent my legs at the knees.

'Don't think so,' he said. 'What does she look like?'

And then I had to think a while, in the swimming-pool room and the Parisian smell, and the shape of Gray, just across from my legs.

'She looks a bit like her,' I said, pointing to one of the photographs on the mantelpiece. The woman was younger than my mother, but had the same shaped face, the same intense dark eyes.

Gray ate his biscuit. He seemed preoccupied.

'Whose flat is this?'

I lifted my feet on to the arm of the couch. I wished Gray would touch some part of me. He was a long way away, on the green leather chair, with his long hands on his knees by the empty fireplace.

'It belongs to my father. But he's in Rome just now.' He broke another biscuit in two.

'What's he doing there?'

The details surrounding the particulars of where I was seemed important; like knowing where your shoes are at a party.

'His girlfriend's Italian. Her mother's ill.'

'Well, my mother looks like that woman, whoever she is.'

He looked at the picture. He smiled and looked quietly back at me. 'She's called Anne Sexton. She's dead.'

He felt in his pocket for his tin and a lighter. The smell of burning dope drifted. He passed the long joint to me when he'd smoked a while, so I took some, then gave it back to him.

'She was an American poet,' he said.

I lay back and closed my eyes and listened to him inhale. My mother looked like a poet because her sister was one, of course. Perhaps Jane looked like a poet too.

'This house has been far out at sea all night.'

That was a poem Jane quoted if it was stormy weather at home. At home Jane would be typing by now. The fire would not be lit. The seagulls would be noisy in the nothing of the sky. *'That upturned bowl men call the sky,'* Jane sometimes said. The ceiling above me was blown with the shadows of vast slim-leafed plants by the windows. *'Glory be to God for dappled things.'* That would be if there were shadows in our woods, where there would be small brown birds with small noises, not seagulls. *'Hope is the thing with feathers'*. I wondered how many poems Jane knew. *'Green green I love you green.'* I listened to her voice in those sounds for a while. Three greens, but six, if you said it twice in a row.

'How many words do you think you know, Gray?'

He didn't answer, and I didn't open my eyes to see if he was still in the room, but I knew he was so I said, 'Are you glad to see me?'

'Sure,' he said. He said sure a lot, so that could have meant anything. 'Sure I am.' Two sures. I wanted a third but none came.

I felt his hand heavy on the bottom of my leg, then the slither of my shoes slipping off my red socks, then the lightness of my feet with nothing between their wrinkles of fabric and the air of the room. Then there were no more words in my head, but the sound of my breath like the sea up and down, on a flat blue day with boats and white sails like enormous flapping and empty blank pages, with the thrum of a Paris aeroplane somewhere high above.

I woke to the feel of sheeted newspaper over my legs. It was *Le Monde*, and across it in large black felt-tip was a message from Gray: 'Gone to the post-office. Sleep well.'

The sun had stopped shining, but the day was still hot. My legs were sticky with sweat, pressed together, and on their underneaths was a rash-like pattern from the couch. The floor felt good and smooth underneath my socks as I went to find water, then through again to a bedroom with half-closed curtains, where books were everywhere. Open on the bed was a paperback of *One Hundred Years of Solitude*. On the bedside table was a stack of assorted spines, slidey hardbacks and musty softer volumes that I lifted one by one. Ibsen: *Four Major Plays*, Kafka: *Letters to Felice*, Oscar Wilde: *Fairy Tales*, Stendhal, Salinger, Wallace Stevens, Flaubert, William Burroughs, Henry Miller, Philip Roth. They must belong there, but the Márquez was Gray's. It said 'Happy Birthday, dear G and love from Clare' on the flysheet. He was on page 102, where cannon shots had opened a hole in the street. Rain had left the ground slippery and as smooth as melted soap and Arcadio was leaving Amaranta with Úrsula. There were pistols and resistance. I stopped reading to listen to a screaming child outside the window and a woman shouting something.

It felt as if it ought to rain here in Paris. There was a heavy feeling, which wasn't simply the folds of the curtains or the squashed-together pillows, or the slight sweet smell of sleep in the room. I sat on a chair piled with soft things and pulled off my socks and decided to wash my hands and face and feet. I put the book that Clare had given Gray back on to the bed and hoped it was in the right place. I was in the bathroom with the door open and water running on to lathering soap when Gray came through. He was holding a baguette. I was standing in the bath with the shower attachment fizzing over my toes, with fine white bubbles like a small shallow wave.

'Good idea,' he said, dragging his espadrilles off.

He sat on the side of the high-walled bath and put his bare feet next to mine, so I sprayed them too. We ate the warm bread, wet from our fingers, and talked loudly, over the noise of water and the sound of car-horns and the round-shaped echoes of what we said.

We seemed to be in and out of echoey places throughout our days in Paris. The rattling Métro made everything filled up but hollow, as it tunnelled from station to station to take us to the Jardin des Tuileries, where we emerged into thunderous light and muted greens, and Gray took my hand along gravelled paths, up wide worn stone stairs into the Orangerie, where a high arched hallway made us whisper, as we bought tickets to see the Impressionist paintings that Gray had decided were the thing to see, when I'd said I wanted to do something French.

There were lots of Americans there, but Gray said that was very French in itself, and had I not read Henry James?

'No. Have you?'

He smiled one of his smaller smiles. 'Well you could try Henry Miller. They like it here. It makes them feel cultured and dirty.'

We stared at Manet's long blue-white lady, with her black maid, her dark eyes and pink roses, until I wanted to stop, so I sat on a red velvet bench and watched people looking, and touching each other and smoothing the pages of catalogues. I wished I was wearing a dress. Gray came and sat beside me, so I stood up and we looked at Monet's lilies with their massed purples and Van Gogh's awkward chair and Pissaro's girl with a stick, which Gray said looked something like me.

When the gallery closed, we walked down the street-wide steps with everyone else. Outside the rain had been and gone and the ground was steamy, the air thick with wet dust, the trees clean and full against the washed-out streaks of the sky.

In a small bar with gold on its windows Gray ordered *vin blanc cassis*. He drank his down in one, and ordered another. The glasses were shallow and heavy. He had small cigarettes with yellow paper around them. Other men in the bar had them too. There was a dog on the floor, like a wolf, I said.

'It's just eaten its granny. We should be OK.' Gray spoke with his Gauloise between his lips, which blurred his words. I said the drink was like Ribena. I liked the way it made my face warm.

'Why did you go to the post-office?'

'Had to make a phone call. Didn't want to wake you up. Besides, I don't like to run up the phone bill there.'

A man came through the door with a beard like Father Christmas. Gray watched me look, and I liked it.

'*Who is Sylvia, what is she?* Do you know that one, Ruth?'

'What one?' My glass seemed to be empty. The beard-man had left the door open, which let in the smell of something sugary roasting outside. Gray had pink fingernails; long and narrow and nicer than any girl's I knew.

'What do you want to do next?' I could feel his knees under the table and wanted to squeeze some part of his long warm-looking shape, but I didn't say that, or do it either.

'Walk,' I said. 'I'd like to walk.'

So we walked through streets with shuttered shops, through buttery restaurant air, where menus swung on blackboards outside places with red-and-white table-cloths, and straight-backed waiters carried baskets of bread, and everybody was talking. We walked through small squares with statues of sitting men and empty wooden benches. Gray took my arm as we crossed a seething street, and told me I must learn about French traffic. Mostly he didn't say much, though, until he asked if I was tired and I said not, but was pleased when we came to what he said was The Select, with swooping chairs crammed on a pavement, and we sat in the dark and he ordered more *vin blanc cassis*, and told me Hemingway might have sat on my chair, although probably he'd have been at the bar by now, drinking stronger stuff than this. I'd never read any Hemingway, and I told him so, and he asked what I did read, and I said *The Bell Jar*, which was slightly made up since I'd stopped just after Esther got food poisoning. I'd have liked to say I was reading *One Hundred Years of Solitude*.

'Well, Plath was a friend of our friend Anne Sexton. Both keen on suicide.'

'Was that because they were poets? Or did writing poems make them suicidal?' I didn't care what Gray said, as long as he talked. He looked straight at me when he answered any question. I spent much of the time he was talking wondering what to ask next, at first.

'Not sure. You could ask your aunt Jane.' He stubbed a cigarette, and frowned into the smoke. 'If you ever go home again.'

'Do you think I might not?' I felt melted enough to ask this plainly. A woman with perfume bumped into my chair.

'You know, Ruth, I don't know what I think.' He sucked at the rim of his empty glass. 'Do you want to read some Baudelaire?'

Then he leaned across the table and took my head in his hands for a moment. 'I wish everyone was like you.'

'Jane says they are. That's the trouble, she says.'

'Well then Jane's been living in Norfolk too long.'

Then he left me alone with other bodies and talking while he went to the *toilettes*, and I thought of Jane's knees with their freckles, pulled up to her chin on the beach at Cley the weekend before, after the thunder-storm, when she told me it was easy to be like everyone else. You just had to want them to like you enough, she'd said. She lay back after that and stared at the sky. I couldn't imagine her not being close to the sea for long. She wasn't the same in London. She laughed more, but didn't smile so much. I hoped Gray was wrong about where she ought to live as he arrived to put his hands on my shoulders. He said something in French and took my wrist in his fingers. We went to the Arab shop on the way home. I carried the bread and he took everything else.

The flat looked smaller in electric light. Someone upstairs made muffled thuds from time to time as Gray and I ate figs and cheese at the oblong kitchen table. We'd bought cold white wine, with stars round the neck of the bottle, which Gray said would rot our insides, but I didn't care. We drank on the couch when we'd eaten enough and I listened to Gray speaking French, with his head down towards a thick paper-back, his mouth more pouted than usual round the up and down of sounds I couldn't understand. It made me think of something soft falling down a long staircase, I said, when he asked if I liked it or not.

'Say this,' he said. *'J'ai plus de souvenirs que si j'avais mille ans.'*

'Say it slowly.'

'I am like the king of a rainy country, rich but powerless, young yet very old.'

He was smiling back into his pages.

'The handsome jack of hearts and the queen of clubs speak *sinistrement*,' he told me.

'What do they speak of?'

My feet were near his knees.

'They speak ominously of dead lovers, Ruth.'

I liked the rhythm of him reading. I liked his feet slipping along on the left of my body, as we lolled now at opposite ends of the couch. I liked the way he rolled my socks off.

'We can't do anything,' I said, when we were on his bed, with my last Tampax still in place and *One Hundred Years of Solitude* under my left knee. His leg lay over mine.

'Like what?'

'Nothing.'

I lay awake long after he left to smoke and sleep on the couch. The queen of clubs moved through my half-awake state. She spoke like Jane, but didn't smile. She asked what I thought I was doing. Gray would never ask that.

My first day in Paris seemed the longest and hottest.

The second and third days felt cooler because Gray lent me some white shorts he found in a drawer, and I wore one of his T-shirts instead of my blouse until we'd had showers at the start of the evenings, which were no different from other bits of the day, except we'd be nearer each other, and talk more than we did together in daylight. We spent evenings wandering around until we were tired enough to sit in the flat. Then Gray read things he found there to me, until we were tired enough to lie on the bed.

I'd never been on a bed with Gray before without other people in the room. We'd never taken our clothes off, and we didn't in Paris, although we almost did, perhaps, on the last night I was there, after we'd been to Versailles, where a policeman had asked for my papers and decided I'd given him my passport in a manner that lacked respect. He gave it back to me and said to try again, so I held the thing again until Gray slipped it from my fingers and gave it back to the *gendarme*. We were allowed to go on our way then, when my face had been scrutinized closely.

'You know what?' Gray said, as we made our way towards a series of arches, through which blocks of ornamental masonry cast sturdy shadows on the ground. 'You know what, Ruth?' He kicked at the gravel so it made a fine arch of dust, and jammed his hands into his pockets. 'We're in another country.'

I thought he meant we ought to go back to Paris, and not stay in this place I had asked to see, like a tourist would. I thought he didn't like this manicured space, this dead king's version of 'the country'. I stared down at long hard straight paths, peopled with slow-moving flocks of clothing on legs and the flat water of a lake, and a cluster of neat orange trees like swollen tennis balls.

'Do you want to go home?' I asked, but he didn't hear me because he'd moved off ahead to stand in front of a balustrade, his hands still in his pockets, his head straight and high. I watched him run his hands through his hair, and couldn't bear the notion that he might be silent, or cross, or apart from me, so I ran and said it again, too loudly, so people stared, as if we were having a row.

'Let's go home, Gray, if you don't like it.'

Then he lurched and locked his hands around my back suddenly and lifted me up against him, and when he put me back down his breathing had changed.

'You can't go home again,' he said. Then he laughed, then stopped and kicked gravel again, saying, 'We do things differently here. And that's a relief. Let's go.'

Back then we went, with my hand in his, through milling people with cameras and German words and the shadows of long-winged birds on the ground and our legs together, to the station where we sat on a warm wooden bench, then into the hot seats of the train, with air through the narrow steel-lidded windows, and his feet up on the seat between my knees, and his eyes in mine in a different way – a way I hadn't been looked at before. I liked it, but couldn't look back, so I watched the up and down of the telegraph wires, criss-crossing as the train swayed us back to the Gare St-Lazare, with its smells of roasted nuts and sweat and soft old railway tickets, which stuck to the soles of our shoes.

'Let's walk for a while,' he said, so we did, through small streets and cafés and shops with dark-bruised avocados piled high and a patisserie where we bought ice-creams and on to the sweep of the Avenue de l'Opéra, where we caught a bus with whooshing doors and had to sit apart until Gray came and stood near me, holding on to the pole so I could see his knuckles firm and shiny in front of my face, until we got off and walked home without stopping at the shop.

'We'll get what we need later,' he told me, as I hesitated outside the door. 'We're going up now. Come on.'

He was at the top of the stairs before I was, because he ran all the way. I heard his espadrilles slapping, two steps at a time, and when I got to the kitchen he'd already left it and was calling me through from the bedroom.

'Did you shut the door?'

I hadn't, so went back and pushed it hard, so it clicked, then went back to the bedroom, where he'd pushed all the books from the bed, so it looked bigger, and softer, with his body along it. I stared until he said 'What?'

'What are you doing?'

He was pulling his shoes off.

'Don't know,' he said. 'Do it with me.'

163

So I lay down with him. He stared at the ceiling.

'My period's finished,' I said.

We listened to cement mixers and a pneumatic drill bursting into sudden noise, then a shouting man. Gray sat up. 'I need a smoke, Ruth.'

He rolled off the bed into a standing position. He reached to touch my head, then bent quickly and kissed my cheek. He left, but didn't close the door.

I lay and watched the light haze the wallpaper. I didn't know how to make Gray come back, but I didn't want to walk through to where he'd be, so I stayed where I was until the front door slammed behind him. I sat up, thinking I'd done something wrong, though I didn't know what. The leaves of the walls were fading into the flowers. The pattern wasn't unlike the big room at Diane's, I decided, then the telephone on the bedside table rang with the small hard noise it made in France. I picked the creamy receiver up, thinking it must be Gray telling me to go and meet him wherever he'd gone, but it wasn't. It was a man with a cigarette voice saying hello in a nice French accent.

'I don't speak French. I don't live here,' I said.

The voice made a small 'mmnn' sound, not unlike the one that Jane made; preoccupied but vaguely attentive too. I waited. I found the switch for the lamp on the book-jammed floor.

'Hi,' the voice said then, in a throaty but definite way. There was a cough and I heard whoever it was sip something before the voice said 'So you're English?'

I said yes I was, but nothing else.

'I'm really calling to talk to my son,' the voice said. 'Have you seen him about in the last few hours?'

I didn't say anything back. There was a London phone number pinned to the wall above a postcard of a Soutine painting with lumps of meat outlined in black. When I'd looked at it I said, 'I don't know. Who are you?'

'Well, you tell me who you are, and then I'll tell you. How does that sound?'

There was a moth trying to get into the lightbulb underneath the shade of the lamp. The lampshade was small and intensely red.

'I'm Ruth. I'm here with Gray.'

'But Gray's not there?'

The moth had got into the lampshade, making flapping sounds with its shadow.

'He's gone to the shops.' My legs were a bit brown, from the sun in Versailles. 'I don't think he'll be long. Shall I get him to call you?'

The man said nothing as I looked at the long ribs of the dark slats of the window, where the curtains would be pulled some time tonight. I was lying on Gray's father's bed, and he didn't know who I was.

'I'm Jane's niece. Jane Myers. She's a friend of Diane's.'

I touched the pillow where Gray's head had been. The silence on the phone continued.

'I mean that's how I know Gray. Jane knows Diane.'

'She certainly does.' He sipped whatever he was drinking. Then sipped again, then coughed.

'So you're Jane's niece.'

I said yes I was.

'So let me get this straight,' he said. Perhaps Gray wasn't meant to have people to stay. I shouldn't have answered the phone. 'You're Ruth Myers and you're staying with Gray. Is that right?'

He made it sound unlikely, and it was beginning to seem so to me, but it was true, and I said yes I was.

'I didn't plan it, exactly,' I said. 'But I went to see Gray in London. Well, I wanted to get away from home, so I went to London and he wasn't there, so I came here on the train. Diane thought it'd be a good idea.' My mouth was dry at the end of this, which surprised me. I pulled Gray's jumper from the floor to wrap round me as the man said nothing. I felt compelled to go on. 'I'm glad I came, though. I'm having a lovely time.'

He didn't speak.

'I think you know my aunt. You went to the launch of her book, in London.'

I knew that about David, at least. I remembered that Jane didn't like him there. But I wanted his voice in my empty room.

'Indeed I did. She's a pretty good poet, your aunt, you know.'

I said again then that Gray would be home soon, and would he like him to call?

'That would be nice,' he said, after a while of breathing and silence.

'Are you in Rome?' I said, for no reason.

'I am just now. But back in Paris tomorrow.'

Now it was my turn to not talk. He must want to tell me he needed his flat.

'We'll be in St-Germain. It'd be nice to meet up.'

My right foot was numb. I'd been sitting on it, without realizing. I rubbed it with the hand that wasn't holding the phone.

'Yes. I think we ought to meet up.' I heard a match strike. Jane always smoked on the phone. 'So tell Gray his dad wants to see him, Ruth. And I'd really like to see you, too.' He drank whatever was in his hand. He smoked. 'Why don't we have lunch? You and Gray and me? How does that sound?'

I heard a phone ring near wherever he was and voices and him saying something fuzzed and fast, with his hand over the mouthpiece, then he was back and saying he'd like to meet me, and should we arrange it now?

'How about it, Ruth? What about lunch? You and me and Gray?'

He seemed to be talking to someone else, as I didn't know what to say back.

'I think Gray better arrange it,' I said. 'I'm not sure how long I'm staying.'

'Don't rush back to London, Ruth. You're on holiday, aren't you?'

I said yes I was, though not what my holiday was from.

'So you can stay in Paris.' He drank. 'How's it going, anyway? How's Norfolk, these days?'

I pulled the jumper round my shoulders. I looked at myself, far away, in the mirror on the wall across the room from the sheets and the bed. Someone outside shouted something I couldn't understand.

'I'll get Gray to call you, shall I?'

'Do that,' he said, and he coughed. 'Do that, Ruth, and I'll see you very soon.'

'It's David, isn't it?'

'Sure,' he said. 'And you're Ruth.'

'Yes,' I said, and I found myself half laughing, like Diane might do to someone unknown on the phone. He'd made it sound like some game we'd been through, and both ended up being perfectly right. 'I'll get Gray to call you.'

'Thanks, Ruth. Nice to hear you. See you soon.'

He put the phone down, and I looked at myself in the mirror again, and decided I wanted to wash my hair. I was pleased to have something from outside to tell Gray. We could talk about lunch with his father when he got back. And I'd have clean hair and it would be all right again. I wandered through into the large room I was getting to know, with its streaked shadows and plants and red rugs, and the sound of a piano downstairs.

I was standing under the erratic stream of the shower, lathering my head, when I heard the front door slam. I listened for Gray's footsteps, but none came in my direction. They moved into the sitting room and something heavy was dropped on to the boards there.

'I'm in here,' I called through, keeping my eyes squeezed against foam slithering over my face. 'I'm having a shower.'

No one moved or came through, so I started rinsing my hair and called out 'Hello' a few times, wondering what Gray would have brought back to eat. He never came home empty-handed. The night before he'd fed me salami, cut into chunks, as I soaked my feet in a bathful of water. I washed a lot in Paris, and so did Gray. Our bodies were soaked in lavender smells from the bar of mauve soap I'd grown very fond of.

'I'm in here. Come through if you like.'

The door opened and a head appeared, with the long body then leaning round. It wasn't Gray. It was Jake. Jake from London, in cut-off jeans and a swirling short-sleeved shirt I'd seen before. He was holding a glass of milk.

'Hi. It's me. How you doing?'

The shower ran boiling suddenly, as it sometimes did, so I moved out of it rather than answering him. No one had seen me naked for years.

'Where's Gray?' I reached for the only towel, which was on the floor so I had to bend over the side of the bath.

'Haven't seen him. He could be in bed, I guess.' He was looking at me curiously. 'So hi. You're here . . . ?'

He'd forgotten my name, but I didn't want to tell him. My hair was dripping and I couldn't rub it, because that would have meant lifting the towel from round my body.

169

'Want some coffee?' There wasn't anything else to offer, until Gray got back.

'Could do with it. Been on a train all day and stuck at Gare du fucking Nord for hours. Clare's still there with Josie. Her bag's been nicked. Those station police are something else.'

'Clare's at the station?'

'With Josie, yeah. Filling in forms and shit. They'll ring if it takes too long, I guess.'

'Do they know the number?' I didn't know what it was. But I hadn't rung Gray to say I'd be here. Jane had done that for me.

In the kitchen I started to show Jake how to light the gas, but he already knew and put water to boil while I went to the bedroom and tied my wet hair back in an elastic band that was lying twisted and soft on the pillow my head had been on before. I dressed in my jeans, without really thinking, and found my crumpled T-shirt under a chair. I stuffed the shorts I'd been lent into the back of the bottom drawer in the bedroom, behind a clump of men's socks. There was a note Gray had left me the morning before, saying 'See you very soon,' tucked into the bookshelves, so I took it down and folded it into my bag, with everything else in the room that was connected with me. I noticed some of my blood on the sheet, and pulled the duvet over it as the sound of Bob Dylan's 'Desolation Row' came from the sitting room. I went through to find Jake rolling a joint. Books that had been on the couch were on the floor.

'Coffee's in the kitchen. Kind of,' he said, pointing to a mug of steam near his feet. 'Couldn't find any sugar, but it's OK.'

He had to shout above Dylan saying Ophelia was 'neath the window, for her he felt so afraid, and I too felt not afraid but apprehensive in his presence. Everything was different now. Clare would be arriving, with her bags and with Josie. Gray could never kiss me properly now.

'Such a drag, this bag thing,' Jake said. 'They're starving, you know?'

He passed me the joint he'd manufactured.

I shook my head. 'I'm going,' I told him. 'I've got to get back to London.'

I knew he wouldn't ask why. 'Why' wasn't a word Jake was familiar with. Things happened, as far as he was concerned. He watched smoke rise as I left the room and came back into it with my bag in my hand.

'Can you say bye to Gray for me?'

Jake's eyes were closed and he didn't respond when I said his name, so I nudged his legs, which slid off the couch. Mine often did that too.

'Hey. Hi,' he said. 'Have some coffee.'

'Tell Gray I've gone to London, can you?'

'Sure I can.'

'And can you tell him David rang?'

'Sure. Good to see you again.'

He didn't even know who I was. The coffee cup had spilled. I picked up my bag. There was a small dark stain on the blues of the rug. There was a biro on the table. I looked for paper, but couldn't see any, so I picked up Jake's hand and wrote David on it, as he almost watched.

'Just so you don't forget,' I said.

'Sure. Gray has to ring his dad.'

He hadn't told me he knew who David was, but there was no reason he should have, I thought, as I crossed the squares of the kitchen floor. Perhaps all Gray's friends knew his father.

'Bye then, Jake,' I called as I opened the door. I wanted to give myself the impression I was leaving somewhere I'd been staying in a normal way. I decided I'd ring home from the Gare du Nord, as I went down the first flight of stairs from the flat. In the squash of the Métro, I decided to find a phone as soon as I got to the station. I'd ring and tell Jane I'd be back the next day. Or maybe my mother would answer the phone. She'd be glad I was on my way. Both of them would be glad. They'd say goodbye back to me when I'd said it to them. I'd ring home as soon as I knew what time a train would be. Then I'd buy my ticket to London, and find a seat by the window and sleep all the way to the coast.

8

Liam took up smoking again the year that Clare died. He bought his first pack in eighteen months when he was in London in mid July, cat-sitting for Fiona and Frank. I told him he shouldn't, and said too that he ought not to be in London, because I needed him by the sea to visit, during this airless and difficult time. The weather was a low-clouded oppression, which looked as if it might require some garment with sleeves when you looked out from indoors, but was really too hot for clothes. Londoners were abandoning theirs at a great rate. The railings of the Brook Green playground were strewn with small sweatshirts; the walls of streets running down to the station were scattered with larger articles.

The best place to be was on a bicycle, by the river, moving out over the towpath towards the west. There the waters slowed to ripple in a stately curve between sweeps of poplars, still and high like a cool green frieze against the sky. That was the way I cycled, on Clare's high black bike (which we had decided I should 'borrow' for now), when I went over to Fiona's place in Barnes. Liam asked me round, to sit in her garden, the Thursday after he got there. He'd been at mine on Tuesday – the evening he arrived – and annoyed me by leaving to feed the cat, before the night was properly dark. I'd been reading and writing about Yeats that day, and felt that Liam should stay to talk about poetry into the early hours, and be more than desultory about our romance. Yeats wouldn't have wandered off from a woman to feed a cat. He might have gone to write '*She is foremost of those that I would hear praised,*' maybe, and reflect on my reflective and pilgrim soul.

'Come into the garden, Maud,' Liam said when I arrived at his sister's house in the claustrophobic heat. 'Come and see the deckchairs.'

Minstrel, the cat, arrived to complicate the wheeling of my bicycle into the bottle-green hallway, where a reproduction Art-Deco figure was standing wax-skinned, with unpainted lips, which made it look ghoulish. Liam shifted the thing backwards to make room for my bicycle, and trod on the cat as he did so. It squealed and ran, so he followed.

By the time I reached the garden, Liam and Minstrel were in a deckchair together, beside an assortment of cups and a teapot, which I leaned to touch and felt was hot. I took my cardigan off.

'It's Earl Grey. I bought it specially.' Liam stroked Minstrel's delicate chin and said there was milk in the fridge, so I went and got it, then the cat was gone and

174

Liam was sitting with his knees together and his navy shorts and a striped T-shirt, like the one he was wearing the day I first saw his tanned legs, exposed to the waiting room of the Natural Health Centre on Brackenbury Road. He'd been holding his head very straight, that first afternoon, which meant he had to look at me when I sat down. There was nowhere to sit but in front of him, unless I'd sat at his side.

'Is that the same T-shirt you've always had? The one you used to wear?'

'Probably. Like it?'

I nodded and wondered whether to mention the day we'd met. He was in the waiting room because he'd done something to his neck and had to see the osteopath. I was there to see a dark-haired therapist, who never said anything except 'And how did that make you feel?'

'You were wearing it when we met,' I said.

'Don't think so. I bought it in Hastings.'

I sat down in a deckchair and drank some tea, which wasn't easy with the way the canvas held my head.

'Is that OK? Would you prefer a cold drink?'

Liam and I had drunk warm orange juice from cartons with straws on the afternoon we met. The fridge was broken in the newsagent's, where we found ourselves after the Health Centre. The shop was the third place we'd been near each other that hot August afternoon. We'd emerged from our respective treatments to stand together in the sweet-smelling foyer and write cheques on the tall wooden counter, then

175

walked towards Hammersmith Grove, one after the other, then into the shop for liquid refreshment. As I followed him out and towards the market, Liam had turned to ask if I was following him.

'I might be,' I'd said. 'It depends where you're going.'

'Down to the river.'

I said I'd be behind him all the way in that case, because I was going there too.

'Want to share the pavement then? There's plenty of room next to me.'

I'd never been picked up on a street before. Liam had passed me his card as we parted, next to the ornamental scrolls of Hammersmith bridge. We had to shout over the roll of the traffic hitting the ramps in the concrete, so I took his card without saying much except thanks. The card didn't say what he did, but he'd told me he was writing film reviews. He went to the pictures a lot, he'd said as buses soared by, and would I like to go some time? His address was in Sinclair Road, around the corner from me. I rang the next morning and he phoned back. We saw a Hal Hartley film the same night, in the Electric on the Portobello Road. Then we sat and drank lager in the garden of the Prince of Wales. He'd walked me home at closing time, but didn't come up for coffee, which my friends thought was a bad sign, but turned out not to be.

Fiona and Frank's garden always smelled of nail varnish, although the varnish Fiona used on her figures was in large tins, rather than small glass bottles. These were kept with paints and brushes and bags of plaster in a dilapidated shed, where Minstrel had her kittens the year before. All but one of them drowned. She was nursing them in a box that filled with rain one night. Liam thought this was the reason Minstrel was nervous and needed a lot of affection.

He was sympathetic about lost babies; had been consoling, and kind, too, when I was briefly pregnant with a baby that would have been his. But he had no interest now in a child of his own. We didn't discuss it any more, except if I was drinking.

'Sure you wouldn't like some iced lemonade?' he asked.

The sun had made a faint appearance and there were fuzzed shadows on the threadbare lawn. Liam watched me watching them. He lit a cigarette. He wondered if Minstrel minded the heat, and if she drank enough water. Minstrel's surviving kitten lived next door, but they seemed indifferent to each other, now they were both grown-ups.

'My mother had an abortion, after she had me,' I said.

Liam coughed smoke out, had a gulp of tea and coughed some more.

'You ought to stop smoking, before you properly start,' I said. 'You'll die if you don't.'

'You're obsessed with dying, Ruth.'

He took a drag and swallowed and looked at me again. I told him Yeats thought sex and death were the only things that could interest a serious mind.

'They all say that,' he told me. 'What do you mean, an abortion?'

'I mean an operation women have to get rid of a baby they don't want. Someone you know had one, remember?'

Liam had had an affair the year before. The woman got pregnant, but it might not have been his baby, and she didn't have it anyway, but the fact that she could have still rankled with me. He threw his half-smoked cigarette into the bushes behind him.

'If you want to talk about that, I don't,' he told me firmly.

There was silence. He pulled at the grass between his feet. I said I was sorry, and I was. I didn't want to argue. I wanted to talk.

'Let's start again, shall we? You say your mother had an abortion?'

'Or a miscarriage, maybe. But she must have been seeing a man when I was small, somehow. She was pregnant when I was three. That's the reason Jane came to stay.'

He asked how I knew, if I'd been talking to someone, and who it was if I had. He sounded aggressive, rather than intrigued. I told him about the letters I'd got from Colette, and how she came to have them. He pulled his nose and frowned at his knees and crossed and uncrossed his legs.

'I think you should throw them away.'

'Why? They're Jane's.'

'You shouldn't read other people's letters. Unless they're dead, maybe.'

I'd read Liam's letters once, which was how I knew about his affair. He never forgave me, but I was glad I did.

'My mother is dead.'

'But Jane isn't.'

'So?'

'So send the letters she wrote to Diane back to her. They're nothing to do with you.'

'They're about my life. They explain a lot.'

'They're private, Ruth. They're from Jane to Diane. You can't have every bit of everyone else's life.' He stood up and ran his hands through his hair. 'Look, I wouldn't read Jane's letters if I were you.'

The cat appeared with a moth in its mouth. She dropped it and batted the fluttering shape, her body taut and long as she stilled its wings, pinned it down, then released it into a moment of frantic low flight.

'But your mother gave them to me. I didn't go looking. Jane doesn't want them.'

'How do you know? Have you asked her?'

I hadn't spoken to Jane for over two years. I no longer knew her address. I'd told her I didn't want it when she rang from New York, the Christmas of 1995, and said she was moving to Boston, and not back to Norfolk, for the foreseeable future.

'You should read them, Liam. Your mother's in some. She went to see my mother when she was depressed and Jane couldn't cope.'

179

'My mother's on the telephone, Ruth. I spoke to her on Friday.'

He stood up as a leaf drifted on to my knee and someone in the next house slammed a window shut. Then there was muffled banging inside Fiona's, followed by a clearer noise. I sensed her presence moving towards us before I heard her voice. She called hi, hello, surprise surprise, and then was there in the doorway in belted shorts, a tight striped T-shirt and her hair up, with dark glasses balanced on top of the pile, on top of her Liam-shaped head.

The cat rubbed itself between her long legs. Fiona picked it up and rubbed her face in fur, while I said hello and Liam asked what she was doing back home.

'Mmnnn, Marlboro. I want one.' He threw the pack over. She came to lift his lighter from his legs. She exhaled with satisfaction, lifting her bare arms as she did so. She said it had been a long hot drive.

'Don't think I can face it again today. Think I'll stay over and drive back in the morning.'

'You don't do things in the morning,' Liam said.

'Not as a rule.' She smiled up into the dense white of the sky. 'But rules are meant to be broken. Guess what? Frank and I spent the night in hospital. He had an accident.'

'Shit.'

'I know. But I'm going to nurse him. It's only a broken ankle. He decided to make a video of his feet as he walked over some rocks.' She laughed without opening her lips, so a squeaky sound came out. 'He's such an idiot.'

'Ruth's come for afternoon tea,' Liam said.

'Nice,' she said. 'Hi, Ruth. How's things? How's your friend?' She moved to inspect the teapot as I said my friend was in hospital.

'Poor thing. God, I hate those places. I felt terminally ill from just breathing the air.'

She took the lid off the teapot, sniffed the liquid and raised her brows to her brother.

'Posh,' she said. 'Earl Grey is it now? My teabags not good enough for you?'

Liam told her it was for me, then looked up into the only tree, so I couldn't catch his eye. His sister went to get herself a cup.

'Liam, I'll drink any kind of tea,' I said.

'I know you will.'

'Well don't pretend I won't, then.'

'Don't be paranoid. Have a biscuit.'

He found a pack of fig-rolls under his chair and gave me two, since they were melted into each other. I bit into the soft and sugary block as Fiona came back to pour tea and sit on the ground with her legs crossed, although Liam's deckchair was free. He was standing up, with the cat.

'Minstrel's missed you.'

'Has she? I missed her too. Can you hang around for a week or so more, though? Frank and I've decided to stay down in Cornwall, since he can't walk any more. I'm taking some work back with me. The Olympia stuff's not due till August.'

She took a teaspoon and used the point of it to dig at an ingrown hair on her calf. Her toenails were painted a greeny blue.

'Stop that. It's disgusting.' Liam sat down in the deckchair. Minstrel scrambled off him to rub herself along Fiona's shorts, then flop outstretched on the earth beside her.

'Well, can you stay or not? Minstrel needs to be fed.' The cat rolled on to her back in a wanton and languorous pose. Of course Liam would stay, for Fiona.

'Minstrel, you're a flirt,' he said.

'She's just glad to see me. Her mistress is back.'

I decided to go to the bathroom.

When I came back, Fiona was in my deckchair, discussing the quality of the Cornwall surf. The barn of their mother's cottage there was full of wetsuits – mostly rotten or split. I'd been twice. Once with Liam and once with Clare and Conor. It had rained persistently both times.

'The Australians have taken Polzeath over, but we like that,' Fiona was saying. 'They're more attractive than the locals. It's terribly exotic.'

'Ruth didn't find it so. Spent most of our time in Cornwall in the bath, as I remember.'

'It was March. Even the dogs were wearing coats.'

Fiona told us she loved Cornwall in winter. That was her favourite time. Frank made fires and they took a hip-flask with them down to walk by the sea.

'I love whisky, late at night on the beach.'

Liam laughed, which surprised me. I thought he'd suggest that Frank's broken ankle might be something to do with a fast-emptied flask of whisky, but he didn't. He smiled and said, 'More tea?'

Fiona answered that she'd prefer coffee. He raised his eyebrows to direct his hospitable question at me.

'I'm fine,' I said. 'I ought to be making a move.' I stared at him as I decided this. He stared back for a moment, and put a hand out towards my ankle, but I stood up to avoid it. I didn't want him to hold my ankle, with Fiona's legs so near us both.

'I'll make another pot anyway. There's no need to rush off. Yeats can wait a while, can't he?'

I hadn't planned on doing anything about Yeats that afternoon, and was aggrieved that Liam thought I might. But he left the garden before I could answer, so Fiona and I were alone and silent, until she said she'd better ring Frank and tell him she'd be back the next day.

'He'll think I've crashed the car. You know how they are.'

I was glad of the cat's arrival between my knees. I stroked her warm neck, and kept my head down as I said I didn't know Frank very well. There was no answer to that, so she said I looked tired, to which there was no answer either.

'Is Liam keeping you up?' she said. 'Shall I have a word with him?'

Then she eased herself on to her feet and went into

the house, where I heard her laugh and Liam saying 'Piss off' in a cheerful way. Then she was in the bay window of the room next to the kitchen. She had the phone in one hand and was wiping the shoulder of a large standing figure with the other. She'd dressed the object in a tasselled shawl and hat instead of selling it to the showroom she worked for, because the nose was missing. I once told Liam it was grotesque. He'd laughed, but he wouldn't do that now. Since his sister had witnessed what he deemed my 'crazy behaviour' in Hastings in April, I wasn't allowed jokes at her expense.

When he came back out again, I told him I was going home.

'Why? Don't be like this, Ruth.'

'Like what?'

'Come on. Relax. Have some tea.'

'I thought we were going to eat together.'

He said we still could. It was only half five. He'd buy some wine soon now, and we could all eat pasta out here in the garden. 'We'll get Fiona to cook. Her bolognese is getting better.'

'I'm tired. I don't feel like talking.'

'Well you don't have to talk.'

'Clearly,' I said, then wished I hadn't because he said to go on then, if I was in that frame of mind.

'I'll ring you,' I said. 'Perhaps we could meet later on.'

Then I kissed him goodbye, and he was kissing me back when Fiona arrived and asked where her coffee had got to. I said I'd see myself out.

'See you later, maybe,' I called from the hallway, as I gripped my bicycle's handlebars.

Fiona called goodbye.

'See you,' Liam shouted. The door slammed behind me, but it often did that, whether you'd planned it or not.

The river was low and green, with a breeze that made the poplars ripple and the sweatshirts of the joggers ruffle behind them as they ran with their elbows working and their heads forward and down. I was alongside a low boat of rowers, with the cox shouting sharp sounds and oars dripping their rhythmic heavy spray, when I realized I had a puncture. The back tyre was flat and bumping over the towpath. I was tempted to lock the bike to a railing and walk on alone, but got off and pushed until the bridge reared ahead, and I thought I might as well keep on, although it was hot and slow and heavy.

I asked a man with two terriers if he had the time, though it didn't really matter. Fiona and Liam could talk for hours. The man's mobile told us it was six twenty-three. He paused as I looked at his phone, and might have been going to ask whether I'd like to use it, but I said thanks and moved away.

I pushed the bike on, over roots and sweet-wrappers and stony ground. A lone man in a yellow boat rowed by, then a squat tug-boat made a rolling wake, which resulted in small earth-coloured waves on the concrete jetty to my left. Yeats must have walked along this path, I thought. He lived in Hammersmith, as a young man. Probably it was this river that he was talking about in the poem of 'mouse-grey waters' and 'cold wet winds'.

'A pity beyond all telling is hid in the heart of love.'

The towpath held a few self-absorbed walkers with curious dogs. Under the bridge at the end of it, small children shouted senseless words to try and make an echo, which wasn't occurring.

The best place for echoes in Hammersmith was under the railway bridge. Some boys on bikes with no mudguards were there as I pushed my bicycle past, about forty minutes after my puncture. One of them asked for a light. He had a half-smoked cigarette in his fingers.

'I don't smoke,' I said. 'It's bad for you.'

'Stupid cow,' he said, so I shrugged and walked faster. Around the corner, I leaned my bicycle against a tree and put on my cardigan. The day wasn't much cooler, but my arms felt bare.

On the crowded pavement of the Shepherd's Bush Road, I wheeled Clare's bike to the crossing and waited for the lights to change. Behind me was the Café Rouge. Three men in dark glasses sat under its awning, talking Italian. Beyond them, at the table next to the off-licence, the local homeless person had seated himself. He had a can of Special Brew and fingerless gloves. He waved at me. He waved at most people. A police car with a siren came through, filling the crowded space with speed and staccato unease. Traffic swerved into the pavement as I stepped back and away and looked into the Café Rouge, where a group of people were about to sit down. Another police car and its siren hurtled through the red lights of the crossing. An ambulance came next, dangerously close to a couple who moved fast then into the Café. I watched the female's slim figure moving into the attractive gloom of the place. Her man's hand was on her well-tailored waist.

As I watched the couple decide where to sit, I saw my old friend Matt at the table on the left, in the window. He had a glass of red wine in one hand and the menu in the other. He was looking more like Robert Lowell than he did when he was sober. I moved myself and the bike backwards to stand on the outside of the glass beside him. I knocked. He looked astonished. He gesticulated as wildly as a man can with both hands full.

'Drink?' he mouthed at me. I nodded. A drink with Matt would be perfect. He'd be intense and garrulous and in love with someone. Matt and I could talk about sex and death. He may be familiar with Yeats. '*Tread softly for you tread on my dreams*,' at least. He'd be sympathetic about my stunted afternoon.

I locked my disabled bicycle to the railings and rushed into the companionable air of a public place, with walls around it to protect one from a potentially violent populace.

'Ruth,' he said. 'Nice dress. Where are you off?'

'Don't ask. I've just been.' I lifted a glass of water

from the mess of his table and drank most of it down in one.

'Sit down and tell me about it. Let's get you a glass. I've ordered another bottle.'

There was an almost empty House Red in front of him and a half-full glass in front of the seat opposite him, where I could have sat.

'Am I intruding?'

I hoped it wouldn't be the German girl he'd been pursuing for months. I liked the Scottish nurse he was seeing much better.

'Sit here.' He patted the crimson banquette beside him. I did so, and he took my arm, saying, 'The thing is, Ruth.' He took a sip of wine, and appeared to concentrate on something in the air, just above his glass. 'The thing is, Ruth,' he went on, still holding my arm, as if I was someone he'd caught shoplifting, 'the thing is I can't remember where Clare is. I mean I was there on Tuesday. But they all look the same.'

'Who do? The patients?'

'Those creepy wards. She was next to a window. There was a bald woman with visitors eating curry. Where is that, Ruth? How do you tell someone exactly where she is?'

'Who wants to know?'

There had been no bald woman there the last time I was. The bed next to my friend had been empty. All the beds were empty, except one, which had a man in it who took the whole length of my visit trying to get his feet to the floor. It was too hot and Clare had a fan, which blew her papers all over the bed. She was writing letters to people she thought she wouldn't see again. She was weepy. She thought she must write to Conor, but I said she'd be seeing a lot more of him. I was bringing him in after football the following day.

'Where's the waiter? God, you could die of thirst here.' Matt waved towards the bar and the waiter came over, as slowly as nurses in the hospital did. He asked for another glass and I said I'd like some tap water, please.

'Have some of this, to get you started.' Matt passed me his wine. It was too sweet and warm, but I was glad of the density, flooding my insides.

'I'm waiting for fags.' Matt took his glasses off. He blew on the lenses and lifted his shirt to wipe them clean. I watched a bowl of mussels being lowered on to the table opposite ours: sharp-edged wings of blue-black against the curve of the plate. The tablecloth looked like a sheet. Clare's current ward was called Six West.

The waiter arrived with a clean glass and a fresh bottle. He poured some for me.

'Cheers anyway,' I said. 'Who's the lucky girl?'

Matt touched his glass to mine and drank.

'Do I know her? Or will I have to be polite?' I pointed to the third glass on our small table, where a pack of Gitanes was crumpled and a cup of espresso abandoned, its teaspoon leaking sticky black, next to a book of matches, all of which were torn out.

'It's not a girl. It's a man. You'll never guess.'

'Matt. I've had a long day.'

'It begins with G.'

'I don't care. Just tell me.'

'You will care. It ends with Y.'

The hand lifting my glass towards my mouth stopped moving.

'Yes, it's Gray.' He chuckled and patted my head. 'He's the one who wants to see Clare. We were going to ring you up.'

Matt laughed down through his nose, then put his glasses back on, then took them off to clean again.

One of my feet was trapped on the other side of the table-leg. I jerked my leg to free it, and as I did my bag slid on to the floor. It spilled keys and my purse and an envelope with Jane's writing looping across it. I dragged the scattered things together, which meant leaning almost under the table. I was bent down, with blood in my face, when I heard Matt: 'Gray, look who's here. Where are you, Ruth?'

His hair was longer. Not as long as it had been in Paris, but longer than it was the last time I saw him, in a pub in Notting Hill, where Liam and I were drinking, in silence, because I'd arrived too late. But Gray's smile was the same as I straightened up.

'Hey,' he said. He could have been blushing. 'We were just talking about you.'

His hair was in waves on his neck, which was finely lined and sunburned at the V in his T-shirt. There were little hairs there, almost white. There was more forehead than I remembered above his eyes, which were the same, as was his voice, saying hello to me, very close, because I'd stood up and he was kissing my cheeks, one after the other.

'Good to see you,' he said. He took my hand in his, which was dry and warm, and kept it there until a phone rang inside his jacket. He took it out and talked French, then walked towards the door and out on to the street as he spoke. He turned to wave to me. He smiled. I took a drink of water. Matt opened the pack of Camels that Gray had dropped, and lit one from the candle on the table.

'Must be his girlfriend,' Matt said. 'She lives in Paris.'

'With him?' I drank some wine. Then drank more, as Matt frowned into his cigarette.

'Patrice. That's her name. I knew a girl called Patrice once. She was married.'

'Is Gray married?'

'Would he be talking to Patrice if he was married, Ruth?'

He looked at me in bewilderment, as if I were a television set that had switched itself off in the middle of a programme. He said he wondered sometimes about my moral compass. Said perhaps I ought to think about marriage myself.

'You need something to centre you, Ruth, you know? Clare thinks so too. We were talking it over last time I saw her.'

'Talking me over, with Clare?'

The idea outraged me, but Gray was coming towards

191

us, so I didn't say what I thought. I watched him sit down, in his long-legged way. He dropped his mobile on the table. I was glad I didn't have one. This was just the sort of moment when Liam might ring and decide to be nice. Matt filled Gray's glass and asked if everything was OK.

'Ruth thinks you ought to be married,' he said.

Gray made a small noise I remembered, which meant he was amused. 'I'll bear it in mind.' He looked over at me. 'And how about you, Ruth? Liam seemed very keen.'

I shook my head. How could he think that? How could he remember Liam's name?

'Course not. You'd've heard,' I said, and might have gone on that Liam wasn't keen in the least. I hardly ever saw him, and if anyone ought to be married it was Matt. And also I hoped very much that Gray was not, now I was sitting so near him, with his hand up towards the waiter, who came straight over and took his order for olives, bread and a jug of iced water.

'And some more of these would be nice.' He lifted the spent book of matches, then let it drop. He lifted the Camels and held the pack towards me. I shook my head.

'Very sensible,' he said, lighting up. 'As is not being married, I guess.' He looked away towards the bar, where a waiter was doing nothing in a long white apron and a waitress was filling a glass. He tapped ash into the butt-filled ashtray, which was unnecessary, since his cigarette was hardly smoked. He tapped it a few times more, though. He did that when he was nervous. Matt and I watched him look out of the window, then back at each of us in turn, then back to his Camel, which he tapped some more. Then he put his elbow on the table and leaned his chin in his hand, so his mouth was half covered as he said, 'Matt tells me you and Clare are friends now, Ruth.'

He ran his fingers over his lips after he'd said it, then smoked again, as I didn't say anything back. I didn't want to talk about Clare.

Matt held his glass in both hands and said that was absolutely right.

'Ruth knows where she is. Ruth keeps her eye on these things.' He smiled and nodded. He wasn't looking at me.

'What things?' I poured myself more wine. 'I don't "keep my eye on" Clare, whatever that means.'

'I mean you visit her. You're friends. I mean you know where she is, OK?'

Matt looked happy as he exhaled.

'You seem to know where to find her when it suits you, Matt.' I tore a match and struck it. It made a narrow white flame that didn't last long. I didn't want Matt to be there. 'I mean the pair of you seem to enjoy discussing me, whenever you can.'

Gray drank from my glass of water. Matt blew smoke rings, as only he could. After a while he told me I was being offensive. He and Clare talked about whatever they wanted, as they always had. That's what friends were for, he said, and I said I agreed entirely.

'I must ask what she thinks of your marital status, next time I go,' I said. He said to shut up.

'For fuck's sake, Ruth,' he said. He stubbed his cigarette and took another from the pack.

The olives arrived with a basket of French bread and Matt took a slice, then a pack of wrapped butter, which he made much of finding his way into. Gray took an olive with garlic stuck to its skin, and there was silence until he took the stone from his mouth and dropped it into the ashtray.

'Sorry, Matt,' I said. He was looking out of the window. 'I know you're Clare's friend. You probably knew her before I did.' He didn't say anything for a while. Then he reached his hand to my arm, on the seat next to his leg, and he held my wrist very hard. Gray wiped the table with the flat of his hand. Matt sniffed loudly, then turned round and said he was sorry too. 'Fuck,' he said. He ran his tongue over his lips and bit them.

'Sorry,' he said, to Gray, not me, which I was grateful for. I didn't want Matt and me to be having a conversation about each other, and Clare, with Gray there to hear it. Matt took his glass, which was almost full, and drank it down, then filled it again. He put his finger and thumb to the bridge of his nose and held them there, with his face down for a while. I drank and Gray ate olives.

I looked at Gray, who was watching Matt, and I wondered how they'd managed to be here together. I wondered if they'd been in touch all the time Gray had been in France. If they often met, if Gray was in London, and how often that might be, and where Gray stayed, now that Diane was dead and her house was sold. I wondered whether Gray knew who'd bought his mother's house. I wondered if I'd tell Gray about the letters, but decided not to, with Matt there, if ever. Matt might decide to leave. He generally had a girl to see.

'Anyway,' I said, in a positive way, 'Clare's in Charing Cross, ward Six West, if you want to visit. You get a lift up, which takes about an hour, and then turn left. She has a bedside phone. I've got the number at home.'

Perhaps Gray would come back to my house to get it. The wine was making me feel warm and stronger. I patted Matt's knee. We smiled. Perhaps Gray would give me his mobile number, so I could tell him Clare's, later on. Or I could give him my own telephone number. Or we could go back to my house. But Liam might ring, or arrive, perversely, and I didn't want that.

'Clare's got a great view,' Matt said. He buttered the bread he'd abandoned. 'If you like looking at sky.'

'I do,' Gray said.

We all looked outside, to see sky, perhaps, but we saw only people with umbrellas, and cars with slashing wipers. When I'd last collected Conor from school it had started to rain ferociously, with large heavy drops pelting the pavement and bouncing up again. 'Like little toys,' Conor had said. I told the men at my table this pleasing simile. It made me think of toy soldiers, I told them, and Gray asked if I saw Conor much, and when exactly he'd said that about the rain. I wasn't sure then how much detail to give about Conor and me. I somehow felt that I'd done something bad in mentioning him at all, although he wasn't a secret.

'Dusty rain is best,' Matt said. 'City rain. That's what I like. Must be nice living in Paris.' He ate a black olive. 'Rue Cherche Midi. So where is that?'

It was just up from the river, as I remembered. A long narrow road that ran into the Place Saint Sulpice, where Gray and I stopped for a drink one night when it was raining hard, like it was now in London. There was a shoe shop on the corner. It was closed the August I was there, but I hadn't forgotten a pair of red leather sandals, on their blue-and-brown box in the window. They were two hundred francs, and my size.

'Ruth ought to know.' Gray looked at me. 'You fell in love with some shoes there.'

I held an olive stone in my mouth and nodded, but did not speak. No one said anything more about the geography of Paris. No one said anything about anything, until Gray asked again if I saw much of Conor these days.

'Are you friends with him?' He took a fat black olive and bit into it, as if it were an apple or a plum, not something that would fit whole into a mouth. 'I mean, do you talk about how he's feeling, at all?'

I wished there were something easy to say, as Gray narrowed his eyes and continued to nibble. I thought how like Conor his face was in profile as he watched the rain then for a moment. I wondered if he had any more children, as he bit the flesh of his thumb and looked away and up to the tea-coloured ceiling. I thought he probably had not.

'Well, how often do you see each other?' Gray sent Conor money at Christmas and on birthdays. Clare put it into a savings account.

'Who?' The stone in my mouth was still salty but dry. I had a gulp of wine.

'You and my son,' he said. His eyes in mine now were Conor's. It was odd to see that intense blue stare, which in Conor's smaller face always made me think of this other version, which was both more and less familiar to me. 'Do you look after him, now Clare's sick?'

I drank more of my wine. Matt was taking another cigarette, having trouble tearing a match from the folded cardboard container our table had been presented with.

'Clare's mother does a lot,' I said. Then, 'I'm writing a book about poets.'

Gray leaned and took my fingers in his. He filled his glass, which he seemed not to have drunk from much, then emptied the bottle into mine.

'Cheers,' he said. He touched his glass against mine. 'Here's to Conor.'

I watched him drink, with his neck coming out of his T-shirt. I watched his hand on the glass, and his forearm, with its fine soft hairs, and his fingers then, with no rings on.

'I do see Conor a bit,' I said. 'I live in the street opposite his school, so I've collected him on and off for ages.'

I didn't say that Clare used to offer to pay me to collect him, in the days when she was still singing and often rehearsed until six, but that I did it for nothing, precisely because Conor was so like Gray, at first. Or how I loved it when she had early-evening shows, and would leave me to give their son his bath, and put him to bed. How I relished the smell of his skin, the pitch of his voice, the slight but essential feel of his arms around my neck. How I'd been part of his school life since Clare arrived at my door after dropping him off on his very first day, because she needed somewhere to cry at the loss of him as an everyday thing. How, after school that same day, he fell off the slide in Brook Green, so I went to Casualty to see his arm X-rayed and put into lightweight and colourful plaster. How I'd come to know Conor better than anyone else, in a way. I'd known Gray's son for all his life, and often wished he could have been mine. But I didn't say that.

'He looks very like you,' I said, and looked into Gray's larger eyes. He bit his thumb. The bones in his jaw moved. His lower lip moved up between his teeth, then was released to tussle with the rest of his mouth. He leaned towards me and held my fingers, like he had before.

'I'd like to see Conor,' he said.

Be careful what you wish for, my mother used to say.

'Of course you would,' Matt said. He might have been slurring his words. 'That's why you have to see Clare.'

'Clare's very tired,' I said.

'Half-asleep when I was there,' Matt said, and I was glad of him near me again. 'Didn't notice my roses. Cost a fortune. Smelled of rubber gloves.' He ate an olive and spat the stone in his hand.

Gray was rubbing his nose, like he used to do. He took his mobile out and looked at it carefully. There was a clock behind his head. It was twenty to nine.

'I should be making a move.' He looked at me again, and it was my turn to bite my lip then, as I watched him get up and saw him standing between the next table and myself. He put a hand on my shoulder, and Matt was standing up behind me to say goodbye.

'I'm collecting Conor from school tomorrow.'

Gray was about to kiss my cheek, to leave. He stopped mid stoop, his hand in mine.

'Come with me, if you want,' I said. 'We can take him to the park.'

I had to look up as I waited for a response. The people at my left were discussing their pets. One of them had a rabbit.

'Great. That's great, Ruth. So where do you live?'

He repeated my address after me, as I pointed across in the direction of Bolingbroke Road, saying how easy it was to find.

'Just over there. But we could meet here if you like.'

'When shall I come?'

'About three,' I said, as if we made arrangements to meet all the time. I watched him walk through the door into the rain, and past my sick bicycle, locked to the railings. I realized without really deciding that I'd leave the bike there overnight. I didn't want it in my hallway when Gray and Conor walked through my door. The rain seemed to have stopped. Gray was turning his collar up, then walking across the road and then not there to see any more. Matt was suggesting we eat. He was saying we needed a steak.

'We've got to keep our strength up, Ruth. We're holding this whole thing together.'

Then he said he thought it was a bit late for Gray to visit Clare tonight, so I assured him Gray was not going there. He asked how I knew. I didn't say because there was no need for him to do that, any more. I asked how he liked his steak. Then I called the waiter, and felt weak – with hunger, I said to Matt. He asked for extra chips.

When I got home it was after ten. There was a message on the machine in my study that said to give Liam a call. He didn't have to feed the cat, now Fiona was home.

'Don't be sulky, Ruth,' his voice told my room, with its white curtain swaying like a sheet on a line in the cool dark breeze.

I deleted the message and wiped my desk, which was wet by the open window, as I listened to message number two. It was Clare's mother. She took it in turns with her ex-husband to be with their grandson these days. She told me that Conor had a tummy upset and would not be at school the next day.

'So you're free tomorrow, Ruth. You probably need a break as much as Conor does. But Clare'd love a visit, if you're kicking your heels. Give me a ring, anyway.'

From my kitchen window I saw the moon, which was a blurred but substantial half-awake shape. I cut an apple in half, and ate it.

'Turning and turning in the widening gyre
The falcon cannot hear the falconer.'

I looked at the clear black sky outside the kitchen, as a plane came into view with its lights and its silence. I bit carefully round the pips in my apple. The phone rang, but I left it. I thought it wasn't too late to do a wash. I wanted my silk blouse clean, to meet Gray at the Café Rouge at three o'clock the next afternoon.

9

I met Matt in my first week at Leeds university, in 1976, when we both arrived at the door of a seminar that was ending when we thought it was about to begin. We went for coffee, then a drink, then a curry. By midnight we were friends. We were both friends with Gray, too, though I didn't know that until a few weeks into the term when my doorbell rang on a mild damp Saturday afternoon. Gray was standing behind Matt on the steps, but was taller than him, so I could see sun-freckles on his nose as I stared.

'Surprise,' Matt said. 'An old friend to see you.'

Then he patted my head, in a way he'd developed, and asked if there was any chance of coming in, so I led the way into my room, downstairs on the right of the large shared house. I wished Joni Mitchell wasn't on my turntable. I should have been listening to Debussy or Miles Davis. I should have been sitting in silence reading *Bleak House* with my new gold-rimmed glasses, with my hair up in some sort of Virginia Woolf knot.

'You should have told me you know our Gray,' Matt said.

Knickers were hanging to dry on the back of a chair in front of the gas fire, so I dragged them off with both hands and jammed them under one elbow, which meant I couldn't embrace Gray as he moved towards me. Socks dangled on the mantelpiece and a jumper hung from a coat-hanger, weighted in place by a Thesaurus.

'Well, I didn't know you did. You should have told me.'

The air smelled of washing powder and fried mushrooms, which I'd just eaten on toast. The Baby Belling cooker was next to the sink, and the electric toaster – a leaving present from my mother – was on the table in front of the window, where Matt sat down, as he always did. I usually sat in the armchair, which I'd covered with a bedspread that belonged to Jane, but I didn't feel like sitting. I felt like leaving the room, which I did, on the pretext of checking that the front door was shut.

'The girl upstairs is paranoid,' I told the men. 'She's always finding it open, and thinks we do it on purpose.'

The front door was closed but I opened it and looked up and down the street, breathing deeply on the autumnal air. Matt's old post-office van was parked down the sloping road, opposite the pub, at an angle that explained the dent over the left wheel at the front. I wondered if Gray and Matt had already been for a drink, or were inviting me for one. I looked at myself in the glass of the unreliable front door, and pulled my hair-band off. I heard Matt's familiar laugh and a low chuckle from Gray that made my stomach turn. He was sitting on the chair in front of the fire, rubbing his thighs, which made the pile of his velvet flares darker. Joni Mitchell sang that someone was in her blood, like holy wine. I turned the volume down.

'Nice one,' Matt said. 'I thought we'd agreed you'd give that crap up.'

I felt myself blush, and went over to the sink, which seemed to take a lot of steps.

'Tea?' I said, and filled the kettle before they answered, which meant I could stand with my back to the room. I let too much water pour into the spout and it gushed through the buckled tin lid, which made me drop it.

'Oops,' Matt said. He was rolling a cigarette. The cuffs of his sweater were unravelled above his slender wrists.

'Sorry,' I said, and Gray stood and came over and lifted the kettle from me with tanned and clean fingers. Now I was pressed between him and the wall and the chair on that side of the table. He had beads on his arm, which banged the tap.

'I'll do it. I feel industrious, here in the North.'

So he put the kettle on as I watched, then we both moved into the limited space of the mottled buff carpet, which I'd tried to disguise with rugs. I couldn't understand how Gray was here, but was waiting for someone to tell me.

'Are you still a postman, Gray?' was the most neutral opening I could think of. Perhaps he'd applied for a transfer to work in Leeds, near me. Perhaps he was looking for somewhere to live. There was an empty room at the top of my house.

Matt laughed. 'A man of letters,' he said, and Gray nodded, smiling a sideways smile.

'And who's been keeping you posted, Ruth?'

I raised my eyes, wryly, I hoped. I'd found out from Jane, of course, and mumbled that she'd mentioned it. He asked how Jane was and I shrugged. I said I supposed he knew she was in London now.

'Well she's based there, I mean. She travels a lot. To give readings.' I found three mugs and just enough milk. 'Where are you living, Gray?'

I decided one of the mugs needed to be washed, as I waited for an answer.

'My mum's place. For now.' Then he said he'd seen Jane a few weeks before, instead of explaining what he was planning on doing when 'for now' was over. He'd been at one of her readings, in fact, and had to say he didn't like it much.

'Bit uptight. A bit too Plath for me.'

'I don't think so.' I looked at his head properly for the first time and saw his hair was longer and newly washed, waving softly on to his scoop-necked shirt.

'Don't get her started,' Matt said. He was pouring tea, and handed me some. 'Maybe we should drive to Haworth. If we're talking poetry, that's where it's at round these parts.'

There was silence as we sipped, until Matt asked if I was up for a trip to the hills. They were thinking of Bolton Abbey, for a change. I was too relieved to think of a relaxed response, so stayed silent as Joni Mitchell told us the last time she saw Richard was Detroit in '68. I wondered whose idea it was for Matt and Gray to ask me to go with them. I wondered how long Gray had been in Leeds.

Matt said we ought to be making a move. He lifted his tobacco from the table to stuff into his back pocket.

'So are you coming?'

'Course she's coming.' Gray reached up and took my hand, which momentarily froze me. He dropped it again. 'We're not going if Ruth doesn't come.'

Matt had held my hand once, after a party, the first weekend of term. We'd walked to my door together, but I didn't invite him in, because it was half three and I was tired, I'd said – although we knew that wasn't the reason.

'Isn't it a bit late?' I looked out into fading light.

'Don't be difficult, Ruth,' Gray said, which pleased me. 'Difficult' was intriguing.

The record-player clicked to a stop. The room seemed less spacious without a melody in it. There was damp on the wall above the sink, and the window paint was peeling.

'We can sing in the car,' Matt said.

'We'll take this.' Gray stretched back to lift my suede coat from the bed. It had been my mother's in the sixties. He stood up and handed the garment to Matt, saying it might turn cold.

'We'll have to share it if it does.' Matt rolled it into a sausage shape to tuck neatly under his arm.

On the street, I stopped walking a few yards from my door, and went back to check it was firmly shut. Gray waited for me, then we moved on down to Matt, who was talking to a man who'd come out of the pub.

'Great,' he was saying as we arrived at his side. 'So can I bring these guys?'

'Sure,' the man said. We were introduced. His name was Dan, and he shook my hand but not Gray's. He was having a party in Victoria Road.

'Number 18,' he called as Gray clambered into the back of Matt's van, over the passenger seat. 'Be there. See you, Ruth.'

He pushed his hands into his pockets and moved away, as Matt's engine started with its throttled gust and we veered off along the empty road.

Matt's van smelled of wood and coal-dust. He lit good fires in his room most nights. On the floor under my feet was a copy of *Art and Psychoanalysis*, a biography of Blake, a ring-backed notebook which Matt brought to seminars but never opened, and a soft-backed roadmap of Britain, which he asked me to pass to Gray. I wasn't quite ready to turn to Gray in the gloom of the back yet, so I said I could map-read.

'I know the way, Ruth. Just thought Gray might want to follow the route.'

Gray said he'd rather look at the scenery, which so

207

far was industrial buildings. He pushed his head forward to jut over the back of my seat. He smelled of oranges.

'Besides, I've got Ruth to talk to. Who needs a map?'

I wound my window down to draw some air between us. The landscape was opening out into fields with mild undulations. The blowing air was earthy and wet. We drove through Otley, with its ragged Saturday market and its steep wooded hills, which reminded me of the woods behind Holkham beach, at home. Gray's hair was brushing my face, until he slid back, saying it was getting too cold for the window, so I shut it and we roared laboriously on towards Ilkley, with its sweeping, dark-rubbled heights. Matt whistled as we passed the Cow and Calf – a cluster of rocks, where children scrambled and adults held hands, and an ice-cream van was parked. Gray asked about my course, which meant I had to turn to speak into his ear. I wished we were driving all night then, squashed in this moving low-lit thing.

The road narrowed and dipped towards the glowering skies of Bolton, which Matt explained he knew well. He'd camped there as a child and tramped the riverbank, looking for places to fish. He knew where to find a shop, when he needed tobacco. He bought a bag of large wrapped mints, which made speech difficult, but were warm on the tongue. He tried the heater, which made a rattling noise and gusted cool blasts on my legs. Gray stretched out on his front in the back, with his left elbow on the top of my seat and his right one resting behind Matt's straggled black curls. I could hear him sucking his sweet. We stopped for a while between the cloud-shadowed moors, to allow a sheep to cross the road. Gray said he thought they moved in groups.

'City boy,' Matt said. 'A sheep needs to be alone sometimes.'

I suddenly wished he wasn't there, interrupting Gray's low voice and the firm warm feel of his chin against my right shoulder.

'How do you two know each other?' My sucked mint was a small and easy thing now. Like a delicate pebble from the beach at home. Matt said they'd met through Clare.

'Did we?' Gray swallowed. 'I don't think we did.'

Matt reversed on to grass to let a tractor pass.

'We did. Remember Sophie?'

Gray did something to move my hair out of his face. The back of my head was too near his.

'She worked in the Albert Hall, with Clare, remember? Took me to a party in Princedale Road. You wanted to walk, so we went to the river, and I took you home for breakfast.'

'Maybe.' Gray didn't sound convinced.

'So when were you in London, Matt?' I unwrapped a mint. I hoped it was a long time ago, and that Clare had moved on by now.

'After A-levels. It was Sophie's idea. Anyway, here we are.'

He pulled on to a verge, just missing another car.

Gray rolled on to his back and made a noise, so I turned and looked and he smiled and rolled over again and put his mouth near my ear, as Matt got out.

'It's nice to see you,' he said.

Matt opened the back doors. Gray asked him where the hell we were.

'Bolton Abbey,' Matt said. He dragged my coat out from where Gray had been lying. It was covered with wood-chips, so I said to leave it. I felt fine as I was.

Our walk began over a fast shallow river with stepping-stones, slippery and dark with moss. I followed Gray, who followed Matt, and they both waited for me on the opposite bank, as I balanced and hoped I looked graceful. Then on up a hill, alive with large cattle, to the cragged black ruined abbey with its shiny cold stone and its central chapel, vast and alarming, with jagged remains of carved windows, like bits of solid torn lace. Trees creaked as light faded, and a soft rain arrived to patter their yellowing leaves. We clambered up juts of collapsed spiral staircases, close behind one another, not saying anything. We wandered over mounds of damp ground, near each other, then scattered again, through ruined dwarf doorways and stunted enclosures, guessing at the use of these long-ago rooms. We came to slats of smooth-topped stones across the noise of a brook. This was where monks bent down to relieve themselves, lifting their robes, on icy mornings, Matt said. Then he needed a pee, and wandered off into huddled bushes, while Gray and I stayed to feel the chill of the water, the shadow-filled bulk of the place. He took my hand, and I gripped his warm fingers.

'How's it going?' he said, and I told him fine. Then I asked how long he was here for, glad that it was almost dark.

'It'd be nice if you stayed a bit,' I said, and he said 'Mmm,' as if he thought so too, then looked away and up at a single slow-moving bird.

'Thing is, Clare has to be back for Monday.'

'Oh.' I turned away, and scrambled for more words as I scanned the shape of a chestnut tree which must have been there for centuries.

'Did you get the train up here?' The dark spindly shape of Matt was moving towards us, his arms out, with his coat pulled wide. He was trying to look like a bird, perhaps.

'We hitched. It was almost as fast. Did it in under three hours.'

I supposed Clare sat on their rucksack, while he held his thumb out. Or maybe she did the hitching. Cars would stop for her. Matt was moving faster. If I threw a stone, I could hit him by now. I started off towards him, not running, because the ground was uneven, but getting away from Gray. He called my name but I didn't look back.

'We're freezing,' I told Matt. He was making a buzzing noise. 'Shall we go home?' I was shivering suddenly.

Matt stopped buzzing and said he supposed I was

right. 'Though I wouldn't mind spending the night here myself,' he called, as I started off in the direction we'd come from.

Gray was at my side, then, taking my hand.

I put my hands in my pockets and stopped to wait for Matt.

'We should have brought your coat,' Gray said. He put his arm through mine. I pulled it free and walked to take Matt's instead. He stiffened slightly, then started to whistle, which he kept up until we got to the stepping-stones, where I disengaged to cross firmly. Ahead, the moon drifted, unformed and porous-looking.

At the van, Matt opened the back doors for Gray so he didn't have to climb over my seat. Rain came harder as we drove away, and the windscreen wipers made a grinding noise, rhythmic and somewhat consoling. Nobody talked.

'I ought to get a radio in here,' Matt decided, when we were almost back. 'Shame you can't sing, Ruth.'

'Clare can,' I said. 'You should have brought her.'

'She didn't want to come.' Matt changed gear for a tight up-hill bend.

I wondered how hard they'd tried to persuade her.

Back in the smeared lights of Leeds streets, Matt drove towards my house, which unnerved me. I didn't want to be dropped off. But I didn't want to go back to Matt's, if she was there. We parked outside the pub on my road, and sat listening to the rain on the roof. Gray suggested we had a drink.

'But there's a party,' Matt said. 'Ruth'll want to change. Shall we meet up later on?'

I poked his leg beyond the gear-stick, and mouthed 'No' when he looked. I wanted to stay with them.

'Actually, Ruth looks like she needs a drink,' Matt said, and I busied myself with the door-handle, then was out in spilling rain to slam the door behind me, and into the Park Hotel's foyer, with its frosted glass and its embracing smell. My hair was wet on my jumper, so I scraped it up, which meant my hands were damp to open my purse. I ordered a half of lager, then turned to say 'A pint?' as Matt arrived at my side. He nodded.

'Long drive,' he said. His hair was blacker than ever, and his eyes more blue in the gloss of his face.

'Nasty night now,' the barman said.

Matt moved over to our favourite table on the right at the back and I followed. The rain traced stuttering lines on the windows. 'Walk On By' was on the juke-box.

'Gray's very quiet,' Matt decided, after a long slow slug of his substantial glass.

'Gray's not here.'

My glass was almost empty by the time he walked through the door. He asked if I'd like another. Matt asked what had kept him.

'Needed a phone-box,' he said. 'She's found a piano stool in a junk shop.'

Matt and I raised eyes at each other as Gray went to replenish our glasses. There was a pay-phone on the bar.

'I told her about the party and said we'll be back in a while,' Gray told us as he sat down with his Guinness. Matt was scratching his stubble. He said Dan drank in the Fenton, and he guessed we should move along there. Gray said Clare wouldn't know where it was.

'We can tell her,' I decided. 'You can ring her again.'

Matt said we could drive and meet her at his place. He wanted to dump the car. I glared, so he made another plan, which was that he'd take the van home then walk back, with Clare, to meet us again. 'No point us all getting wet,' he said.

Gray smoothed his flattened hair, which stayed pulled back as he ran his hands on down to the top of his spine. His forehead was finely lined with tentative sketches of what could be wrinkles.

'Not sure about that.' He gulped at his glass. 'Although it makes sense on paper.'

The lager was making me feel energetic and mellow, and the drips down the front of my jumper were warm.

'Yes. You get her, Matt, and we'll meet up in the Fenton. How does that sound?' I said.

Gray looked at me and didn't look away, as Matt told him I was right, for a change, and the plan would suit everyone fine. It was only seven o'clock. He stood up, feeling for car keys.

'Will you ring Clare, or what?'

Gray considered. He asked Matt for a roll-up, and when it was made he said he thought he needn't bother.

'You tell her,' he said, striking a match.

'In the Fenton in an hour or so, then?'

'An hour exactly,' Gray said.

When Gray and I walked through my front door, so I could change my clothes, about half an hour later, the girl across the corridor was playing *Pretzel Logic*. I was pleased. Steely Dan made my room a sophisticated and airy place.

'Don't take all night, Ruth. We've got an arrangement, remember.'

In Paris, Gray used to say I dressed as if I'd never done it before, every time. I'd speeded up since then, and told him so.

'Well it's so cold up here, you'd have had to.'

He bent and put the fire on, full, then asked if the toaster worked. I explained it was new, and where the bread was, as I stood behind the open door of my wardrobe to locate my old silk dress. It used to be beaded, but was not much any more. As I wriggled out of clothes, and Gray made toast beyond the wardrobe door, I didn't ask why he hadn't been in touch, except the one postcard, since Paris. I talked about the objects around us, and how I came to have them, now that I'd left home. I told him too about the day I'd left Norwich, when Jane came to say goodbye and keep my mother company.

'Does she miss you?' he said. I heard him scraping toast. 'Are you going back for Christmas?'

'Suppose so. Will you send a card?'

He laughed, and said he wasn't really the Christmas card type. 'Every card not sent, Ruth, is a relief to postmen everywhere.'

I hunted through clothes on the floor of my wardrobe as I asked why he was a postman. He said he'd thought it would give him time to write, although the play he was writing had been in scene three for a month. He laughed unconvincingly. My plastic belt must be with the clothes at the other end of the room, but I didn't want Gray to see me without it. The dress looked like a sack, unbelted, Jane said.

'Perhaps you should write a novel instead.'

'Yeah. Or perhaps I shouldn't bother. Perhaps I should leave the country.'

I decided to use a ribbon, and forget the belt.

'Leave for where? I mean, why?'

He said he needed a change. He was thinking of France for a while. He could do some translation, and pick up some teaching.

'I've got a few contacts. And the Paris flat's empty. I need to get away. I'm jammed.'

I heard him rooting round the cutlery tray. He wanted a teaspoon, and found one.

'Must be nice to have somewhere to go, I suppose.' I concentrated on finding my shimmery tights, to stop asking when he'd be back, and who else would be there and if it really had to be Paris. A cottage on the Yorkshire moors would be a good place to write.

'Well it's good to speak French, I guess.' He bit into

his toast. 'I mean it's nice to have something you can do without really trying.' He gave a tired laugh. 'Which writing definitely isn't, in my case.'

'Doesn't your father ever need his flat?' I was dressed. I closed the wardrobe door.

'My father had a stroke, last November.'

'God. How terrible. I spoke to him, when I was there. In Paris.'

I held the lipstick I'd picked from the mantelpiece in my hand. I couldn't put it on, now.

'Yeah, he said. It was a shock.'

Then he came over and felt the fabric of my dress and said 'Amazing.' I said I was sorry about David, and that I'd have liked to meet him, to which Gray gave a wry smile. Then he told me we needed to focus, and asked if I was planning on shoes, so I turned to the mirror and applied lipstick, twice, as he stood behind me and I saw his face in the mirror, and below that the clock that said ten past eight.

'He'd have liked to meet you, Ruth.'

I nodded, and watched myself do it. I was glad Gray's father had liked me.

'But let's not talk about him.' Gray had his hands on my waist.

I turned and wiped crumbs from folds of embroidery at his neck. I licked my fingers and got lipstick on them, so rubbed them on my dress as he watched.

'Oh well,' I said.

'What?' He was looking at the ribbon round my waist. I folded my arms, which made them seem more

217

in the way than they had before. He put his hands on his head. A car went by, through a puddle.

'I don't know.' I unfolded my arms and pulled at my fingers. 'I mean you won't live in Paris for ever, will you?'

He arched his back, dropped his hands, then lifted them high and said he wasn't planning on living anywhere for ever.

'Don't say that, Gray.' It came out like a whisper.

I cleared my throat and felt slightly weak, so sat down, but he pulled me up, with a hand under each of my elbows. I concentrated on keeping my legs rigid as we looked at each other, and I couldn't move closer because he said, 'We're late. Better not keep Matt waiting.'

It wasn't Matt Gray didn't want to be late for, I supposed, but since we were still together, alone, I smiled as well as I could.

Cheerful music drifted through my walls. Gray whistled along as I found shoes. My coat was still in Matt's car. My umbrella was underneath the table. It didn't open and close properly, but was better than nothing.

'Party time.' Gray looked happier, so I tried to nod, in a normal-looking way. Clare would be there next. I hadn't seen Clare since I was sixteen, when she'd backed out of Diane's kitchen as we watched in stunned silence. Gray followed her, as I remembered.

'The toast was good,' he said. 'Thanks, Ruth.'

'Thank my mother,' I said.

The front door slammed behind us as we stepped down side by side into rain.

The Fenton was surprisingly empty for almost nine on Saturday night. Dan wasn't there and neither were Clare and Matt.

'Perhaps the car broke down,' I said, as we sat at a large table with a full ashtray on it. My folded umbrella fell between the chair-leg and my tights. It was heavy and wet.

'Maybe.' Gray was looking towards the bar. He decided to buy some tobacco, though he'd told himself he would not. 'But this is a special occasion.'

I watched as he waited to be served. His shoulder blades gave him a delicate but solid shape, now that he'd removed his jumper again, and I liked the way he angled his legs, like a girl might, I remembered. The girl standing next to him looked at his head. They exchanged words and she laughed. I'd seen her in the corridors of the university's English Department, where she carried a school satchel. I wondered what Clare looked like now, and found myself watching the door, which opened twice before Gray came back, but not to bring Matt and Clare in. As Gray rolled a cigarette between long confident fingers, I looked at his watch and saw it was after nine.

'Are you worried?' he said. 'Missing Matt by now?'

'Matt and I aren't like that.' The lager was sweet. 'But it's not like him to be late.'

'Well it's very like Clare. Her sense of time bears

219

little relation to any objective reality.'

It sounded annoying to me. I asked what she was doing now, trying to sound relaxed. Trying not to demand any facts of her life and Gray's place in it, exactly. He inhaled, then put his elbow on the table between us and his chin in his hand, which brought his face nearer mine. He said she was meant to be doing art history at Warwick.

'But she's mostly in London. At singing lessons. You'll have to ask her why that is.'

'Don't they mind?'

'Who?'

'The people at Warwick. Don't they care she's not there?'

'They may do. Or they may not. You know how she is.'

I said I didn't really know her.

'I suppose you don't.' He smiled lightly, looking into my eyes. I must have looked as apprehensive as I'd sounded. He put his free hand over mine. Then there was a heavier hand on my shoulder and I turned to see Matt, with Clare behind him. She was wearing a wide felt hat over dense but drifting waves, which reached almost down to her elbows. I remembered what she looked like with something like fear. She glowed, as if a spotlight were inside her somewhere, or on her, although she wasn't shiny. She had a red mouth, with no lipstick on it. I thought of Thomas Campion: '*There is a garden in her face.*'

'Ruth, tell Gray not to be cross.' She stretched to touch his head, so a sleeve of damp red fabric brushed my face. 'Matt wanted fish and chips, but I could smell coriander on this weird little alleyway so I made him track it down and eat curry.'

She turned her smile on him. 'And you're not sorry, are you, Matt? It was delicious.' She sighed happily, remembering deliciousness, I supposed. 'Let me buy you a drink, Gray. Ruth, I'm sorry.' And she looked from him to me, as if we were both in a painting she was considering, then dragged a suede bag from her shoulder and asked what we'd like.

'Well, it could have been worse,' Gray said, when she'd moved off to the bar and Matt was sliding into the bench seat next to me. 'At least they're still serving. That's pretty good for Clare.'

She took some time to come back, and when she did there was a man behind her carrying a pint and a half of Guinness, which he put on our table.

'Thanks,' Clare said. 'That's really kind.'

Gray said thanks too. It must be what Clare did, instead of asking for a tray. She stayed standing to pull her outer garment over her head. It was a cloak of some sort, which she dropped and kicked under the table, before dragging a Fair Isle jumper up and off too. Now we saw antique lace, which must have been hand-dyed because it was darker in patches. She pushed handfuls of hair back and sat down between Gray and me. Her satin skirt draped on to my knee as she crossed long legs. She was wearing green boots with crepe soles which I knew came from the King's Road, because I was saving up for some.

'So, Ruth,' she said. 'What a fabulous dress. I almost got one like that at Portobello last week, but some American guy squeezed in first.' She reached for Gray's tobacco and papers. 'I hear you had a wet walk.'

I nodded. My mouth was dry.

'You would have loved it,' Gray said, wiping tobacco she'd spilled back into his pack. 'Very Gothic.'

Clare said she didn't much like the idea of monasteries. 'I mean I know they look nice, but I always get a horribly masculine vibe. I think of buggery when I go to those places.'

She gulped Guinness, surprisingly thirstily, then wiped her mouth and I saw the turquoise ring on her thumb. My Shakespeare tutor wore a ring on her thumb.

'Did you like it, Ruth?' She turned and smiled. I nodded, then wanted to say some words, to make sure I still could.

'But I like being in Matt's car, anyway.'

'She likes the sweets,' Matt said. 'Ruth will go anywhere if you buy enough sweets.'

I glared at him and his remark. 'I'm not going to Haworth again.'

Clare said she wished we had gone to Haworth. She would have loved that, she said, and asked if Matt had read *Villette*.

'Some of it.'

'That's what Gray says when he hasn't read something.'

'Which is rare,' Gray said. 'Have you read it, Ruth?'

I shook my head. 'It's Jane's favourite, though.'

'Who's Jane? Diane's Jane, you mean?'

I nodded as Clare said that surprised her. 'I'd have thought a poet would like Emily best.'

Jane didn't like people who called female writers by their first names, unless they were friends, so I was glad of a burst of noise from the door area. Oddly glad too to see that Dan had arrived with a group of people with plastic bags. Dan wouldn't ask about novels I should have enjoyed. One of his party was hitting another with a loaf of French bread. Matt stood up.

'I'd better say hello, or they'll come over.' He squeezed past my back, which knocked my chair into Clare's. She put a hand on my shoulder and one on my waist to ease me back where I'd been. Then she rolled herself another cigarette, with Matt's pack.

'I'll make it up to him,' she said. She licked the paper delicately.

She leaned back in her seat, blowing smoke. She rubbed her free left hand up and down Gray's arm, in a preoccupied way, then left it to rest on the back of his neck, before asking if he was OK.

'Tired?' she said. She pulled a strand of his hair. 'You look worried, Gray.' She put a hand on his and stroked the fingers, briefly. 'You're not cross, are you?'

He took his hand away. He said, 'Ruth was asking about Warwick.' He looked at me, seeming agitated rather than cross. I wished I could hold his hand, then, and tried a smile that didn't feel right.

'Poor you,' she said to me. 'Has Gray been boring

you with that? I'm thinking of leaving, to tell you the truth. I'm thinking of going to Paris, and singing in some smoky bar.' She made a happy face that stretched her eyes. 'Have you been, Ruth? There are so many jazz clubs.'

I didn't have to answer because Matt was back, with the girl who'd talked to Gray at the bar. He introduced her as Sue and we all said hello and she sat down where Matt had been, as he went to buy more drinks. She was on rum. I was beginning to have a headache, with the lager mostly and the smoke on all sides. Everyone seemed to be laughing. Or talking at the same time. Gray asked Sue if she was at Leeds and she explained how her part-time degree worked.

'Matt's sweet, isn't he?' Clare asked her. 'Have you been in his post-office van?'

I didn't want any more of my drink. Matt came back with more, though, as the bell for last orders rang and the pub surged to a new wave of shouts. Clare's back was towards me, as she and Gray talked. He was frowning, his nose wrinkled up. Matt and Sue were discussing Bolton Abbey. She preferred Fountains Abbey, which he hadn't been to but would love to drive to some time. She'd like that too, she shouted. You had to shout by now, as I discovered when Dan came over and asked if I was up for the party. I nodded, and he put his thumb up, saying see me there, and moved away. He had two bags of beer, which impeded his progress.

When I got back from the ladies', where I'd

discovered I'd lost my lipstick, everyone was standing up. Clare was holding Gray's arm and Matt was holding Sue's. I bent to get my umbrella and felt a rush of blood to my ears, which throbbed unpleasantly when I was upright again. Gray said I looked pale and I nodded.

'I might skip the party.'

Matt and Sue were moving towards the door. Clare had her jumper over her head. I watched as she gathered the folds of her cloak, then dragged her hair out of the fur round the neck. She looked slightly more flushed than she had, but still quite garden-like.

'Shall we go?' She took Gray's arm, and mine too, as if we were walking through a park together, with herbal borders to discuss.

'What a lovely pub,' she said. 'I wish I lived in Leeds.'

Outside, bodies huddled. Clare walked us to Matt, who was smoking. The rain had stopped, but the air was damp and had a whiff of fireworks in it. Bonfire Night was the following week.

'I think I'll go home,' I said, but Gray was the only one who noticed, so I said it again.

'I'm not feeling too well,' I explained, loudly. Various people looked at me. Clare put her hand on my shoulder and said I ought to be wearing a coat.

'You poor thing. Do you live near here?'

I nodded, said just round the corner and down the road. I felt Gray watching, then Clare, who had sensed his attention on me.

'I'll be fine,' I told them both. 'I've done it loads of times.'

I reached for my umbrella, which Gray was holding, but he held it firmly and said he'd walk me back.

'She can't wander about at this time of night.' He said that to Clare.

'Well how will you get to the party?' Clare ignored Matt, who was now close by, saying we ought to be moving along. Gray asked how to get to where they were going from my place. I could have told him, but didn't want to seem keen.

'It's dead easy.' Matt waved a hand. 'Walk along there, then take a left. Number 18. You'll know where it is by the noise.'

Clare was taking my umbrella from Gray. She said she'd come with us, if it was as simple as that. I didn't know what to do with my hands. They felt like things I should have in a bag, to ask someone else to look after. I watched Clare smiling and thought of Jane: '*My heart is like a singing bird.*'

'I just want to go home,' I said, and Clare said of course I did, and they'd walk me there. Gray took my umbrella back.

'This is crazy,' he told her. 'It's raining. I'll take Ruth. You go with Matt. OK?'

'So you don't want me to come?' Clare's voice was cool.

'Do you want to come?' Gray wasn't shouting, but he might as well have been, and for a moment I thought Clare would say yes. Her body was taut for an instant, like a racehorse, or a greyhound, maybe. But Matt called her and she relaxed. Gray put up my umbrella and pulled me under it with him, looking at her as he did so.

'Take care of her, then.' Clare touched his shoulder. 'And come straight back. No fish and chips.'

Then she turned and took Matt's arm. They moved away before we did, without looking back.

Gray didn't say anything as we walked until we were at the corner of my street, then he asked if I'd mind if he stopped for a fag. It seemed a strange place to pause, but I said OK, and held the umbrella while he crouched and rolled one, then sat on a step and took his first drag.

'Sit down,' he said.

'But we're almost there.' The stone steps looked cold. I thought of Bolton Abbey, being there without us, jagged and black. The umbrella felt heavy, so I folded it, although it was still raining. The dark fabric flapped in a sinister way and I was glad Gray was there as men passed, drinking from bottles. They turned into my road ahead of us and we heard glass smash and shouting. Gray threw his glowing cigarette up into the air.

'Idiots,' he said. 'Why is the world so ugly?'

'It's not.' I pointed up to the moon.

'Sure. But how do we get there?'

He took my hand, then started off at a run and we zigzagged from one pavement to the other, until we got

227

to mine, where uncurtained windows reflected street-lights in wide orange stars on their shiny black. There was no one else in. Gray dropped my hand.

'A safe landing,' he said, and I stood for a moment.

'Quick cup of tea?'

I walked ahead of him up the steps, then stopped, as my insides lurched in a shot of violent heat. The front door was open. It was about a foot ajar, swinging into the empty dark hallway. I gave a small cry, or a scream maybe, and he was behind me, pushing past, banging his hand on the door with an incoherent shout. I grabbed his arm and pulled him to one side, expecting someone to run out and past us.

'Don't, Gray. Stop it.' My heart was too fast. We stood quite still for a while as nothing happened and the door stayed gaping open. I could see the gloss paint on the radiator in the hallway, and the stripes of the torn wallpaper.

'I'll go in,' he said, but I said not to.

'We'll call the police.'

'What, and wait till the morning, when they turn up?'

He was moving towards the door and pushing it lightly, then inside, and I couldn't see him any more so I followed to find him at the foot of the stairs, jabbing the light-switch that didn't work.

He pushed the door to my room, which stayed firmly locked, so they weren't in there, whoever they were. There was probably no one, I said. It was probably just the hopeless door, but he said we'd have to see, and started up the uncarpeted stairs. I moved behind him, touching the back of his jumper with one hand and the smooth bannister with the other. We ascended together, up the first flight, then stopped for Gray to try the two doors on that landing. I stopped breathing when he did that. His breath came loud and slow in the silence. The doors were locked and so were the three doors on the floor above. Next was a short passage to the final flight of stairs, where a skylight cast long shadows. Gray's breath seemed slower and louder as he stopped for a moment. Then he put his finger on his lips, as I looked. He peered up and on to the final landing. The door of the room there was ajar, but since no one lived there, it might always have been.

Gray put his hand back to still me as he moved on up, but I followed close behind, the hem of his jumper bunched in my fist. The bannister was narrower now, and rough. We walked across planks and rolled underlay, springy like damp turf, then to the panelled door, which Gray kicked gently. It swung, to bang the wall of the room. Gray's hand went inside and found a switch. Pale light flooded, and he moved forward and didn't come back, so I went in too and we stood a few feet apart in a small sweet-smelling room filled with stacked chairs, and a large bed with a drooping stained mattress.

I stood just behind Gray, against the wall. He turned. The sleeve of his jumper with the smell of Matt's car on it touched my nose as his hand reached over my forehead to switch the light off. The moon was bright momentarily. When it was shadowed by cloud, and darker again, I reached out with both hands for his waist and pulled him as close as I could. I wanted to be squashed. We were safe now and together and he'd led us to that place, miraculously. I lifted my head as his hands moved down from my hair to finger my neck, and then at last we were kissing.

We leaned together against the wall, then moved hand in hand past chairs that fell over, and on to the length of the bed by the window. We knotted our fingers, and breathed each other's warm skin. I felt I hadn't properly breathed all day until then, as the moon lit his face, and I was utterly weightless. I might have floated, without his limbs on parts of mine. Without his hands on my dress, and my legs, as we breathed into each other with rhythmic noises that seemed to echo themselves in the compression of the room's musty quiet. And then the front door slammed. We stayed very still. Someone had come in, not gone out, of course. Ours had been the only two bodies in this house we'd searched, a long time ago.

The girl from downstairs screamed. Gray sat up, but I didn't. I held his arm, and lay on my back, with my knees pulled up against the plane of his shape.

'Whoever you are, fuck off out of my house. Leave now, whoever you are.' She sounded scared, rather than angry.

The bed creaked as Gray stood. He didn't move for a moment, and his hand stayed in mine. Then the shout from downstairs came again, as a scream, and Gray left the room. I heard his feet, fast down the stairs, then a shrill howl from the girl, then the slam of the door. Gray had left. I knew that because his voice came then, from the pavement outside. He called my name and I knelt on the bed and strained to open the window. He was waving up from the other side of the road. The window was painted shut. He called my name again and the whole street must have heard it, but the girl coming upstairs towards me seemed oblivious. She was calling my name as well, closer now, and her boots were loud as she walked up and into the room. She switched on the light. She came over and held me, because I was sobbing. She said she was calling the police, right now, but I told her not to.

'I know him,' I said. 'He's someone I know.'

'Bastards,' she said. 'All of them.'

I didn't see Gray again that weekend. He and Clare left early Sunday morning. Matt told me Gray didn't go to bed. Gray had stayed up all night and got wrecked, Matt said when he came round the next afternoon.

'Odd bloke, Gray. But I like him.'

'So do I,' I said. 'I like him a lot.'

'Well I'd never have guessed.' He stubbed his cigarette and stood up in the sunlight. He said he fancied a drive.

10

It was different visiting Clare at home when her father was there, not her mother. The mother took up more space. She wasn't substantially larger, but she tended to be in the kitchen, which was small. And unlike my mother, she talked, a lot. At the sink, at the cooker; wiping, beating, shaking or stirring, her voice took up more room than her body. It followed me around the place, disregarding walls or corners, and I'd call back, out of uneasy politeness, so between us we filled everything – the folds in the curtains, the gaps at the back of bookshelves, the airing cupboard, the drains; bits of the garden, probably, too.

The garden was where the father liked to be. He seemed small compared to that, which was long, unkempt, and large for West London. He'd come to the door to let me in, and smile rather than speak when he saw it was me. Then he'd maybe comment on the weather, before returning down to the foliage outside the precarious wooden steps at the back. Clare's flat was on the first floor. Her father didn't make tea, as the mother did when I arrived, so I used to go through and make a pot. He lived alone, since his second wife was dead. He had the look of a solitary man; someone unused to another body close to his own, which had the effect of making me hold things like the sugar bowl out towards him at arm's length. He never took my hand, like his ex-wife would, but held my gaze, occasionally, as he explained Clare's current state, before he went back outside. He discussed his daughter's mood in terms of physical height — 'a bit low', 'quite up today', once 'up near the ceiling', when she'd had a blood test that showed what turned out to be a brief remission.

Clare's father was a semi-retired book-dealer, never without a plastic bag of hardbacks somewhere nearby him, which she made fun of, if she wasn't 'low'. She made fun, too, of the fact that he always wore the same green waistcoat, with the same grubby trousers. And of the fact that he'd started smoking a pipe instead of cigarettes. He hadn't told her he had emphysema. He didn't tell me either, but the mother did. She told me also that he was fond of Eccles cakes, as she crumpled an empty packet of them into the bin one afternoon, so I sometimes brought some to have with our tea. He'd accept graciously, as if he were merely a visitor there, now that a female had arrived to supervise the afternoon.

From Clare's bedroom window I could see the old cane chair her father liked to sit in. Sometimes his head would angle forward and his hair slip into the neck of his shirt, which meant he'd fallen asleep. If Clare slept too, as she increasingly did, I felt nervous of the silence of the place, with its lowering sick-room smell and the bedside table's array of self-important medicine bottles, with their cheerless pills and sticky liquids which the household relied on but mistrusted. Sometimes the telephone rang as I sat on the bedroom chair, alongside unworn clothes and towels and Conor's plastic figures. Clare would wake at the gurgling ring, but mostly shake her head if I held the handset towards her. Mostly it was her mother. She rang every time I was there and was insistently breezy, which she wasn't if she rang me at home. In my house, I wasn't with a man she used to be married to, who'd left her for someone else, which allowed her now to find him mildly ridiculous. Or maybe she'd always found him ridiculous, which was why he'd left her, years ago.

She'd always ask where the father was, on the phone at Clare's. If I said 'in the garden' she'd say 'It's well for some.' If he'd left the premises, to buy tobacco or the *Evening Standard*, she'd give a small hollow laugh and say 'Put Clare on the phone.' She'd then spend a conversation with Clare checking that she was being well attended to, in spite of her irresponsible father. Clare would raise her eyes, say 'Yes, Mum' or 'No, he doesn't have to. Ruth's here.' Or sometimes, closing her eyes, 'I don't want to talk about it.'

One afternoon in mid August, when I'd arrived later than usual, having delivered Conor at a friend's, a

234

phone call between Clare and her mother went on for some time. The topic was frozen food.

'I think Dad knows how to defrost sausages,' Clare said. 'And if not then I can tell him. I have managed to feed my son for the last eight years.'

I looked out of the window. The garden chair was empty. Clare was raising her voice, which was an unusual and pleasing sound. She must be feeling well. 'I don't need this,' she said. 'No, don't. I'll ask Ruth. She's probably opened a freezer before. Do you like running people down, or are you just bored?'

Clare lifted the phone away from her ear to hold it high above her gingham-covered duvet and throw it across the room. It landed near the window. As I straightened up from collecting it, I saw Clare's father move out from underneath trees at the garden wall. I stayed to watch him stroke the cat, stretched on a lozenge of sunshine underneath an easel, which held a small oil painting which hadn't changed since I'd first seen it, a month or so before. He was painting a view of the garden, with the pear tree, his chair and Clare's bedroom window strung together by the washing line. He put this artwork beneath his daughter's bed every time he left. Clare called it 'our little secret', meaning a secret she and her father kept from the mother. It was my secret too, of course, like most in that house. Like the fact that Clare smoked, which the mother wasn't supposed to know, although she did, because she knew — as Clare did not — that her father had given up cigarettes, so the butts in the bedroom couldn't be his.

Money was another secret matter in Clare's bed-ridden life. Unbeknown to either parent, I used to collect her Social Security payments from the post-office in Shepherd's Bush Road, before she got round to claiming the more respectable 'disability allowance'. I don't know what the family thought Clare lived on before, since she hadn't worked much since she'd moved back to London. She used to sing in bars from time to time, and at parties and weddings occasionally. But she told me not to mention my trips to the post-office, so I never did. I'd slip her an envelope with her money inside it when we were alone, and she'd wink contentedly. She obviously liked the pretence that she was still an independent person, despite being unable to dress herself.

'You know what I hate most about all this?' she asked, after the sausage conversation. 'It's having to talk to my mother every day.'

I put the offending telephone handset back in its cradle, which had something viscous spilled on it.

'There's no escape from her now.' She closed her eyes. Tears appeared as she squeezed them tightly shut, then squeezed her whole face and put it down between flat palms and sniffed. I didn't know what to say. I'd been reading Adrienne Rich.

'*They gave me a drug that slowed the healing of wounds.*'

We heard footsteps in the corridor.

'And now he'll be wanting me to tell him what she said. Can't we send him out? I need a break. I need a cigarette, Ruth.'

She wiped her eyes, looking more cross than sad now.

It was too early to collect Conor, and there was nothing else I could ask of the man so I suggested we shut the door of her room, so she could smoke in peace. I opened the window. I'd done that before, and we'd both enjoyed the conspiracy. She'd said it was like being teenagers again, though Clare probably did what she liked as a teenager and never bothered to hide it.

'If Dad comes in, you take the cigarette,' she instructed, as she slid a pack of Marlboro Reds from the bedside table's top drawer, where she kept ear plugs and mints and a watch with no strap, and folded papers with handwriting on them.

'But I don't smoke.'

'Well pretend you've started. The strain of my illness has driven you to it.'

I did feel strained. It was tiring to be always remembering what I was and was not supposed to know, or do. I hoped the mother wouldn't ring back. If she did, I'd say Clare was asleep.

*'A conversation begins
with a lie.'*

I hadn't lied to Clare as yet, but I'd been economical with the truth about Gray being in London. She didn't know he was there.

'It's at times like this I wish I had a husband,' she said, leaning back on red pillows, which made her look paler than the blue ones did. 'If it wasn't for Conor I'd tell them both to leave me alone.' She pulled at her hair, which came out in wisps. I almost said she should ask me to do more for Conor, but did not. She disliked my being in a position to be with her son more than she was. It had led to silences in this room in the past.

'And you know what tonight has in store? My mother is washing my hair. I'm a wreck.' She sniffed and wiped her cress-coloured eyes, then looked up at me, biting her lip.

'I'll do it. If you'd like.'

It was only a quarter to five. I was supposed to be going round to see Liam at Fiona's, but not until half eight. Clare's eyes were more black than green again now, on her shadowy side of the room. She smoked and shook her head. She sighed.

'Tell me something, Ruth.'

I couldn't think of anything to tell, since we couldn't talk about Gray.

'I'm just working, really. Just getting on with the poetry. I mean that's what I'm meant to be doing.'

It sounded as if I resented being there, with her, when I ought to be working.

'I'll be writing about Adrienne Rich later on.' That wasn't true. Though I might be thinking about what to write, that evening. I spent a lot of my time with Liam thinking about things he had nothing to do with.

She made a snorting noise. 'Who's Adrienne Rich?'

I said she was American, and I liked her, but I'd only just started reading. There was a poem called 'Diving into the Wreck', I said, and she laughed and asked how it went. I said I couldn't remember.

'I came to explore the wreck . . .

I came to see the damage that was done.'

'It's about finding treasure. I think.'

'That's nice.'

She held her left hand out and still for a moment. She looked at the stone of the ring that I'd seen on her left thumb for ever. She rubbed it with the fingers of her right hand, which still held a cigarette.

'I think you might as well have this, Ruth. I'm always having to take it off for some bloody scan or another.' She started twisting it over the knuckle before I could register what I felt. Her ash was precariously balanced. I lifted the saucer that served as an ashtray to put between us, but she snatched it from me.

'I am capable of not setting the place on fire, Ruth.' She pushed her ring back into place and glared. 'I was trying to give you something.'

I felt the muscles in my neck tighten. I didn't want a friend who gave me things.

'I mean Conor only comes in when he has to, you know. He thinks it smells in here. I heard him saying it yesterday night.'

I thought of Conor's smiling eyes when Gray and I arrived to collect him from his play-scheme now.

'Sorry,' she said. 'It's not your fault.'

She looked at me more than I liked, those days. There wasn't much else she could do, as I moved around and she did not.

'It's so unfair,' she said.

I was nonplussed, as I often was by shifts in the mood of our conversations, which seemed to veer into culs-de-sac rather than going anywhere. I pulled at my own hair, which had been cut and coloured the day before, in Kensington High Street. It wasn't fair that I'd walked through hard-edged blue light to a place of fast-moving, glossy-haired people to have a lean young man who smelled of raspberries massage shampoo-foam around my head. Nor that I'd be leaving this crumpled stasis to cycle through neon, alongside the diesel-licked river, to see Liam and eat fish in a garden, while Clare had her hair washed by someone she didn't want near her. I rubbed dust from the window and was struck by the lushness of outside, by the random easy movement of the trees out there, as the phone started again. Clare ought to change the ring tone.

'Tell her I'm out. And I won't be back.'

It was her mother. I said Clare was fast asleep. I watched a man on a ladder wash the windows of a family house beyond the garden wall. There was a climbing frame on the lawn there with a swimming costume hanging from it and several bikes and a large doll, spread-eagled on the grass. Clare's mother said she was glad her daughter wasn't awake, and how good my company was for her.

240

'You really perk her up, Ruth. She's always happier after you've been.'

She might have been happier to be left alone for a few hours, I thought, but I'd mentioned that before and been met with silence. Clare's garden was in shade now, except for a ribbon of light threading the slats of the neighbour's fence. The days were shortening fast. I'd bought some lights for her bike, the weekend before. Her mother seemed to want our conversation to continue, but wasn't saying anything. I could almost hear her breathing.

'And Ruth, I've been thinking.' She left a gap, as if I might help her articulate something. I probably knew what it was. She'd mentioned Gray every time we'd been alone together, by then. She liked his voice, she'd told me. She wondered what he did, and who he stayed with and if he looked like Conor. She'd offered me wine, instead of tea, the last time I'd stayed until after six.

'I was thinking, Ruth,' the mother continued. 'This isn't the best time to mention Gray to her, is it? I think we might wait until after Friday. She's got radio-therapy, and that always exhausts her. And Conor knows not to upset her this week.'

I'd imagined that Conor would tell Clare about our meetings with Gray, but could see now that he wouldn't, unless she asked directly. He had an instinct for what he should not say. Perhaps he cast spells around the flat, like I did as a child, to improve the atmosphere without having to speak to anyone real.

He seemed by and large more resilient than the adults in his life. I rarely asked how Conor felt about things, because I remembered the discomfort of questions about my emotional state when my mother was absent or ill. It was easier to pretend to be happy than to admit to Jane that I wasn't. If I ever strayed on to the subject of Clare with her son, he'd talk about football or trainers or a fight he'd almost been in. If I asked, 'What does your mum think about it?', he'd tell me what his grandmother thought and how other people disagreed. He seemed more comfortable with stories of arguments than tenderness, just as people are more comfortable watching a public brawl than a passionate embrace. But he seemed less uneasy with affection lately. He'd allowed Gray to fold his fingers in his to cross the Shepherd's Bush Road that afternoon, when I went ahead to buy stamps. I watched as they waited, hand in hand, to come to me, and as I saw their four legs moving almost together, and the look on Gray's face as he looked down at his son, I couldn't think it was wrong to bring them together. I was going to tell Liam about that moment when I saw him later on. He'd say it was sentimental but I didn't care. He'd say we should tell Clare that Gray was seeing their son. He disapproved of what he called my 'meddling'. He thought secrets were bad for people.

'Secrets wreck lives,' he'd told me at the weekend, over a drink. 'You can't build anything on lying to someone.'

I'd said that I hadn't lied to anyone. And if secrets

ruined lives, then Conor should know who his father was.

'And you think it's your job to tell him, do you?'

'Don't be ridiculous.'

'Exactly.'

It had been last orders in the Black Bull, and my turn to go to the bar as our conversation reached that point. I'd changed the subject when I got back to our table. I didn't want to talk about Conor and Gray. Liam would be bound to accuse me of being over-involved. He often did that now. But I'd been thinking about secrets lately, and how useful they were or were not. Adrienne Rich wrote about secrets and silence, between women especially.

'We stayed mute and disloyal
because we were afraid.'

I wasn't afraid of Clare. But I was nervous of what she might do if she found out her son saw his father, with me. Being as ill as she was gave her a new if unacknowledged authority.

An aeroplane roared overhead, like some vast vacuum cleaner hoovering up the clouds, as Clare's mother ended our conversation. She said I must take care and Clare must rest, which seemed superfluous advice. Apart from hopping to the bathroom, there wasn't much my friend could do to tire herself. As I turned from the phone call, Clare was sitting up straighter.

'I had a dream last night.' She patted the bed to the right of her legs. I stayed standing where I was. 'It was a birthday party in the Schoolhouse, and Ted Hughes was there. He was sitting at the kitchen table, digging candle-wax off it with the end of a pencil.'

I sat down while she held the ashtray towards me. As I reached for it we misconnected and the contents spilled. Clare wiped the pale dust violently, smearing it into the yellow sheet.

'Get something. Get a wet cloth.'

There was panic in her voice, whether because of the miniature cremation or the mess her mother would guess the origins of, I wasn't sure, but I felt it too and ran to the kitchen, bumping into her father. He sensed emergency and ran towards the bedroom. I heard, 'Get out for God's sake. Just leave me alone,' then he was coming towards me as I made my way back to her room. I touched his shoulder as we passed, and saw his small brown eyes were moist, but went on to wipe the duvet clean. When it was done, I turned to take the cloth away but Clare said to leave it. She patted the space I'd sat on before and asked what I thought of her dream so far.

I didn't know what to think yet. Ted Hughes made me anxious. I should have done him by now, but was putting it off. It felt like having to write about some-one's father whom you haven't met, but know you're not supposed to like. I watched Clare slide another cigarette from her pack and thought of Jane's copy of *Ariel*, which I saw every time I went upstairs in my childhood home. Her Plath collections were on a bookcase with no sides on the landing, held in place with a large oval stone from the shore. I thought of having to read 'Daddy' at school, and how the word 'bastard' in the last line made me hot, and how my mother complained to Jane that it was inappropriate for a fifteen-year-old girl with no father, and threatened to ring the headmistress, and Jane had grabbed the book from her and read it, sneeringly, loudly, as my mother left the house and Jane read on, until *'Daddy, daddy, you bastard, I'm through.'* And I burst into tears.

Clare was waiting for an answer.

'Well, did you like Ted Hughes at your party?'

'Kind of. He was handsome. But mostly I thought it was odd that he'd come since he wasn't invited, and nobody knew him. I didn't actually know it was him until you told me.'

'I told you? Was I at the party?'

I began to feel nervous.

'You were with Gray.' She looked at me and bit her lip. 'You and Gray were on the couch by the window. You were eating crisps and you told him that Ted Hughes liked me and you thought we ought to get married.'

I looked at the telephone. I'd given the number to the man in charge of the football Conor was playing, in case of accidents. I said whoever I was in the dream was nothing to do with me, in that case.

'His wives killed themselves,' I said. 'He wasn't a man to marry.'

'No, but you weren't really you in the dream. Well I

245

knew it was you, but you were only about twelve. I thought you'd come to keep Conor company, except Conor wasn't there.'

'Whose birthday party was it?'

I didn't like the dream. And liked it less when she said that Jane was there and she thought I ought to go home, but no one wanted to take me, so Ted Hughes said he would, but Diane said he couldn't.

'Diane? What was she doing? She's dead, you know.'

I wanted to get back to reality, away from myself as an unwanted guest at a party, too small to go home alone.

'I know. I think that's what the dream was about. Colette rang me up, a few days ago. She was talking about the house she's bought. She thought I'd like to go there. As if I could.'

I was horrified. Colette was offering Diane's things to everyone, then. Gray must be told about this largesse. And why would Clare want anything there, I asked her.

'She thought there might be something I'd like Conor to have. Diane was his granny, Ruth, after all. I thought it was rather sweet of her.'

Clare looked wistful then for a moment, before shrugging and turning to face me. 'But Conor's OK without any of Diane's old junk. She left him some money.'

'Really? How much did she leave?'

'A lot. Which is a good thing, in the circumstances. But he can't have it until he's eighteen.' Clare's face clouded and she bit a nail. 'Which means he won't be able to spend it on me.'

'Mmm.' It wasn't a noise I often made, but it seemed the best one. 'So the dream was about Conor's granny, you think?'

She nodded. She looked quite pleased. 'I've thought about it all day, and that's what I've decided. It must be something about Diane's house. I was thinking maybe you could go there. Just out of interest. What do you think?'

She looked like she used to, when she was in a pub somewhere, making connections that nobody else did concerning people nobody really knew. She seemed alert, vivacious and capable, in her ruthlessly whimsical way. I could see why Gray had been in love with her then. Why he still might be, if he saw her again.

'I could ask Colette if you could go for me and find something small for Conor to keep. I'd love to know what's still there.'

I asked if she'd been before and she said only once on Christmas Eve, when Conor was four. She'd never mentioned the visit to me. I decided I needed water, and offered her a hot drink, which she thought she'd like, which was a relief.

As the kettle boiled, the father came in from the garden. He said Clare seemed rather down.

'She needs her mother here, not me.' The kettle clicked itself off. 'You look well, Ruth,' he told me, so

I said he did too, which made him look sad. Clare wanted mint tea. I needed a cup. They were all on the draining board, waiting for her mother to wash them up.

'How's your painting coming along?'

He frowned. 'Keeping me busy,' he said. He took a glass from the counter behind him and gave it a token rinse before filling it with water. He sipped it leaning against the outside door, which swung open, so he closed it and turned the key in the lock. He took his pipe from his waistcoat pocket and pressed inside it with his thumb. He had a wedding ring still on his finger. I took a clean-looking mug and dropped a herb teabag in it.

'She's OK then, is she? Drinking OK?'

I nodded, then turned to him and nodded some more.

'He needs a father around, that boy.'

I nodded again. Then I looked at him, which I hadn't been doing till then.

'Have you met Gray?' I said. 'He's really nice. I think . . .' I hesitated, but just for a second. 'I think Conor likes him a lot.'

He was tilting a match to the bowl of his pipe. 'Women are odd,' he said, and I laughed.

'I'd better take her this.'

I hurried back to Clare.

Her mint tea was too hot to hold without something around the cup handle, so I found a box of tissues and took a wad of them to wrap around it before I handed it to her. She seemed happy with the arrangement.

'Clare,' I said, 'I've been talking to your father.'

That was cowardly and beside the point, so I started again, as she concentrated on the steam rising between the cup and her mouth.

'Clare. I've got something to tell you that you might not like.'

'What? I won't see Christmas?'

'It's not about you. It's about Conor, and me.'

Then I left the room. I'd seen an open bottle of wine on the table next door, and I thought I might have some, but then decided I wouldn't. It wouldn't stop my pulse going so fast. I'd have a glass after I'd told her, maybe. I went back into her room and sat down, forcing my head up and my eyes straight into hers. She stared back at me. The phone rang but I left it and she didn't react.

'Do you want a cigarette?'

She shook her head. I took a deep breath.

'Gray's in London, Clare. I met him with Matt. He's staying for a while.'

I felt a bit sick. She didn't speak. She stared with wet-bark-coloured eyes, narrowing then wide and green again.

'Has he seen Conor?'

I nodded.

'Does my mother know?'

I shook my head, which was a lie, though silent.

'Have you told Dad?'

I shook my head harder. I felt as pale as she was. I wished she'd stop looking at me.

'But you've told Liam, haven't you? I bet you've told him.'

'But only him, Clare. And he hasn't told anyone. He wanted me to tell you.'

She seemed to be grinding her teeth. The hand nearest me was clenched into a fist. 'Who do you think you are, Ruth? God?'

I stood up and went to the window, where there were no shadows on the uncut grass. The cat walked slowly towards the house and the window-cleaner had gone. I didn't know what to say, but I wanted to say something true.

'Gray wants to know his son.' My back was towards her and my face very hot.

She burst into tears then, in a way she hadn't for months. Not since she'd learnt that it would be pointless to operate on her spine. I went and held her and she didn't resist, but crumpled, her backbone under my fingers, her thinning hair against my own, which I pushed away from the heat of our faces.

'He wants to see you, Clare. He wants to make it all right.'

She sobbed, then sniffed as her body stiffened and she pulled away from me. 'Well I don't want to see him,' she said.

I watched her wiping her eyes with her fingers, stretching the skin, so her cheeks looked taught and smooth like they did years ago, then she dropped her hands to pull at her ring.

'Do you mean that?' I said, after a while of silence. 'You really don't want to see Gray?' She shook her head, but she didn't look up. She had the duvet between both hands, and her head was moving, like a mechanical thing that doesn't work well.

'Why not see him for Conor?' I said.

She looked up at me then with her whole face wet. 'He left me,' she said. 'He didn't want to know.'

Then she sobbed in a way I hadn't heard before. I didn't like the noise. And I didn't believe that she didn't want to see Gray. I couldn't believe that at all.

11

Conor was born in November 1989, the weekend the Berlin Wall came down, but I wouldn't have known he'd arrived in the world if I hadn't been about to go to Amsterdam with a man who decided he couldn't come with me. He was married, and rang just before eight in the morning, as I was brushing my teeth with the radio news in the bathroom. François Mitterand talked of 'these happy events'. My paramour said I should go anyway and enjoy myself, but I tore up my ticket before I put the top back on the toothpaste.

It was a glittering morning, with sunshine turning patches of my walls into panes of light, so I put on the clothes I'd planned to wear on the plane and set off by bike to the Goldborne Road. I'd have breakfast in the Lisboa Café, where everyone would be talking Portuguese, which might be something like being abroad. It was market day in the Portobello Road.

By the time I'd arrived at the secondhand stalls under the roar of the Westway, I'd acquired *Stories from The New Yorker 1950–60* and a pair of faded red-leather gloves. I was trying on a pair of old sun-glasses which reminded me of Jane, when I heard a particular voice from behind draped velvet. When the voice laughed, then said, 'It's lovely, it really is,' I was certain who it was.

Clare was sitting behind a laden trestle table. She looked like someone in a play about someone in a flower-shop, but instead of flowers there were swathes of patterned fabric on all sides of her, and blooms of bright objects in delicate clusters on a green lace cloth on her table. A paisley wrap swirled on her shoulders and from her rolled felt hat her hair hung in a pale density of reflective waves. I watched as a girl at her stall passed a bag to a man behind her, who barely noticed, because he was looking at Clare. Then I moved towards her, with something like pride in our acquaintance.

'Ruth. My God. What are you doing here?'

She looked not older, but softer, somehow.

'Looking for something to change my life.'

'You might find it on this stall,' the girl with the boyfriend said, then she moved away and Clare and I were left to say how strange it was to meet there, where neither of us came much any more. The immediate present was easier to discuss than the time we'd last met, about three years before, at a party. I'd been leaving as she arrived. I didn't ask what she'd been doing since then, because I thought I knew. Everyone knew she'd been living in France. We assessed each other in curious glances while agreeing

253

that we used to come to the market every week. Clare said she'd never missed a Friday when she was in London full-time.

'Which is how come I have all this junk to get rid of.' She smiled at a red-head who was holding a scarlet kimono up to her shoulders.

'That's a fiver. It's good with your hair.'

The girl moved to look in a tilted mirror as another arrived in a shot-silk jacket that I'd seen on Clare in the past. It had looked better on her, of course.

'Can I have it for eight?' The potential customer lifted both arms above her head to show the fabric straining. 'It's not going to last too long, is it?'

'Not if you do that.' Clare sucked in her lips, then blew out with a bubbling sound. 'It's ten, I'm afraid. Someone the right size'll take it like that.' She snapped her fingers. She looked at me and asked how things were, but I didn't answer because the girl buttoned the jacket and handed a note to Clare, who stood to put it into a purse. It was then I saw she was pregnant.

'When's the baby due?' The customer asked the question, which gave me time to stop staring. Clare's coat of soft corduroy had the two middle buttons undone.

'This time next week, supposedly.' Her left hand moved to pat where the baby was. She was wearing two rings, but none on the third finger. 'But I'm hoping he gets bored and comes out sooner.'

I wondered if Clare knew it was a 'he', or if she was guessing, as she said she was longing to see his face. I scanned the near-distance for male-shaped clues.

'You'll see enough of that.' The woman laughed. Clare raised her eyebrows, with her cool look that brought her chin forward, and may have been going to say something contrary, but the kimono girl came back and said she'd take it; it would be good in bed.

'Gosh, that's not far off now, is it?' She pointed to Clare's stomach.

Clare put coins in her purse and zipped it shut, then turned to me. 'You know what, Ruth? I'd love a hot chocolate. Could you watch the stall for a minute?'

'I'll get you one. I need a coffee.'

In fact I needed something much stronger.

When I returned with Clare's hot drink, she was groping inside a cardboard box.

'Damn,' she said, as she dragged a collection of glass shapes and newspaper on to the table. I watched as she untangled the various strands of what I was beginning to recognize as a small chandelier. It used to hang in the top landing of Diane's old flat. It didn't light up, because it was meant for candles, but I'd seen its dusty colours in the daytime, many times, by the light of a high window outside Gray's room.

'I should have had this out at six o'clock. The dealers would've loved it.'

'What is it?'

This was becoming increasingly obvious, as her slim fingers worked beads free to spread in a circle around the turquoise-and-pink central bowl. It was nice to see it again, but somehow disturbing, like seeing a person you were once in love with, but can't remember quite why. I reached out and rubbed a red glass frill between my thumb and fingers.

'I should have stuck it in some soapy water. Most people can't imagine how it's meant to look.'

She frowned, then stopped and smiled at me, and asked how I was, which I didn't respond to, since she was absorbed in rubbing her chandelier clean.

'Tell them someone'll come along who knows how to wash up, and they'll take it like that.' I snapped my fingers and she smiled again. She glowed, like a birthday cake, maybe.

'Faster than that, if they know anything, Ruth. It's Victorian. I think.'

I watched as she sipped her hot chocolate, inquisitively, as if she had no idea what to expect of the taste.

'You look lovely,' I said without thinking. 'It suits you, having a baby.'

She made a wry face and said that would surprise her, in such a way as to make me want to ask why, but a man came and lifted a teapot from her wares. He blew into the spout, as if he was blowing a pipe.

'It's a good pourer,' Clare assured him. 'I used it every day for five years.'

'So why did you stop?'

'I started drinking coffee.' She winked at me.

'Very continental. How much?'

She said five. I looked at the chandelier. The man was looking too. 'Give you ten for that,' he said.

'Times ten, and you're on.' She gave him a 'dare-you' sort of smile that made her eyes shine more greenly. She had lots of smiles.

'Can you stick it under the table while I get some cash?'

Clare considered. She said she'd keep it an hour, with the teapot, if he paid for that now.

'Mmm. You're tougher than you look.' He handed her a fiver and went off, saying he'd be back very soon, but Clare told me they all said that.

'I've been keeping this for someone since eight.' She brought out a quilt I hadn't seen before, with hand-stitching round tiny diagonals of printed fabrics and little pieces of velvet.

'How much is that?'

'I said fifty, but I won't get that now. It's going to rain any minute.' The sky had darkened. Her table looked shabby without sunlight on it, and she herself seemed somewhat diminished, sitting with her plastic cup.

'I'll buy it.'

'Seriously? It's damaged, Ruth.'

'I'll give you fifty, Clare. A quilt is what I wanted.'

She laughed, somewhat wryly. 'Well you'll find a better one than this if you wander around. I couldn't take fifty from you.' She was folding it up. 'And anyway, what if the man comes back?'

If he did, Clare would say she'd sold it, and he

wouldn't care, if she was nice to him. I took a note from my wallet.

'Take this and I'll go to a cash machine.'

She rubbed her large front and frowned into the air to her right. Her eyes seemed grey rather than green when she looked back and said no, really, it wasn't worth fifty.

'He was rich and you're not, Ruth.'

My face must have registered surprise at this assumption, because she said what she meant was that I was her friend.

It began to rain very slightly. Clare blew into her hands, as if being cold was her main preoccupation. I realized that the hat she was wearing was very like one that Gray used to wear.

'So you won't sell it to me?'

'This isn't about me and you, Ruth.'

I scrunched my empty coffee cup. 'Do you need any help packing up?'

She said someone was coming for her with a car at one. I wondered who it was.

'Look, what I'll do is I'll give you my number. Do you still live round here?'

I told her Bolingbroke Road, and she said great, she was camping out at the Schoolhouse for now.

'Give me a ring tomorrow, and if the bloke doesn't show you can have the quilt for forty. Come round and get it. Come round anyway. I owe you a cup of hot chocolate.' She smiled a wide affectionate smile. 'OK?' She wrote on a piece of yellow paper and handed it to me. 'Let's talk tomorrow. Come round on Sunday. I'll give you tea.'

She stopped her smile, and looked not lonely, but separate from the rest of the day. She'd always had a way of seeming oddly apart, even when surrounded.

On Saturday I was in the bookshop in Camden where I worked four days a week. At lunchtime I rang Clare's number. If Gray picked up I'd put the phone down, but there was no reply. After work I went to a party, which I left early to get a bus home, to sleep and dream that Gray was in my local shop with a pram, with no baby in it. He was buying aubergines and gave me some.

On Sunday morning I rang Clare's again. I couldn't go round because my Amsterdam man was taking me out, but no one answered anyway, nor again at three, when I was in a pub on the river. I realized I was worried.

'What's to worry about?' my companion said. His wife had two little girls.

'Clare said she'd be there and she's not.'

I was then subject to an explanation of the unpredictability of birth. Babies can arrive before they're officially due, I was told. Clare could be in labour. Or just out, enjoying herself.

'Maybe she's having a drink by the river with someone charming. Like I am.'

That annoyed me more than his knowing about babies. Clare probably had forgotten she'd asked me to visit. She could be out buying a cot or a pram, or aubergines, for all I knew. I decided not to ring again and didn't until Monday lunchtime. The bookshop was quiet and a woman came in with an infant and asked if I'd mind if she breastfed. I told her she'd be more peaceful downstairs in the Cultural Studies section, and when she'd gone I phoned the Schoolhouse. No one answered, or again at three, but at five a woman picked up and said 'Clare's phone.' I knocked a coffee over a pile of pale hardbacks.

'Can I speak to Clare? Is she about?'

There was no reply, so I asked again.

'Who is this?'

'I'm Ruth. Is everything all right?'

'She hasn't mentioned a Ruth.'

A man came to pay for a John Berger, but I waved him away to the till at the back and explained that I was a very old friend. The woman lit a cigarette.

'Well, she's in Queen Charlotte's right now. I'm only feeding the cat.'

I tried to sound casual as I asked if it was the baby or something else. The woman inhaled before telling me. The baby'd been born on Saturday morning. Everything had gone smoothly.

A pale girl asked where she could find a biography of Gurdjieff. I pointed her in the direction of the Women's Studies desk.

'Was anyone with her?' I sounded suspicious. 'I mean, does she want people to visit?'

The voice said Clare had gone in alone. 'You know it's a boy, I suppose.'

I said yes.

'When's visiting time? I'd like to see it. I mean him. I'd like to see him.'

The woman smoked and said there was no rush. The baby wasn't going anywhere. Then there was a moment of silence, after which she apologized for being uptight.

'I mean, if you're a friend that's cool. But you know how things are. I mean she doesn't want . . .' She inhaled, then exhaled slowly. 'I mean, I said I'd keep certain people in the dark, that's all.'

I paused before making a noise which I hoped meant I knew what she was talking about. She made the same noise back to me.

'That's great, though,' I said. 'That's wonderful.'

By Wednesday Clare was home, and answering calls.

'He's beautiful,' she told me.

I said I bet he was.

I arrived to meet Conor on a misty afternoon that made me think of Norfolk. The air was like something a soluble aspirin had just been dropped into. Clare opened the heavy-looking door. Her face was pale, and her eyes very dark. The baby was asleep, she said, as we climbed up to the top of the building. The hallway smelled of candle-wax and paper, as it always had. The sound of an electric guitar came through from the middle floor, where parties used to start.

'Is that Justin?'

Justin had taken over the room that Matt had lived

in for a while, when there were parties every Saturday
night, and I went there a lot.

' 'Fraid so.' Clare stopped, her hand on the bannister
ahead of me. 'He's not meant to be here, but neither am
I. The council wants the place empty.' The guitar playing got louder as she said she liked the noise of it. She
looked vaguely into the space of the once-baronial
stairwell. 'The place seems more empty since I came
home with Conor. Which is strange.'

We continued on up, past the door of the bathroom,
into the lighter air of Clare's landing, which had been
painted since I'd last seen it. There were yellow walls
and dark doors, with what you could see of the floorboards brick red. She pointed to a half-open door and
took my arm then, to draw me towards her and into a
room with drawn curtains and a basket on a bed,
inside which was a bundle with a small nose and eye-
lashes and a damp open mouth. I watched to see his
breathing. Clare ran a finger down the side of his face,
then waved the same finger towards the door. I
followed her out of the room.

In the cream-and-blue kitchen she told me to excuse
the chaos, and I said 'Amazing,' and she smiled and
nodded and bit her lip.

'I can't believe it, Ruth.'

She looked so different than she had at the market
that I stared, until she noticed and said 'Tea?' and I
said I'd make it because I thought she should be sitting
down, but she said I was the guest, and it was lovely
to have one.

The kitchen had the same floor as the hallway, but there was less of it showing. Old clothes spilled from bin-liners, a large chest of drawers lay on its back, and the dilapidated three-seater couch seemed to have spread.

'I know.' Clare turned from the sink. 'It's a mess. I dumped my stall here on Friday, then started contractions. There's nowhere to put it anyway.'

She pulled the floral curtains then lit the gas, which I remembered the noise of as it blew on only one side of its ring.

'We have a choice of teapots.' There were three on the table, one of which was the one the chandelier man was supposed to have bought.

'So he didn't come back?'

She shook her head. I had a cake in my bag, but there was one on the table already.

'Cake?' she said. She cut herself a hunk and explained that the woman feeding her cat had left the fridge full of fruitcakes. 'New mothers are supposed to eat sugar.'

'Has your mother been yet?' Clare's mother lived in Acton by then.

She rubbed one of her breasts and frowned, saying she wished he'd wake up because she was leaking.

'My mother thinks I'm bonkers.' She laughed, seeming pleased as the kettle boiled. The teapot was filled and placed on the table. Clare sat on a chair, then moved to the couch.

'Stitches,' she explained. 'It's not much fun, sitting down.'

I poured tea and put sugar in hers.

'Are you taking anything?'

'Hot salt baths are meant to be good, but Conor seems to wake whenever I run one.' She pointed at the cake, but I didn't feel hungry.

'It's nice to see you, Ruth. You're my first quite voluntary visitor. Your quilt's in that pile, by the way.'

I said I hadn't come for that.

She pulled a cushion from behind her and arched her back. She explained that she'd been trying to get rid of everything because she wanted to get out of London. She was thinking of moving to Wales.

'Though I'm nowhere near ready to go.' She gulped her tea thirstily. 'And I can't see myself at the market for a while.'

She breathed and bit her finger. The sound of the guitar downstairs came mutely through the floor. A siren went past on the Shepherd's Bush Road. Then the baby made a small bleating sound, and Clare was up and out of the room as the doorbell rang through the whole house, as it always had, no matter which of the people inside anyone was coming to see. The guitar playing continued as the bell rang again, then Clare was back with a shape at her breasts, trailing a lacy shawl.

'Ignore it,' she said.

. I stood up and saw the face of the miniature creature.

'Don't say it,' Clare said. 'I know what you're going to say.'

An interior door slammed and footsteps echoed down the lower stairs. The baby looked exactly like Gray.

'It must be weird for him,' I said. 'A perfect little clone.'

'He hasn't seen him. And won't, if I have anything to do with it.'

She looked at her baby, not me, and I was glad she couldn't see my face. My expression must have been odd. She unbuttoned her blouse and moved towards the couch. She seemed absorbed then, making soft noises, crooning and low.

I put my cup on the table and asked if I should come back another time, but she didn't reply. She may not have heard. She was stroking her baby's head. I asked if she'd like more tea, but she didn't answer that question either, so I listened to the silence for a moment until it was broken by footsteps on the stairs, getting louder as someone moved towards us. Clare didn't react, but I was aware of the door and felt myself stiffen as it swung wide, to frame the body of Diane, with a large teddy bear clutched to her front and a bottle in tissue-paper under an arm, with folded gold foil at the top. She saw me before anything else, but only paused for a moment.

'Well, well, well. What a lovely surprise. I'd hug you, Ruth, but I have my hands full.'

Diane moved into the room as elegantly as always, if

slightly more slowly, around the upturned chest of drawers and over towards Clare, whose uplifted face had drained. Diane's hair was a glamorous ash-blond grey. The familiar smell of her cigarettes was on her clothes as she passed. I sat down involuntarily. I hadn't seen her since the day of my mother's funeral, two years before, when she was swathed in black velvet, with a large-brimmed hat. Jane told her that she wasn't invited, before we all went into the church. Diane had come in anyway, and sat on the other side of Jane from me. By the time the service was over, my aunt was clutching her arm. My last memory of the day was the pair of them leaning against the wall together, next to the table with Jane's typewriter on it, as people filed past to say goodbye.

'I know, I know, I should have rung, but I had to come as soon as I heard. And I'm due round the corner in fifteen minutes, so you'll only have me for ten.'

Diane dropped the teddy she'd brought on one side of Clare and sat down on the other, folding her long legs in their tan slacks. She dropped a large bag to the floor, and kicked it away with low-heeled suede shoes.

'God, what an angel. And he's having a drink. What a good idea. What a perfect relation to have.'

She lifted the bottle she'd brought towards me, her painted fingernails startling against the foil.

'Ruth, I don't know how you got here before me, but thank God you did. You can open this, while I adore this astonishing creature.'

She bent to rummage in her bag, where she found an

envelope, which she asked me to put on the table, before she forgot. 'Because that's a present for Mummy.'

Clare hadn't looked up from the baby since Diane sat down, but at this she did. 'Diane,' she said, 'there's no need. Please.'

'Does Ruth know where to find glasses? Should I have brought paper cups?'

She bent to inspect Conor more closely as Clare looked up at me. Her face was flushed and her eyes very wide. I spread my hands and attempted a question-mark with my face. I pointed to the door. She shook her head violently.

'And what have you two been plotting? Do I need a drink before you tell me?'

The bottle Diane had brought was lifted in my direction again. I took it and stood with my back to them both and forced myself to inhale through my nose very deeply. Clare said there were glasses above the sink, but she didn't know what state they were in.

'I think I can guess.' Diane winked at me as I turned to look at Clare, who was curved around Conor and looking at him.

'But as long as they're water-tight I don't care. What about that young man who let me in? Would he like to join us?'

'He doesn't drink.' Clare looked at me hard. 'Does he, Ruth?'

I shook my head. 'It makes him sick.'

Clare looked at the oven, down low to her right,

smiling for the first time since Diane had arrived, and I found three glasses, of different sizes, as Diane uncorked the champagne. I was glad she'd realized I wasn't going to do it for her. I took one of the fizzing glasses to Clare, then took one for myself before she had time to hand it to me. She leaned meticulously against the table. She seemed slightly shorter than she used to be, as I stood almost beside her then moved to sit on the upturned chest of drawers. If she was standing up, I wanted to sit.

'Cheers, Clare,' I said. 'Here's to . . .'

'Little boys.' Diane took a mouthful, 'And their mothers, of course.' She tilted her head and narrowed her eyes to Clare. 'And their fathers, perhaps?'

After a while of silence I said the teddy bear was a nice one and Diane said yes, Gray had one just like it. Clare stood up with Conor, swaying slightly from side to side, like she used to between dances at parties. She raised her eyebrows at me.

'In fact, it was Jane who gave Gray his favourite teddy, now I think of it, Ruth.' Diane drained her glass, then ran her hands round it and down the stem, as if assessing its value. 'She arrived at the hospital at some unearthly hour, with roses, the teddy bear and a flask of Irish coffee. I'd never been so glad to see her in my life.'

She poured herself another drink and gazed vaguely at the pile of mostly open bin-liners on the floor around my feet. She wandered towards them and picked a silk scarf from a knotted pile of woollens, heaped next to an invertebrate angle-poise lamp. She said the scarf looked familiar and shook it out, then fingered the fringe, which was silky and long and caught on one of her rings, whose cold diamonds had confused me when I was a child. I stood up and moved nearer Clare, so as not to seem to be watching. The scarf did look familiar. Clare was swaying in a different rhythm now, her face strained, as if in vague pain.

'I need a pee,' she whispered. 'Can you hold him for a bit?'

The warmth of his shawled form was in my arms before I could answer. I was surprised at its weightlessness.

'I could have done that for you. That's what I'm here for, you silly.' Diane was over beside me, her perfume mingling with the smell of new skin near my face.

'He's used to Ruth.' Clare kissed her son's slight cheek and left the room. I moved to the couch, in what I hoped was a casual way. Diane watched as I tried to position myself where Clare had been, and to hold Conor like she did. He stared up at me, milky blue and unfocused, and worked his soft wet lips. I stared back, and noticed a nick in the top of his miniature ear, like a bite taken out by some fastidious mouse. Gray had one the same, on the same side of his head.

'Strange, isn't it?' Diane said, with her glass in her hand and the scarf she'd found draped around her cashmere neck. 'He suits you, Ruth.'

I touched Conor's head with its soft unformed dip,

269

which made me think of cakes before they're properly baked.

'How does it feel?'

I found I couldn't reply. I swallowed hard. I hadn't wept in front of Diane for about twenty years, and I didn't want to now.

'God, you're like your mother, Ruth.'

I looked up, to see what she meant by that. She was squinting at me, the way Jane used to.

'Am I?' I said. 'She thought I was like my father.'

Diane paused. 'Well that's because she saw too much of you to realize you were the image of her. Jane would know what I'm talking about.'

She smiled, to herself, not me. She lit a cigarette, which I thought she ought not to, but didn't like to say.

'Jane's a poet, Ruth,' she said, as if I didn't know.

Jane's latest book was called *Stone*. The title poem was 'For Diane'.

'And have you heard from your aunt at all, lately?'

I would have liked to say 'Have you?' but didn't want to give that pleasure. Diane must know I wasn't speaking to Jane. I hadn't spoken to her since the day she'd asked me to meet her in Norfolk to decide what to do with everything there. She was letting our house, which my mother's will had left to her as long as she lived. When I arrived, in sleet, the week before Christmas, the place was full of boxes. The kitchen smelled of bleach and the bookshelves were bare. My mother's cupboards were empty and her bedroom stripped of everything except two pictures I'd made for her at primary school. She'd framed them herself, and Jane thought I'd like them, but something about them on the unmade bed upset me more than my mother's coffin had. Jane was appalled at how angry I was that she'd organized everything without me there. She gave me a drink. She told me that I'd said I was working every day, which was true, but that didn't excuse her destroying our house, I said. Jane gave me another drink, and asked me to stay the night, although she was planning to leave, which she did. I told her I'd rather be alone.

Diane was staring. 'She misses you, Ruth. You know that, don't you?'

Clare's baby wriggled. He twisted his head.

'Do you think she'll come back?' I said. 'Do you think she'll move back to Norfolk one day?'

'I doubt it. She saw enough of that place to last several lifetimes.'

Jane wrote me a letter after the house was let. She said it would be well loved, and that she hadn't been able to face life there alone, but it was where she'd written so much, and where she'd been happy. She hoped I had too.

'I mean would you go back to somewhere you'd been miserable for fifteen years?'

I looked up to say something, but the words wouldn't come for a while. I swallowed. I told Diane that Jane was not miserable, living with us. Diane then explained that since I'd been a child, I couldn't have known what anyone felt.

'But Jane expressed herself to me, my dear. I wish I'd kept more of the letters she wrote. She wrote beautiful letters, your aunt, Ruth.'

I watched her sigh and look contentedly about her, then seem to stiffen, somehow.

'Now, Ruth.' She exhaled and put her head on one side, in a way I knew well. 'You of all people must agree that a child is best brought up with a father around.'

Conor was now curling and uncurling his fingers, so I put my smallest one into his reach and felt his cool grip. I stared at his thumb, like a freshly shelled prawn.

'I mean, you know what it's like not having a dad.'

She made the word 'dad' sound like some exotic piece of underwear. I could feel myself blushing in its intimate sphere.

'Well it seemed fine to me.'

One of Conor's hands moved into his mouth. I adjusted him in my arms, stood up and rubbed his back, as I'd seen Clare doing.

'And anyway it's nothing to do with me, Diane. You'll have to talk to Clare about . . .' I couldn't quite say Gray's name, while holding his baby. 'It's up to Clare what she does,' I said.

'Clare won't listen to me. She didn't want me to know she was pregnant.' Diane laughed her inscrutable laugh. 'Have another drink. Shall I take baby?'

I moved back towards the couch as champagne was

held in my direction. She dropped her cigarette butt into a vase of roses and took another from the pack on the table.

'You know what, Ruth?' She sparked an unsatisfactory lighter, until she got a flame and drew the thing in her mouth to a sustaining glow. 'You don't get what you want by asking people for it.'

'Well then why are you asking me?'

My backbone seemed too long for my body. I could feel it at the top of my skull.

'Because you're sensible. And because you and I know that it was wrong of your mother to get Jane to bring you up, the way she did.'

If I hadn't been holding a baby, I might have left the house, slamming the door like Jane did the last time we met. Conor must have felt my tension. I stood up and swayed, which felt good.

'Nobody got Jane to bring me up, Diane. She wanted to be there. She wanted to help. And what's that got to do with Clare and Gray, anyhow?'

Diane raised her eyebrows, in a way that would have silenced me years ago, but I carried on talking.

'Why not go and tell your own son about what's best for babies, since you know so much about it?'

Diane had been more than happy to do whatever she wanted, with or without Gray's father around. David had never lived with Diane and Gray, as far as I knew, but I didn't point that out just then, because Conor's small cries grew more urgent as the bathroom door slammed and Clare's footsteps ran up the stairs.

She came directly to me, dragging her blouse apart.

'Poor little hungry.' She sat down and fed him. The noise he made changed to a barely audible grunt.

'Could you not smoke, Diane?'

I should have said that. I was glad to be sitting near Clare and a breastfeeding baby. I watched his cheeks and tried to calm down. My mother had looked after me as well as she could. Jane helped, that was all. And she did what she wanted, in doing that. Jane always did what she wanted.

Diane moved to the sink, with the soft scarf still round her neck, and ran the tap on her cigarette before looking round for the bin, which she found was full, but squashed the butt into anyway.

'Do you know, I think this scarf might be mine.'

Clare didn't look up. 'I don't think so, Diane. But it's for sale if you want it.' She winked at me. 'Everything on the floor is for sale.'

'What a good idea. Have you got your eye on anything, Ruth?'

Clare coughed. I smiled in her direction. 'I buy everything new,' I said. To which Diane said, 'It's well for some.'

Clare and I focused on Conor.

'Don't throw this away by mistake, will you, Clare,' Diane said, to make us look up. She patted the envelope I'd placed next to the vase on the table, what seemed like a long time ago. 'I'd like you to buy the baby something nice with his old granny's money.'

I hoped that meant she was about to leave. Clare

must have assumed so as well, because she was saying the teddy was quite enough and there was no reason for Diane to feel she need do anything more, when the telephone rang in the hallway. Diane was out of the room and answering it before I could move. We heard her laugh, and the word 'grandmother', in a sort of squeal, then Clare stood and moved fast to the door, then came back and handed me Conor and went again to the hallway, where she said, 'Don't answer my phone,' and something else I couldn't make out.

'Well my goodness,' Diane said loudly.

'Look, I don't want your money and I don't want your son. Do you understand that?'

Footsteps started down the hard stairs, then stopped as Clare shouted, 'You can both just leave me alone.'

The footsteps started again, moving slowly, as Diane left, calling back that Clare ought to calm down. 'Shouting upsets a baby,' she shouted. 'You need to calm down, young lady. You need help.' She must have been down on the second landing when she shouted back up, 'And I don't mean Ruth.'

I gulped at a glass left on the table, holding Conor with one arm. I'd forgotten to worry about how to hold him, and he seemed not to mind as I refilled my glass. I would have gulped that down too, but Clare came back, with the scarf in her hands. She sat at the table, then stood up, then put her face into the scarf and wept.

'Sorry, Ruth,' she said between sobs, which subsided into sniffs as she blew her fine nose on the scarf, then looked across at me, with hot cheeks and bright wet eyes. 'Sorry, Conor,' she said. She drew uneven breaths. 'He's four days old and I'm having a breakdown. God, Ruth. What have I done?'

I passed her my glass, but she shook her head, smiling wanly. 'Better not get drunk as well as hysterical.'

'Conor doesn't mind,' I said. 'Look.' We looked at his steadfast, unseeing gaze. 'He's fine. He's glad to be here.' I smiled down at him, and he didn't smile back, but didn't weep either. He seemed to be getting used to me. I was getting used to him. 'You sit down now and hold him and I'll make more tea. Or would you like coffee?'

Clare nodded. 'Yes. Very continental, but there's only instant.' She sat down. She stroked Conor's face. 'He hasn't a clue what's going on.'

I wasn't very clear either. I wondered if I wanted to know, as the kettle boiled and she told me to give her the pink mug. That was the one she used when she needed cheering up.

'Which is a lot of the time, in this kitchen lately.' Her eyes met mine, greeny-grey and sad. She told me the Schoolhouse was so different now.

As I made coffee I tried to think neutral thoughts.

'Diane thinks a baby needs a father,' I said.

'Yeah. Like Gray had. In boarding school.'

I opened a new carton of milk. I cut more cake. 'Where is Gray, Clare?'

'In Brussels. I think.'

'Does he know about Conor?'

She shrugged. She picked a sultana from the table and pressed it on to her tongue. 'Bound to, isn't he? Now Diane's found out.'

'Didn't he know you were having his baby?'

She pressed her lips together. She touched Conor's head. 'He knew I was pregnant.'

Her hair was falling out of its clasp. I'd never seen it unwashed before.

'But did he know it was his?'

She nodded.

'So he didn't want a baby?'

She didn't respond, so I went on, not knowing what I wanted to say, or to hear her say either.

'Well, plenty of men probably don't want . . .' Not 'their babies'. I didn't think that was true. 'Well, they don't like the *idea* of babies, perhaps . . .'

'It was me he didn't like the idea of, Ruth.'

I drank some champagne, which was warm and less fizzy by now. I thought of Clare watching Gray as he leaned on the bar of the Brook Green pub, years ago, and the way she narrowed her eyes if he stayed there too long. 'But he adores you. You've been in his life for ever.'

She hadn't been in it as long as I had, but I wasn't looking for facts.

'Can we not talk about Gray, just now? I'll start drinking again.' She lifted her chin. She pulled at her lips with her teeth. 'He's a shit.'

'Is he? I mean, why is he, now?'

She took my glass from my hand and had a sip, then passed it back to me. 'He's a liar.'

I looked at the pattern of the curtains, which I'd looked at many times before. If Gray was a liar, then he was a good one. I got up from the table and got a cup, then poured more brown liquid from the teapot on to milk, and watched it turn murky. It was cold and bitter, but gave me something to swallow.

'He lied to me, Ruth,' she said.

I tried to imagine Gray's part in the story, not to think of him as someone I knew.

'Did he say he wanted a baby, then change his mind?'

'Not exactly.' She took a sip of champagne. 'But he didn't say he didn't want one. Until I told him I was pregnant.'

'But when he sees Conor he'll want him. He'll want to be with you both.'

'Gray's out of my life, and that's that.' She chewed her lip. She stroked Conor's head. She said Gray was living with a French girl, now, and was when she got pregnant.

'I knew what the score was, Ruth.'

I looked at the curtains again, and the way the leaves looked like part of the flowers, until you squinted and saw their darker lines. If she knew what the score was, then when had Gray lied?

'I mean I thought I did. I thought he'd leave her. I don't know why.'

Because he always had before, I supposed. Anyone would leave someone else for Clare.

'He must have said he would,' I said.

She nodded. Then shook her head. Then looked down at the baby again.

'Well he wouldn't leave when I asked him to, eight months ago. I gave him a chance, Ruth. I said I was having the baby and if he wanted to be in its life then he'd have to be in mine. I won't share Gray. And neither will Conor.'

My hands were cold. 'Shall I light the gas?'

She nodded, and I bent to blow the flame into place. I'd done it often before, often with Gray in the room.

'He's not coming near us, anyway, now. He'll take Conor to France, if he gets a chance.'

She seemed to be crying. She said sorry. She said she was tired.

I sat on the upturned chest of drawers and lifted a torn silk blouse, which I started to fold.

'He wouldn't do that, Clare. Gray's not like that.'

'You don't know what he's like, Ruth. You don't know what he's like any more.'

I realized the blouse I was holding was the one Clare wore in a pub in Leeds, many years ago. I could see her in it, almost, still. I wondered if the Gray she knew had ever been the same person I thought he was. I realized he couldn't have been. Gray had always been someone I didn't quite know. Someone Clare must have known much better.

'And now Diane wants to take over, of course.'

'Well you can deal with her. She'll get the message.'

'But I'm so tired, Ruth. Conor wakes every

two hours. I mean he's gorgeous, but it's exhausting.'

I dropped the blouse. 'You know what, Clare? You just need a rest.'

I lifted Gray's baby from Clare's slender arms and rubbed his fine back, thoughtlessly. She yawned. She smiled. She looked alone.

'You go and lie down for an hour or so.'

She stared. I nodded. Conor and I would be fine.

'But only if you're certain, Ruth.'

'I'm certain, Clare. I really am.'

I needed time to think. What I thought mostly, after she'd gone to bed and I heard her snoring lightly, was how pleasant it was to be with two breathing people, both of whom were asleep. I thought too, as I looked about me, that the scarf Diane wanted was like one my mother had, years ago. She used to wear it to take me to school. She kept it in the car, because Jane wore it if she found it in the house. It was one of the few things in Norfolk, apart from me, that they'd both liked equally well.

12

Six days before Clare said the last words she spoke, I collected a prescription for her mother, who'd rung about lunchtime and left a message, which I could have interrupted if I'd wanted to talk. I was staring into the house across the street, where two figures moved between a well-lit table, scattered with fruit, and the darker reaches of the back of the house. One of them was a child, who followed the adult, as I watched through the gloomy September day and listened to Clare's mother's familiar voice saying the not unfamiliar words, 'Could you do me a huge favour, Ruth?' I nodded in blank affirmation before I heard what my task was to be. I didn't much care, since I was doing nothing much, really. Robert Lowell was my poet that week.

'Everyone's tired of my turmoil.'

I'd been reading him the evening before, while waiting for Liam, who'd arrived on time but left early, after a row. He'd said he was tired, in a way that made clear it was me he was tired of. He'd said I was impossible.

About midnight, I'd turned on the television and watched the end of Ken Russell's *Women in Love*, and wished that Liam was like Burkin, who longed for the love of a man. He could have bonded with Gray. I wondered what Gray thought of Lawrence. Perhaps he was watching the movie too. Perhaps he'd been to Switzerland and walked the snow, with great wide woven trays attached to his feet and a thermos full of bilberry liqueur. When the film ended, I watched snooker, and after that I made camomile tea, which I drank until almost dawn, because I couldn't sleep. Not simply because Liam had left, again, but because of a letter I'd read, from Jane to Diane, in which she'd cleaned the bathroom because David was dead. Diane had rung my aunt with the news and Jane cleaned the house then walked on the beach then she and my mother went out to the pub.

Clare's mother's prescription was for her high blood pressure, and she hoped I might drop it in to her some time, if it wasn't too much of a bother. It was no bother to collect it, though I needed a raincoat and wore my new wide-brimmed hat. The surgery was empty except for a woman sitting on the far side of the room, with the community nurse by her side. She must have been in an accident. She was weeping and rubbing her legs. I listened as she stopped crying to say, 'I'm scared.' The nurse said, 'Is there anyone you'd like us to ring for you?', and I turned to see the woman shake her head. I wondered who I'd have asked them to ring, as I walked out into rain again to pass the playground and the muddied grass of the adjacent field, where Gray brought Conor after school. A man wiped wet leaves off the slide as a little girl waited. Conor used to like to pile autumn leaves, then stamp the pile flat and start all over again.

'You were kissed so much you thought you were walked on.'

I couldn't ask anyone to ring Gray if I'd been in an accident, unless Conor was with me at the time, of course. Then I'd be taken away in an ambulance, which neither Gray nor Conor would feel obliged to climb into. They might visit, if I stayed in hospital. They'd been to visit Clare together the week before. Gray had gone up to her bedside with their son, and his flowers, and she'd said hello, then been violently sick, so he took Conor down to the café. He liked the hot chocolate there.

Clare wasn't in Charing Cross any more. She was in a hospice up off Ladbroke Grove. I knew Gray hadn't been there yet, though I hadn't asked him. I tended not to ask Gray about Clare directly. I liked us to talk about Conor, because he was connected to me, through habit, if nothing else. Gray said it was great to find him so pleasant, so gregarious, so oddly familiar. He wanted to take him to France at Christmas, which caused me anxiety, which I tried to disguise. I was happy with them both in my kitchen, eating doughnuts with muddy feet and flushed faces after their after-school football, which Gray had turned into a neighbourhood game. Small boys knew his name by now, and called to greet him as he arrived on Brook Green with the leather football he insisted on bringing, though Conor found the plastic one better to kick.

'Gray's here,' they'd call. 'Let's have a match.'

'I'm in goal.' Conor would drag off his coat and bundle it over to me. Gray had bought him gloves and pads, of which he was proud.

I'd walk on home through drifts of leaves. The children didn't know my name. I was the woman who hung Conor's coat on a railing, and took his school bag off in the direction of Tesco's.

I was the person who sat with Gray in my kitchen, after the doughnuts were eaten and twilight arrived. Conor played the games he'd by now installed on my computer, as Gray and I talked in the darkening kitchen, with the breathing gas fire, discussing mostly whatever poet I was on at the time. Gray knew more about most of them than I did, though I was catching up. Talking was easy with Conor next door, shouting results through, or demanding assistance when my machine refused some complex command, or crashed completely. The first time that happened, I'd rung Liam to ask advice, and he'd said to turn it off, then on again, so that's what we always did, with variable results.

'Shame he couldn't arrange to come by some time and give us some tips,' Gray said one misty afternoon, when we'd struggled to install a racing game. I felt myself blush. I didn't discuss Liam with Gray.

'He's not in London much, during the week.' I pulled yellowing leaves from some flowers on the table. 'And he's not that good at teaching computers.'

I decided not to mention the many rows we'd had about there being too many games on mine of late. I said Liam wasn't used to children.

'Neither was I.' Gray smiled, and looked tired, but not unhappy with the fact. He lit a cigarette, and watched smoke drift. 'Which is a shame,' he said. He tapped his ash on the plate that had held our doughnuts, which was streaked with liquid jam. 'Nearly ten years. And I can't get them back.'

I rolled dead leaves in my fingers into a soft withered ball and said that Gray had had other things, surely. It didn't sound very convincing. But he'd been the one who didn't want a child, as far as I knew. He stared, his blue eyes wide and dark, and said I must be joking. Could I imagine, he asked, what it was like to be banned from your own son's life?

'Can you imagine that, Ruth? If Clare wasn't . . . well, I mean if this hadn't happened, I'd still be banned, I assume. God knows what'd be happening if I hadn't met you with Matt in the Café Rouge that night.'

He stubbed his cigarette and stood to rinse the plate. He often washed up when he was upset. He said he didn't know what I'd said to bring Clare round, but whatever it was, he and Conor had me to thank.

'Gray. Gray, come here. I'm on five hundred already.'

I watched him wipe his hands on his jeans and rush

through to his son, which was a relief. I hadn't done anything to 'bring Clare round', except not tell her what I was doing until after it was done. She was resigned to it now, but only just, and Liam still blamed me for interfering. Liam thought it was none of my business whether Gray saw Conor or not, and that I should have left the situation to everyone else.

'Well then no one would have arranged it,' I'd told him.

'Don't be ridiculous,' was his reply. 'People can manage their lives without you, sometimes, Ruth.'

'Well, you certainly seem to, most of the time.'

Soon after that Liam had said I was impossible, and left me to read alone until dawn. He must have gone to spend the night at Fiona's place. She had a couch he found comfortable, which I was beginning to forgive her for.

When Gray came back through from talking to Conor, he looked pleased with himself and the world.

'What a boy. That machine of yours might explode in the face of his genius, some day soon.'

I hoped it didn't. I needed a computer that worked.

He ruffled the top of my head. He said he really appreciated these afternoons. And thought Clare was beginning to approve of them too.

'What d'you think? Think she's softening towards the idea of me as a dad?'

I nodded, but couldn't quite say yes. Clare didn't discuss Gray with me any more.

'Almost six,' he said. 'We'd better be making a move.'

At six o'clock I usually walked Conor home, and Gray went off to the Tube. He'd kiss me on the cheek, and Conor too, which made us all seem connected in an easy way that I loved, but didn't mention to anyone else.

When I got back from the doctor's surgery with Clare's mother's prescription on my Robert Lowell afternoon, I went into my study without removing my coat. The woman from the house across the street was on her doorstep with a pushchair, and the rooms of her house were unlit. All I saw now in her uncurtained windows was the reflection of my own. I waved my arms to see myself, but was too far away for the movement to show. I pushed a key on my keyboard and read what I'd got so far, which was a quote from someone else: 'Lowell's poems tell us more of what it means to live painfully and difficultly in our century than any other writer has previously dared.' Gray had laughed when I'd read that out.

A taxi pulled up on the street with its warm and pleasant throb. Lowell died in a taxi in New York, on his way to see one wife with a picture of another one under his arm. I watched a woman get out of the taxi and thought of Colette. She'd been on my mind somewhat since Clare had asked me to visit her new house. On my mind more since the last old letter I'd read. Colette must know a lot that I wanted to know. And the fact that she hadn't been to see me for months made me wonder if she knew that was the case. I lifted the phone and pressed her number. The answering machine wheezed its chesty welcome for what felt like minutes, before I was asked to leave a message after the beep, which took a long time to come.

'It's Ruth, Colette. Can you give me ring?'

I hoped I'd said it loud enough, and that she'd listen before too long. A car outside attempted a three-point turn. The rain had stopped, but the pavement was shiny and some of the large wet leaves there held water. I buttoned my coat without really thinking, and pulled the belt tight and went down the stairs and out. I didn't want to work. I wanted to walk, to Clare's at least, with her mother's prescription, and then on somewhere else that I hadn't been to before and didn't know how to find, but would move towards and hope for the best.

At the top of Hammersmith Grove, a light rain began. I crossed the courtyard of an abandoned garage, where a man and a boy were kicking a punctured ball. I skirted their shouts and avoided puddles like rock pools, with reflections of sky the colour of murky sea-water. On the Goldhawk Road, buses sped past, with fine arches of mist spraying from the black of their tyres. I could have been on a beach, on some lowering grey day of my childhood, trailing Jane and my mother, with her bundles of seaweed slithering brown and wet from her red felt coat. She thought it was good for the garden we didn't really have. Her sweet peas in pots were rampant, however, so maybe the seaweed-collecting was not as pointless as Jane insisted it was.

On the Askew Road there was a 'cottage' for sale, and blocks of flats with small high windows, white and square. I passed Askew Mansions and the Orchard Tavern, and a funeral parlour, with a green marble clover-shaped headstone displayed. There were no houses with visible attics which could once have been Diane's. There were shops selling paint or wet second-hand fridges. But the house was near by, and I wanted to find it.

Next to a church, there was an empty house with dead geraniums on every sill and several old baths out in front. I went to inspect, but saw nothing but empty dark rooms. A cat jumped almost under my feet as I swerved to make way for a pushchair to pass. There were no more domestic dwellings to see, so I crossed the road to a newsagent's, where I bought a Toblerone from an Irish man, and was about to bite the first chunk when I came to a mews branching off to the right, and saw a small corner house with no curtains. A bare central bulb glared over a ladder, with a man on it painting the ceiling. He had a cloth tied over his head in a sort of turban, I saw as I got closer. A radio was playing blurred classical music, and the man was whistling, which I'd never heard Frank do before, but there was no doubt in my mind that it was him. I banged on the window. He turned, waved his paintbrush and smiled.

'Door's open,' he shouted. 'Shove hard. It needs a good push.'

The smell of wet paint was stinging but pleasant. Stairs ahead were piled with boxes, and the corridor narrowed by a stack of radiators with useless stunted pipes.

'Come through, but mind the carpets.'

The door to Frank's room was jammed with rolls of underlay. Moving in over them was like clambering on to, then off, a soft narrow bed.

'Great. You made it. I should've told you to put on the kettle, before you came in here.'

Frank was balancing a paintbrush across the top of a can of emulsion. Then he turned and saw me and stared with wide eyes. 'Ruth.' He clung to the top of the ladder, as if expecting turbulence. 'It's you.'

'Yes, it's me. Want some Toblerone?'

He shook his head hard. 'Liam's not here yet. He's in town. I think.'

The way he said it made it clear that Liam was not in town, and perhaps never had been in his life.

'I wasn't expecting Liam to be here.'

'Ah. Well, he might be. Fiona said.' He nodded his head, so the cloth on it slid further down. 'Think he's in town just now, though.'

He sat down on the top of the ladder, and put his head in his hands.

'Shall I make some tea? Where's the kitchen?'

He pointed vaguely behind his head. I held the Toblerone up towards him and he reached down for the packet and took half the bar. He nodded his head as he chewed.

'Have some tea,' he said, through chocolate. He pointed again towards the back of the house. I went along a damp corridor to find a stained porcelain sink with one working tap, and a kettle without a lid on a greasy two-burner stove.

'Milk's in here,' Frank shouted. 'You just need a cup.'

I found a cloth, crisp with paint, to protect my hands from the steam, and took the kettle back in to Frank. He was kneeling, busy with teabags. I poured boiling water and he added milk. He said there was no sugar and I said that was fine. We drank, blowing into our mugs. I looked at the ceiling and wondered out loud how long it would take to paint.

'Few days,' he said. 'Needs three coats. She must have smoked quite a bit.'

'She did. Diane loved cigarettes.'

'You don't, do you? I've run out of baccy.'

I shook my head. 'My aunt loved smoking too. Still does, I suppose.'

'Your poet aunt, is that?'

I nodded. He said Fiona had a book of Jane's poems, and I must have looked surprised because he went on to explain that it had been a present from Liam, which irritated me, somehow, though Jane's books weren't mine to give away.

'Is Fiona fond of poetry?' It sounded sarcastic, so I said I knew Liam was, hoping to imply warm approval of this worthy trait.

291

'Is he?' Frank seemed nervous. 'Look, Ruth, I really need a fag. Mind if I nip out?'

I shook my head. I hadn't come to see Frank. I wasn't sure why I'd come, now I was there. The thing to do would be to go upstairs, if Frank didn't mind. He picked a heavy coat from the floor and was slamming the front door before I had time to ask. He ran off towards the Goldhawk Road. I studied the ivy on the high opposite wall, which shone a Christmassy green in the darkening afternoon. My head was reflected in the window, with my face pale and indistinct above the bundle of my scarf.

'I rowed for our reflection, but it slid between my hands . . .'

Diane and Jane once took me rowing on the Serpentine. Between them they lost an oar, so we had to sway aimlessly for ages until another boat came and somehow got it back to us, slippery dark and smelling of weed. I was wearing a dress with lumps of embroidered flowers which had been made from something of my mother's, and the sash got soaked and dragged cold on my legs, as we walked somewhere for tea.

Diane's room was cold, and seemed more so with great cans of white emulsion open round the floor. Frank seemed to be using three pots at once, including the one on top of the ladder. An armchair draped in sheeting lolled by the fireplace, where lumps of burnt coal rested with a sandwich-wrapper and many cigarette stubs. I sat down with my tea and waited.

Then put the mug on the floor and my hands in my pockets. Frank was being a long time, considering how close the shop was. But I didn't feel like going upstairs yet. I wondered why Liam was coming, if he really was. It was pleasant sitting there alone.

When the front door opened, it wasn't Frank or Liam, but Fiona. Her voice arrived before she did.

'It's me. I made it. Frank? Liam? Is anyone home?'

She shouted as she moved towards where I was, then stood quite still as she saw me in the chair by the fire.

'Hi, Fiona.' I looked into her startled eyes. 'Want some tea?' She didn't answer. 'Frank's gone to the shops.'

My hands seemed unfamiliar as I got two teabags out of the pack, and pulled them apart, for something to do. The back of my neck ran hot to prickle the hair there. Everyone was meant to be here together this afternoon then, except for me.

'We don't have any sugar, I'm afraid.'

I seemed to be making Fiona tea in my cup. Milk splashed heavily from its badly torn carton. Fiona didn't speak. I picked up the cup and turned to pass it, but it slid as I caught her eye. The floor ran pale brown, which felt something like a relief.

'Why's Liam coming, Fiona?' My voice was hard and louder than I'd expected.

'Well, it's complicated. I mean, he wanted to see Frank, and he's painting here.'

'So do you all meet up here often?'

293

Perhaps this was what Liam did, when I minded Conor. I thought he was always in meetings with the people he worked for in Turnham Green.

'Almost never. I've got a show in ten days to get ready. Though Frank gets bored, by himself. You know how they are.'

There was a knock on the window, and his face was there. He was waving another Toblerone. His smile faded as he looked from me to Fiona. She shrugged. The front door jolted open, then was carefully closed.

'Fiona. You made it.' Frank didn't unbutton his coat. 'Anyone fancy some choccy?'

Fiona came past me and lifted a cloth from the mantelpiece to wipe up the drink I'd spilled. She was moving differently, now he was here.

'I was telling Ruth how you like company, Frank.' She left the rag on the floor to soak up the liquid, and sat down on the edge of the chair that had my bag on it. 'We got fifteen models into the window. Now I just have to paint them.'

Frank dropped cellophane from his tobacco towards the floor. It landed on the lip of an open paint tin.

'So what brings you here, anyway, Ruth?' Her lipstick was freshly applied.

'Nothing, really. I mean nothing for me, particularly.' I took the chocolate Frank offered, and snapped a chunk, but kept it in my hand. 'Colette thought Clare might like something for Conor, so I said I'd come round and see what there is.'

I ate Toblerone, as they both didn't look, then she

asked Frank for a cigarette. He passed her his pouch and stayed by her side as she rolled one. He lit it for her. A child outside shouted 'I want a bell,' twice. Fiona picked tobacco from the inside of her lip. She leaned back in her chair, felt my handbag there and pulled it out to drop on to the floor. I picked it up, and wiped a smear of white from the black leather with a licked finger. Then I wiped the finger on my coat. Then wiped that with the palm of my hand, which made it worse.

'So why is Liam coming round?'

Frank threw his butt into the grate. He sighed. He got out his tobacco again. Fiona stood up and put a lid on a paint pot and banged it in place with her fist, which was robust and workman-like.

'It's not our fault, Ruth,' she said. 'We didn't ask him to come.'

She stopped banging the paint pot and sat down on it now. She drew lines in the spilled tea that was still wet on the floorboards. She seemed to be drawing a star, which she spattered away with the flat of her hand, then started on another. 'He went to see Colette last night. I mean, he came round to us, and he was really upset, and we thought that'd be the best thing to do.'

I tried to lick my lips, which were coated with a sticky dry chocolate taste. Frank scratched paint from his fingers.

'Why?' I said.

'Why what?'

'Why did he go to see her? What's Colette got to do with anything?'

Fiona smoked, then looked up at me, and her look was not unfriendly.

'Ruth,' she said.

Frank decided he needed hot water, but didn't say why. When he'd left the room, Fiona stood up and walked to the window, then back to me. She put her hand on my arm. 'The thing is, Ruth, Frank and I've been here quite a bit. And Liam's been upset about you and Conor and everything. He's been really confused.'

'What's Conor got to do with Liam and me?'

Fiona dropped her hand from my arm. She kept her head towards the floor and said, 'Well not much. That's the problem.'

Then she sat down suddenly and looked at me. Her stare was even and cool. I looked at the window, which was black by now. Our two figures were clearly defined in it, under the bare bulb which made hard shadows. My feet were freezing and so was my nose. Fiona sniffed as Frank reappeared. He must have thought someone was weeping, and that it had to be me, because he started in a gentle tone to say that what was happening, he supposed, what they needed to tell me, was that Liam was kind of upset at the moment.

'He's confused. He needs people to talk to. I mean this kid – what's his name again?'

Fiona told him Conor's name.

'Yeah, well this Conor thing's been bothering him. I mean, I'd be the same if Fiona decided . . .'

Fiona coughed and pulled at her hair.

'If Fiona decided what? To look after her friend's little boy sometimes?'

Fiona was tying her hair back into something elastic she'd had on her wrist. My heart was banging, which I hoped didn't show as I explained my need to go upstairs. I'd come to see what Diane had left there. What Liam did was his own affair, I said. Fiona shrugged. She said I must know how he was and I said not really, why didn't she tell me, since she'd been seeing so much of him lately. Frank climbed the ladder and began painting the ceiling, which made a good rhythmic sound as no one spoke for a while. Fiona decided it would be much brighter in here when the white was done. Then she said again that Liam was worried.

'About this Gray thing, you know? About you and his son, and being with them both all the time. He doesn't like it, Ruth.'

'He doesn't have to. And why shouldn't I spend time with a person I've known all my life? Liam spends time with you.'

She put a hand on one of Frank's feet, at her shoulder level, firm on the ladder, and she told me she was married, which I said must be nice, but had nothing to do with Liam or me or Gray either, and what was she trying to say?

'Well if you can't work it out, I'm not going to tell you.'

She moved her hand up to Frank's ankle and

wrapped her fingers around it. I saw her wedding ring, pressed into the red of her fingers.

After a while of silence, with the brush and its paint going back and forth in it, I asked if I could use the bathroom. Frank said sure, if I didn't mind obstacle courses. Fiona rubbed the tops of her arms. She asked if there was any available heat. Frank shook his head. She pulled her coat closer round her.

'Shall we all go for a drink? It must be time you clocked off. Let's take Ruth to the Orchard.'

'So where is the bathroom?'

Frank looked at his watch. Fiona scowled.

'Oh, come on. She needs one. She's pale as this bloody emulsion. We'll leave Liam a note.'

''S only five fifteen,' he said. 'What if the dragon arrives in my absence?'

As I reached the first landing, I heard them talking quietly, then Frank's slow laugh as the light-switch worked and I saw dark walls with pale patches where paintings had been along the narrow hallway.

I sat down on the landing and was glad to be alone again. I lifted a strip of paint-spattered negatives from the floor at my feet and held it up to the light. It seemed to be pictures of nothing. The end of a roll or light in the camera. I slid it into a box stacked to my right, which was filled with newspapers and a hard-backed notebook, which I pulled out. The pages were empty. A box to my left had hand-painted tiles in it, which had been round a fireplace in Diane's Highbury house. Further along was a jammed chaos of plates, with pale stencilled lemons and oranges on them. Their chipped blue rims took me back to the kitchen at Diane's, with its high fridge and its humming and its regular ice and Diane's long legs and bursts of short laughter and then Jane and her voice saying, 'Ruth's good with eggs.' I leaned back into the cold damp of the wall and could almost feel Jane's hand on my head, as I wandered past her long ago, to leave and go up to Gray's room. Jane would be there again always when I came back down, with her drink and strong fingers, and fine long back, and her smoky rounded voice. 'Ruth's good with eggs,' she used to say. 'Ruth can do that, Di.' 'Let's leave that to Ruth. Ruth can do anything, really.'

I put my head in my hands then and sat very still. I hadn't heard Jane's voice for too long. I reached to touch the old plates that I'd washed up so often. A dog barked in the next-door house. Something clattered downstairs and Frank laughed. Then the front door jolted open and footsteps came into the hall. It was Liam, I knew. His shoelace must have been undone. I felt the time it took him to bend to tie it, before I heard his voice.

'Cash machine's empty,' he shouted. 'No notes. You'll have to lend me some.'

Now his feet moved in towards them. They'd be whispering, I assumed, and pointing up in my direction, beyond the dirty ceiling. In the bathroom, I flushed the chain, with its Victorian gush and its hollow after-spill trickle, and then I went quickly and loudly down the uncarpeted stairs.

Frank and Fiona were both on the ladder, coming down or going up. They looked at me as I came in. They both said nothing. Liam was smoking by the window. He tried to smile, but I didn't bother. I lifted my bag from near his sister's legs and moved to the door, then stopped and turned.

'Don't let me interrupt your evening, anyone.'

I slammed the door behind me. I had nowhere to go that I wanted to be.

I was just past the undertaker's when Liam caught up. I didn't have to turn to know it was him. He took my arm, and his breathing slowed.

'Where are you going?' I thought I'd better ask, before he had the chance to, because I had no definite plan.

'Hastings. Eventually. In a while, that is.'

A bus went past, so I waited a moment.

'Did you go to Colette's last night?' I didn't look at his face, but could feel him closing his eyes. 'Did you really stay there?'

'I really did.'

'But why? You could have stayed with me.'

'I couldn't. Ruth, we need to talk.'

The pub we went to was white-walled, with large polished tables and a picture of Beckett above the bar, where a man was talking Spanish to a dark-haired girl. He lifted her hand to kiss, as they spoke. Between kisses, he twisted a ring on her finger. I didn't have any rings, and neither did Liam. I paid for our bottles of lager, since he still had no money. Frank and Fiona hadn't had any to lend. Before we sat down he bent to tie his lace.

'Why did you come to Diane's?'

He poured his lager and said it wasn't Diane's. It was his mother's, and he'd gone there to talk to Fiona and Frank. 'They know more than you think,' he said.

A waitress walked by with a large basket of long stumpy chips, for a table of young men under the window. Liam noticed her waist in its shiny belt, and asked if I was hungry. I shook my head.

'You know, this is really morbid, Ruth.'

I said I'd had bacon and eggs for lunch, and he said he didn't mean my lack of appetite.

'I mean this obsession with death and dying and dead people's letters and houses. It's crazy. And crazy-making, too.'

He drank with his head back and I watched his neck, which I used to like to kiss. I poured lager so it foamed, and I drank the head down and all the pale liquid too, and then I poured some more. Liam lit a cigarette. His fingers weren't steady.

'So what do we need to talk about?'

I wished we were in Hastings alone, suddenly, and it was a long time ago, when we talked to each other in bed, before Clare was sick and Gray arrived. I wished we didn't have to talk about that. But I expected now that we did.

'I think you know that already, Ruth.'

He drank again. I tried to think of something to tell him about something active and real and not about me. I told him about the doctor's, that morning, and the woman who didn't have anyone to ring after she'd been in an accident. He smoked, in a maudlin sort of way. He said there was no need for me to worry about that happening to me, if that was the point of the story. 'Which it is, of course.' He turned his chin towards the bar, in an angry way he had. 'They'll be there, don't you worry about that.'

He lit another cigarette. I said I didn't know what he was talking about and he said I did, I knew very well. He laughed, without any sound, in a way that made his lips blow out. He finished his beer and banged the bottle. I wondered what time he was thinking of getting a train.

'Do you want another?' He pointed to my half-empty glass. I shook my head.

'It seems to be making you cross,' I said, which was a mistake, because he took my purse and went to the bar, where there was no one to serve, so he shouted his order into emptiness, and two barmen arrived at once. Back in front of me he held his drink between blunt fingers on the table top. He sighed. His shoulders relaxed. I reached to touch the top of his head. He took my hand. He put it back on the table, over on my side, and said he wasn't cross.

'You seem it.' I knew him well enough to say that, at least.

He was tired, he said. Not because he'd been up till three with his mother, then up again at eight and writing something he had no interest in, then walking back to the Askew Road, because the buses were crap and the cash machines broken.

'No,' he said, wiping his mouth. 'It's not that, Ruth. It's you. I'm tired of you and your crazy involvement in something you shouldn't be anywhere near.'

I swallowed hard. I bit my lip.

'Well if you've got something to say about how I behave, then say it to me. Not your sister and Frank. Or your mother.'

He slammed his hand on the table. People at the bar looked over, so I stared, then they stopped and Liam dropped his voice.

'Ruth, I went to talk to Colette because I didn't know who else to ask. And Fiona and Frank have been in that house every day for three weeks and they've just tried to help me make sense.'

He drank. He breathed. He looked at me.

'What sense? I don't understand.'

He took my hand again then, in a way he used to.

'I don't want us to not be straight, Ruth. I think you know what I'm talking about.'

He drank more of his beer, then put the bottle down, quietly. Something about him being more calm made me nervous and hot and pulling my fingers, which he leaned to hold in his and said not to do.

'I know your friend's sick, Ruth, and I know that's hard. But Clare's not the person you want to be close to now, is she, really? This Conor thing's not about her, and it never has been, has it?'

His face was near mine, but I didn't pull back. I didn't speak, or swallow, either.

'Tell yourself the truth, Ruth, for once in your life.'

He drank. He said 'The truth' again, quietly, with a look of disgust, as if I'd asked him to eat it and it had been out of the fridge for months. 'You know the truth. You know why you want to be near Conor, and don't pretend you don't.'

'Well, why do I, then?'

He drank a lot, quickly, in long thirsty gulps.

'Because he's Gray's son.'

He took a cigarette from his packet, lifted it to his lips, then lowered it again. He did that a few times, then finally lit it, looking right at me, and blew smoke as he said, 'And you know about Gray, really, don't you?' He nodded slowly, then faster, then stopped and was still. 'About Gray and David and your mother and you.'

He put his lips round the neck of his bottle, tilted his head and drained the dregs. Then he stared back at me. 'Colette's told me everything.' He pulled his shoulders back, then relaxed them to be nearer me. 'You're Gray's sister, Ruth. Half-sister, I mean. You must have known, Ruth. Or tell me you didn't.'

He stood up and lifted his bag from the floor, then dropped it to wipe his hand on his leg, then picked it up again. 'That's what this Conor obsession's about.'

He stood with his bag in his hand. He wasn't looking at me.

'Don't,' I said. I pulled the hem of his jacket. 'Liam. Don't go.'

I stood to be nearer him but my legs wouldn't hold me, so I sat and coughed a lot. I couldn't stop coughing, and I flapped my hands towards the bar to make him get water, which he did and smoothed my back as I took breathless sips, then he was at the bar again, and back with two whiskies. I drank mine down in one. I still couldn't speak, so held the glass out towards him. I needed another. He pushed his own towards me, and went to the bar, coming back with two more. I drank one of them, before I asked him then why no one had told me who I was. How come it was left to him to find out?

'Jane, I mean. She should have said. Or my mother. Or . . .' And then I was silent. Everyone knew except me. And maybe Gray. I couldn't ask Liam what Gray knew.

Across the table, Liam held my hands and said it wasn't that simple. There was no point in blaming anyone now. My mother decided it all, he told me, between smoking, and drinking, and holding my hand. David and she had an affair, then split up when I was a baby. He stopped wanting to see her when she got pregnant again, and Jane did know, of course – she came there to help when it all got a mess – but what could she do? My mother was determined that I wouldn't know. Everyone else just wanted to make her all right. To help her get on with me, by herself.

'Ruth,' he said again, as I couldn't move my tongue round my mouth. He'd run out of things to say, so he could only say my name, as I breathed through my nose and bit the flesh of my hands.

'I need to talk to Gray. I need to see him, and talk.' I stood up, then sat down again.

Liam shook his head. 'He's on a train to Paris tonight.'

'Why? Why's he gone there? How do you know?'

'He needs to sort some stuff out.' Liam shrugged. He drank. He looked at me. 'I tried to ring him earlier on.'

'What?'

'Well nobody told him either, Ruth. Don't blame Gray.' He tried to smile. 'Though I have for a while.'

I squeezed his fingers in mine then. I took his hand with mine to my face as I wiped my eyes and cried more than I had before. People at the next table stared, and Liam disengaged from me, and stood up and said 'What?' at them loudly, as I put my head down on my arms.

'Better get you home,' he said, from behind me. His bag was still on the floor.

'Can I come with you?'

He shrugged. He looked very tired. He smiled.

'Sure you can.' He picked up his bag, without dropping my arm. 'Some sea air will do you the world of good.'

As the wet of outside hit me, I felt woozily drunk. Liam put his arm round my waist. He said we needed a taxi so we got one to Victoria Station. Our train was delayed in Battle, but I didn't know, because I was fast asleep. I wasn't used to Scotch. Whisky was my mother's drink. Perhaps David liked it too. Maybe my father was fond of the only drink that both Jane and Diane disliked.

13

The last time I saw Clare I arrived where she was at three thirty-five, and waited for her to wake up. The clock was above the television, which was on high grey brackets, across the room from her bed and the large firm chair I sat on. The room was small but not cosy, despite soft-focus wallpaper and long floral curtains, which were partly drawn across glass doors which led to a patio, where late chrysanthemums bloomed. There were flowers inside the room too, in vases which seemed either too big or too small for the stems they held. A plastic pot near my feet held wilted heather. On the bedside table were yellow roses, browning at the edges. It was too hot for flowers here, and too dry, Clare's mother liked to tell me. She was trying to find somewhere to park, as I sat with Clare's steady breathing and noticed a large homemade card that hadn't been there before. It said Get Well Soon in fat felt-tip. Clare's father was with Conor that afternoon. Gray had been to view some houses for sale near by and was now in the day-room, next door to Clare and me, waiting.

When Clare woke up she asked what time it was. She looked not at my face but at my hand, on the arm of the visitor's chair in front of her face. I told her it was nearly four and she sighed. I asked if time went quickly for her.

'Very slowly,' she said, and I wondered if that was a good or a bad thing and couldn't think what to say next. I asked if anyone interesting had been that day.

'Hazel came this morning.'

I didn't know who Hazel was, and said so. Clare said she hardly knew her either. People were always coming to see her now who she hardly knew, she told me. They usually knew someone else who'd died, and liked to talk about how they should have been to see those people more and how the funeral could have been better.

'Her husband's crazy,' Clare said. 'A paranoid schizophrenic, by all accounts.'

She rolled her eyes, and I did it back, like I would have if we were in her red-painted sitting room, with her cigarettes between us, and Conor eating chips and watching TV, and all the time in the world to discuss other people's mad men.

'Roll me a cigarette,' she said.

Her face was extraordinarily pale, and her eyes not as green as the week before.

'Sorry,' she said.

I looked at a bruise on her right wrist, above a lucky charm on fine red string, which her father had put there at the weekend. The skin on her arms was white, with pinkish blotches. I rolled a cigarette as well as I could. Liam would have done it better, but Liam was at my house. He'd decided we ought to go out that night. He thought Gray might come too, for something to eat.

'Are you hungry?'

'I don't think so.'

I'd brought some nut chocolate. There were Polo mints beside her bed. I took one and sucked it, then took another, as I always did.

'Have as many as you want,' she said. 'But you'll have to buy your own pretty soon.'

'Shall I open the curtains a bit?'

She shook her head, as I stood up to do it. She said she liked it being mysterious, so I sat down again and looked for something to say. There was a moulded grey sick-bowl on the arm of my chair, which blended well with the pale blue of the paintwork that Clare disliked.

'I suppose I should be saying something significant.' I took another mint.

She smiled and said she supposed I should.

'Or you could take a photograph. Some people do.'

I found that hard to believe, but she assured me they did and went on to explain that her mother had made her change her pyjama top for the last picture shoot.

'Did you wear make-up?'

She shook her head. Said it was a bit late to start new habits now.

'Want coffee?' she asked. 'You'll have to make it yourself.'

I didn't. I wanted to talk.

'Colette came to see you, Liam said.'

Clare nodded. She smiled. 'Like a ghost,' she said. 'Or do I mean a saint?'

She drank something out of a glass through a straw, and the noise it made was hollow and loud. I pretended not to notice. Pretended not to notice too that she couldn't smoke the cigarette I'd rolled, and not because I'd done it so badly. I lit the crippled-looking thing when she moved it back to her mouth, but she gave it to me to put in the ashtray after her first faint puff.

'Pretend it's yours,' she said. 'If my mother arrives.'

She smiled, but I didn't smile back.

'Clare,' I said. I took her hand. It was cold.

'What?' she said.

'Are you scared?'

She shook her head. 'Don't think so.' She turned to look out of the window. 'But it seems a lot to have gone through, to end up dead.'

The clock moved on to ten past four. Outside a pneumatic drill started. They were rebuilding the car park, to make more room for the mental-health unit.

'I mostly hate leaving Conor alone.'

A man outside called that they needed to pull back. A noise stopped. Another began.

'We'll look after him, Clare. He'll be OK.'

'Who will? You and Gray, you mean?'

My left leg was numb. I pulled off my shoe and wriggled my foot as I said yes, Gray and I would look after Conor. 'And your mother and father. And Liam. I mean everyone will. We'll all help Gray.'

She picked up her cigarette. Her nails were bitten. I found matches in the folds of my clothes.

'You won't move away, will you, Ruth? You won't fall out with Gray now?'

I didn't say 'Now what?' I asked her to tell me what happened when Colette had been. She said she hoped I wasn't expecting a Hollywood ending.

'Everyone who comes expects something. But it's mostly just boring. Except if I think about Conor.'

The bed was high and bulky with contraptions to protect her legs from the weight of the blankets. The room smelled vaguely of something burnt.

'Did Colette talk about me?'

'A bit.'

She took a sip from the straw in her glass and shifted the top half of her body. She breathed deeply. She looked at me, her lashes long and very black against the unlined shadows of her face in the soothing gloom.

'I know who you are now, Ruth, if that's what you mean.'

'Did you know for a long time?'

'Never,' she said. 'Did you?'

I shook my head.

'So what's it like, having Gray for a brother?'

I heard drills outside, and a siren. It was hard to say. Gray was the only brother I'd had.

'I suppose it's a sort of relief,' I said. That's what I'd told Liam on the beach in Hastings, where we'd found a piece of wood like a bird that I'd brought home to keep. 'Although we haven't exactly trawled it through. I don't think we want to go over the past, just now.'

Gray and I had talked about Conor, that morning when we'd arranged who would come to see Clare and when. He'd been sick in the night and Gray was worried, but I said he was over-tired. It's what my mother and aunt used to say about me. I was an aunt now too.

Clare bit her lip and looked out of the window. She said she was sort of relieved as well, to find out what was what.

'You know, Ruth, Gray liked lots of women. He liked lots of women a lot. But I was always jealous of you.'

She reached for my hand.

'Well, you don't have to be any more.'

'No. I won't have to haunt you.' She smiled. 'That might have been tiring.'

The door opened and Clare's mother's head came through. She gestured for me to go near to her.

'I need a favour, Ruth. Have you got a twenty-pence piece? I'm moving the car.'

The wood of the door smelled new and sweet. I went to my bag and found one. She said she'd owe it to me, and I could see she wanted to mean it.

'I'll remind you,' I said, as she backed away, after kissing me goodbye. We kissed each other goodbye a lot now, and she often moved her car, from one time-limited pay-and-display space to another. She said it kept her busy.

'You won't leave London, will you, Ruth?' Clare said as I sat down and pulled up my legs to rest my chin on the knees. 'You'll stay near Conor, won't you?'

I nodded. I didn't say that Liam would be near us both too, because it seemed unkind to mention my future and his, which we'd decided we would share in my flat for now. Fiona and Frank were moving into the Askew Road house, which Colette had decided to give them now that Fiona was pregnant. The expected new baby was part of the pull of London for Liam now, I knew, but that seemed fair enough. Since I had a nephew, he ought to maybe have one too. Perhaps we'd have a baby ourselves one day, we'd decided, on the train back from our weekend in his house. We'd had sex again, which was a good thing. I wondered if I should tell Clare about that, but decided not to, though sex and death were clearly connected. Yeats thought so, anyway. Probably most poets did.

'That momentary peace which is a poem.'

When Clare closed her eyes, I said I might go and she nodded. She told me not to say goodbye, so I didn't say it out loud. I walked away from her backwards at first, then thought that was silly so turned to face the way out. I was carrying my bag, my shoes and my jacket. Gray's coat was hanging on a hook to the right of the door. A tissue drooped from the pocket. I touched the fabric as I moved out into the corridor, to see the sliding glass of the doors which opened by themselves to let you through, when your body got near enough.

* * *

In the building-site of outside, a man in a yellow hard-hat on a ladder was holding a drill. Beyond him an ambulance moved between a lorry and a vehicle with caterpillar tyres, which scooped stacked clots of red wet earth. A man in a fluorescent jacket asked if I was all right and I said 'Thank you,' as if he'd given me something. Outside the gates was a silent sound, though mothers at the entrance of a primary school collected yelling children. The sun was bright and streaked the pavement leaves with vivid crimson and lime and yellow-pink gloss. A range of straining poplars scrawled a fast-clouded sky and a whistle in a playground shrilled as I turned to cross a street of moving traffic. Horns blared but I didn't look back. I walked on through my silence and sunshine on walls, which flashed gold, then were plain again and blank. A woman in front of me was wearing high-heels which tapped a clean and pointed noise, then stopped as she saw the stretched figure of Christ on a cross outside a church which looked a bit like a spaceship. Its spire was fine and very high. The woman in heels kissed the feet of Jesus, then bent to rub them up and down with both hands, as if they might need warming up.

When she walked on again, I followed and came to a bus stop, where a double-decker was waiting. I got on, then off at the stop before mine, where a man in dark glasses chewed gum in a fur-collared coat. I walked down a street that held nothing but shadows. I watched my feet on the plane of the pavement and

315

thought of all the feet that had walked along it, and were no longer wearing shoes. On the Shepherd's Bush Road a car blared country music, its roof back and chair-legs sticking out of the top. Girls in coats came towards me, and a man with one arm. I turned past the launderette. No cars had headlights yet, and there was only one street-lamp lit along the stretch of pavement ahead. I walked underneath and saw the bulb inside, with its cool blue glow, burning pale and strong in its smooth glass shell. I walked on then past a skip, and the house with the rosemary bush.

When I got to my own street I was glad. I knew the cracks in the paving stones. I knew the shape of Liam on my doorstep, but not why he was there. When he waved, I didn't wave back. He stood up before I was near enough to hear him, but when I got close I could see he was saying my name. He was holding an envelope, square, padded and brown.

'Ruth,' he said. 'Ruth, this has come.'

He looked pleased. He was reaching his arms.

'I had to sign. It's from the States.'

The package had a battered and hopeful appearance, so I sat with him there on the steps of my house and tore the envelope with my teeth. I knew it was from Jane. The book that slid out was her *Collected Poems*. I handed it to Liam as I looked at her letter, which said Jane very much hoped she would see me soon. She was giving a reading in London. She was also going to Paris. There were more names of cities she was planning to be in, and I said them out loud until Liam put a hand on my leg and said 'Look.' It was his right hand, and with the fingers and thumb of the other he was holding Jane's new book open. He told me to read it, but it wasn't a poem. It was a page with four words on it.

For Ruth, with love.

I took the book from Liam with both hands and stared.

'Pleased?' he said.

I didn't answer.

'All right?' he said.

I must have nodded at that, because he was in front of me then, with his hands under my elbows, to lift me up and turn me round.

'For Ruth, with love,' he said.

Then we unlocked my front door and moved together, inside.

THE END

THINGS TO DO INDOORS
Sheena Joughin

'AN EXCITING NEW TALENT'
Sunday Telegraph

Sisterly sharing is taken beyond the pale when twenty-six-year-old Chrissie finds a postcard from her boyfriend to her sister signed, 'Kisses, Nick'. Within moments she severs her two central relationships and looks boldly forward to the haphazard pleasures of an independent life.

Her lyrical journey, from lovelorn waitress to self-contained mother, takes us through the pubs, parks, parties, patisseries, peeling houseboats and rackety flats of west London to the shores of Lisbon, Ireland and Brighton. But Chrissie's attempts to escape the emotional convolutions of London only ever seem to lead to encounters that intensify rather than dispel her growing sense of how knotty life can be.

'SHEENA JOUGHIN HAS AN UNUSUAL CLARITY OF VOICE AND A CRAFTY DUALITY, SOMETHING BOTH BROODING AND LIGHT, IN HER WRITING. THE HURTS AND NASTINESSES BETWEEN HER CHARACTERS ARE PARALLELED WITH A CASUAL PERSISTENCE OF GOOD NATURE AND GOOD HUMOUR IN THIS FUNNY, PIERCING BOOK ABOUT LOSTNESS, CHILDISHNESS AND GROWING UP'
Ali Smith, *Times Literary Supplement*

'SHE WRITES LIKE AN ANGEL AND THINKS LIKE THE DEVIL. JOUGHIN IS A MAJOR DISCOVERY'
Fay Weldon

'[JOUGHIN] IS ALREADY A MISTRESS OF MORDANT COMEDY . . . A TALENT TO WATCH'
Daily Mail

'VERY FUNNY, VERY EDGY, VERY ACUTE. I LOVE THIS BOOK'
Julie Burchill

'JOUGHIN HAS A MERCILESS EYE FOR UNFLATTERING DETAIL AND FOR THE INSECURITIES OF BOTH SEXES . . . EXTREMELY FUNNY'
Daily Telegraph

0 552 77153 8

BLACK SWAN

THE FAMILY TREE
Carole Cadwalladr

'HALF DELICIOUS ROMP, HALF CALAMITOUS CHRONICLE
OF FAMILY BREAKDOWN . . . EVERY TWIG ON THIS
FAMILY TREE QUIVERS WITH LIFE'
Sunday Times

'A SUBLIMELY FUNNY AND CLEVER FIRST NOVEL, I PREDICT
THAT IT WON'T BE LONG BEFORE THE EXTREMELY
TALENTED CAROLE CADWALLADR IS REQUIRED READING'
Daily Mail

On the day of Charles and Diana's wedding, Rebecca Monroe's
mother locked herself in the bathroom and never came out.
Was it because her squidgy chocolate log collapsed? Because
Rebecca's grandmother married her first cousin? Or can we
never know why we do what we do?

'HOW MUCH ARE OUR LIVES DICTATED BY OUR GENES? IF
WE COME FROM A DYSFUNCTIONAL FAMILY, ARE WE
DOOMED TO FOLLOW THE PATTERN LAID DOWN BY OUR
ANCESTORS? FOR REBECCA MONROE, THESE QUESTIONS
HAVE PARTICULAR IMPORTANCE AS SHE STRUGGLES TO
UNDERSTAND THE LIVES AND CHOICES OF HER RELATIONS
AND ATTEMPTS TO FIND ANSWERS TO HER DILEMMA.
CAROLE CADWALLADR'S CLEVER AND MOVING DEBUT
EXAMINES THREE GENERATIONS OF THE MONROE FAMILY
AND EXPLORES NATURE VERSUS NURTURE . . . THOUGHTFUL
AND IMMENSELY ENTERTAINING'
Observer

'SUCH A PLEASURE TO READ. UNPRETENTIOUS AND
SERIOUS, FUNNY AND MOVING. A RARE FIND''
Monica Ali

'OSTENSIBLY, *THE FAMILY TREE* IS ABOUT THE MONROE
FAMILY: THEY BICKER, GO ON CARAVANNING HOLIDAYS
AND THROW PARTIES TO CELEBRATE THE WEDDING OF
CHARLES AND DI. BUT DEMONS ARE LURKING BENEATH
THE CHINTZ . . . IT'S READING-ON-THE-ESCALATOR STUFF'
Time Out

0 552 77269 0

BLACK SWAN

A SELECTED LIST OF FINE WRITING
AVAILABLE FROM BLACK SWAN

77084 1	COOL FOR CATS	*Jessica Adams*	£6.99
77115 5	BRICK LANE	*Monica Ali*	£7.99
99313 1	OF LOVE AND SHADOWS	*Isabel Allende*	£7.99
77243 7	CASE HISTORIES	*Kate Atkinson*	£6.99
99860 5	IDIOGLOSSIA	*Eleanor Bailey*	£6.99
77269 0	THE FAMILY TREE	*Carole Cadwalladr*	£7.99
77220 8	GEOGRAPHY	*Sophie Cunningham*	£6.99
99767 6	SISTER OF MY HEART	*Chitra Banerjee Divakaruni*	£6.99
99954 7	SWIFT AS DESIRE	*Laura Esquivel*	£6.99
99898 2	ALL BONES AND LIES	*Anne Fine*	£6.99
99890 7	DISOBEDIENCE	*Jane Hamilton*	£6.99
77179 1	JIGS & REELS	*Joanne Harris*	£6.99
99871 0	PEOPLE LIKE OURSELVES	*Pamela Jooste*	£6.99
77153 8	THINGS TO DO INDOORS	*Sheena Joughin*	£6.99
77104 X	BY BREAD ALONE	*Sarah-Kate Lynch*	£6.99
77203 8	NOBODY LOVES A GINGER BABY	*Laura Marney*	£6.99
77190 2	A GIRL COULD STAND UP	*Leslie Marshall*	£6.99
77093 0	THE DARK BRIDE	*Laura Restrepo*	£6.99
77166 X	A TIME OF ANGELS	*Patricia Schonstein*	£6.99
99960 1	WHAT THE BODY REMEMBERS	*Shauna Singh-Baldwin*	£7.99
77301 8	HAVE LOVE WILL TRAVEL	*Lucy Sweet*	£6.99
99952 0	LIFE ISN'T ALL HA HA HEE HEE	*Meera Syal*	£6.99
77173 2	BROTHER & SISTER	*Joanna Trollope*	£6.99
99864 8	A DESERT IN BOHEMIA	*Jill Paton Walsh*	£6.99
77221 6	LONG GONE ANYBODY	*Susannah Waters*	£6.99
77102 3	RAINY DAY WOMEN	*Jane Yardley*	£6.99

All Transworld titles are available by post from:
Bookpost, PO Box 29, Douglas, Isle of Man, IM99 1BQ
Credit cards accepted. Please telephone 01624 677237,
fax 01624 670923, Internet http://www.bookpost.co.uk
or e-mail: bookshop@enterprise.net for details.
Free postage and packing in the UK. Overseas customers: allow
£2 per book (paperbacks) and £3 per book (hardbacks).